BROKEN SOULS

BROKEN SOULS

EVAN GRACE

Broken Souls
Paperback Edition
Copyright © 2025 (As Revised) by Evan Grace

Dark Wolf Books
An Imprint of Wolfpack Publishing
1707 E. Diana Street
Tampa, FL 33610

www.darkwolfbooks.com

Edited by My Brother's Editor

Paperback ISBN 979-8-89567-930-2
Ebook ISBN 979-8-89567-929-6
LCCN 2025941849

BROKEN SOULS

BROKEN SOULS

ONE
BRYLEE

After disembarking from the plane, I make my way slowly down the tarmac. Everyone around me is rushing, probably rushing to family or friends waiting for them. No one's waiting for me, of that I'm sure. My mom did offer to pick me up, but my father is still recovering from the heart attack and needs her more than I do.

I should've come sooner, but I just couldn't. Don't they realize how hard it is for me to come back to Barton? No, of course they don't, because as far as they've been concerned, I should just get over it—I should move on, that it's time for me to start my life.

At baggage claim, while I wait for my suitcase, I look up Uber on my phone and arrange for a ride. My thoughts start to drift to the past, but like always, I try blocking them out. Great, just thinking about having those thoughts has me scratching at my wrists.

I drop my hands to my sides as the buzzer goes off, signaling the arrival of our luggage. My gaze follows the bags as they move down the belt until they're on the track that goes round and round. I spot my suitcase and grab it off the belt. Toward the end of the line, I spot my suitcase and grab it, pulling the handle out so I can drag it through the airport and out the sliding doors. I spot the red Camry and make my way toward it.

"Hi there, you're here for me." The man is old enough to be my grandpa.

"Hello. Can I take your bag?" Taking my bag, his leathery skin brushes mine, and I cringe. Contact isn't my thing, but as always, I push the thought down. Moving from the trunk, he opens the front passenger side door. "You're welcome to sit up front…if you want."

"Thank you," I whisper and climb in.

The airport is twenty minutes from my home. I'm glad for the quiet as he maneuvers out of the parking lot. It gives me time to mentally prepare myself for my family reunion. Don't get me wrong—I love my parents and they love me, they're just different. They've just never been people who show a lot of emotion.

Cornfields fill my vision as we drive along the highway toward my hometown. The place where, up until my sixteenth birthday, had been my home. My haven is now a place I dread being—so much so that I haven't visited in a long time.

"Do you live in Barton?"

I turn to look at the driver. "No. I used to, but I moved to Chicago a while ago."

"What brings you back?" So much for silence.

"My dad had a heart attack." I tug my sleeve lower on my wrists. "I wanted to come home and make sure he's okay. They've already sent him home from the hospital, which makes me feel better." What is it with this guy that's making me talk? I've spent the last eight years keeping to myself and being invisible—just the way I've liked it, wanted it, and needed it to be.

"It's amazing how quickly people can recover and be home. I'm sure having you home will make the healing go that much quicker too."

I don't reply, just nod my head and gaze out the window.

Ten minutes pass, and he pulls onto my street. Nausea settles in my belly, and a lump forms in my throat. The gray ranch-style home that I grew up in comes into view. As always, there are beautiful flowers lining the walkway up to the house. The garden gnome that I painted for my dad when I was twelve still sits in the flower bed next to the steps.

My driver pulls into the driveway and shifts the car into park. My heart thunders in my chest.

I climb out and move toward the back.

He hands me my suitcase. "I hope you have a good visit."

"Thank you," I mutter. Sweat drips down my spine and a shiver racks my body as I wheel my suitcase up the walkway to the front door.

I ring the doorbell, and a minute later the door opens.

"Brylee, you're here." My mom smiles and then steps back as I enter. Most parents would hug their children at this point, but instead, I get an arm squeeze. "How was your flight?"

"It was good. Luckily it's a short flight." My throat is scratchy. "Should I take my suitcase to my old room?" I'd rather stay at a hotel, but I should be here for my dad.

"Yes, I put clean sheets on the bed. Go get your stuff put away and then come visit with your father."

"Thanks, Mom." Turning to head down the hall, she stops me with a hand on my arm.

"We're so glad you're home. It's time to put the past behind you." She reaches up and tucks a loose strand of hair behind my ear. "I knew it would take you some time, but that you would finally get over it and come home for good."

They have always thought I should get over it. They will never understand why that day still haunts me. They don't get why I can't ever forget. Why I won't let myself forget. I've tried for years, but it has never worked.

Numbness wraps around me like an old blanket, and I welcome it. Anything to keep from breaking down. Answering Mom, I nod and turn down the hall to my room.

Opening the door, images of my youth bombard me, and I step inside and stand in front of my white wooden desk. Pictures of my friends and me cover the wall. On the desk, I pick up my sophomore yearbook. I open it, and the pages are smooth and cool to the touch as I flip through each page until I find the page with his photo, Chase Foster. Back then he wore his dishwater blond hair long. His ice-blue eyes stare back at me with a familiar twinkle.

My fingers trace his full lips that are curled up in the corner in that familiar smirk he always wore. *Wait, what am I doing?* I slam the book shut and toss it in the trash can.

Sitting down on the end of my bed, I stare blankly at the photos of my past.

"Brylee, come here." My best friend Kaylee waves *me over. The spunky blonde has been my best friend since kindergarten.*

I wrap my arms around her. "Hey!"

"Are you excited about Friday?"

I nod. On Friday I turn sixteen, and I'm pretty sure my parents are getting me a car. Then I'll be able to do whatever I want, within reason, of course. My parents are on the strict side, but when I get a car, I can get a job and start making some money. Then I'll have more freedom.

"I'm totally excited. I'm just dying to know what kind of car they got me. You, me, and Tiff can go driving around Saturday."

"It's so not fair that you're turning sixteen first." She glances behind me. *"Chase is coming down the hall right now."*

Chase Foster has been the star of my fantasies since I started having them. He's two years older than me and the most beautiful boy I've ever seen, but he doesn't even know I'm alive. All the girls want him, and he's got a reputation for sleeping with anyone, but I've never been able to get his attention.

This past year I've learned how to wear makeup to highlight my favorite features and how to style my wavy chocolate-brown hair. It's helped me get noticed more by boys at school, but they still don't want me like that. I know it's because of my body. I'm rather tall for a girl and also skinny with barely any boobs. I pretty much have the body of a young boy. I hate it, but what can I do? I've tried everything.

I casually turn around to see where he's at. He's standing in front of the gym doors. His muscles on display give me a queasy feeling low in my belly. Chase is wearing basketball shorts and a T-shirt that molds to his muscled body. His hair is pulled back in the cutest ponytail.

I know I should look away before he catches me, but I don't care. Something compels me to keep gazing at him. I hug my books to my chest as I watch him turn his head in my direction. My body freezes. Chase's eyes meet mine, and he holds my stare. I know I'm blushing right now because my cheeks feel hot.

"Oh my god," Kaylee says behind me.

Chase walks toward me. He's got this lazy swagger that is so hot. He's almost to me when a couple of his friends stop him. Disappointment fills me, and just as I'm ready to turn around and head to my first class, he walks past me.

"See you around, Brylee." Then he winks at me. He freaking winked at me.

Once he was out of sight, I looked at Kaylee. "Did that just happen?" I whisper excitedly.

"He looked at you like he wanted to eat you up. Maybe he's going to ask you out." She starts clapping and jumping up and down.

"Maybe." We make our way down the hall to our English class, and I can't help but smile. Things are starting to look up.

TWO
CHASE

"Chase, your mom's on the phone." I look down at the back of the girl's head in my lap and sigh. She wasn't doing it for me anyway.

"Honey, get off my dick." My half-hard cock slips from whatever-her-name's mouth, and I stand up, tucking my flaccid cock back into my pants. The bleach blonde pouts as she stands up, but I don't care. I don't look at her as I step around her and move toward the bar. If my mom can't reach me on my cell, she usually calls the clubhouse.

I sit down at the end of the bar, signaling Jared. "Need the bottle of Jack and the phone."

"You got it." Jared turns and moves down the bar. When he comes back, he sets the black-labeled bottle in front of me and hands me the phone. I grab the bottle first and tip it back letting the whiskey slide down my throat, welcoming the burn. Taking a couple more deep swallows, I feel that familiar warmth that spreads through my body.

I tap a cigarette out of the pack after picking it up

off the bar top. Placing it between my lips, I quickly light it, blow out the smoke, and then pick up the phone, holding it to my ear. "Hey, Mom, whataya need?"

"Chase Alan Foster, is that any way to talk to your mother?"

Scrubbing a hand over my hair, I sigh into the phone. "Sorry, Ma. What's up?"

I hear her sniffle into the phone and roll my eyes, staring at the ceiling, taking a drag of my cigarette. "Nothing, I just miss you. You haven't been by to see me lately."

"I know, I'm sorry. I promise I'll stop by this week. We'll order pizza." I take a drink of Jack. "Have you heard from Dad?" Eight years ago, my dad up and walked out on us. I can't say that I don't blame him, even if he did leave twenty-year-old me to look after my mom. We all fell apart after Kyle died, but Dad took it the hardest.

Every now and then he shows back up, but only to get my mom's hopes up, only to disappear again and again.

"No, not recently. I was hoping he'd be home for Kyle's birthday." Every year she makes me celebrate my brother's birthday. He'd be twenty-three this year. She'll make all of his favorite foods and a chocolate cake with vanilla frosting.

I know I shouldn't be encouraging this behavior, but it gives her something to look forward to. "Maybe he'll show up."

My boss, mentor, and best friend, Loco, and yes, that's his real name, waves me over. I don't like the look on his face; his brow is furrowed, and his mouth is pinched tight. "Ma, I've got to go. I'll call you tomorrow."

"Okay, honey. I love you so much. You know that, right? Don't ever think that I don't. You and your brother have given me so much joy." She sniffles again, and I close my eyes. I fucking hate this time of year.

"I know, Ma. I love you too. I'll talk to you tomorrow." I hang up and hand the phone to Ryan, one of our newbies. I snuff out my cigarette, lighting another as I move through the bar toward the hallway that leads back to Loco's office.

"How's your ma?" Loco is a full-blooded Apache Indian. He always wears his hair in a braid that hangs down past his shoulder blades. The man is pushing fifty but is built better than guys half his age. Hell, a couple of years ago, he helped me get in shape after I got sober. *Fuck*, I had let myself go for a while there, and it fucking showed. I'd had the beginnings of a beer belly, a puffy face, and constant bloodshot eyes. Now, I still have my Jack, cigarettes, and the occasional joint, but the hard drugs are done, and I'm in pretty good shape, if I don't say so myself.

"Eh…Kyle's birthday is coming up, so she's getting sad. Nothing that I can't handle. What's going on?"

He leads me into his office, and I don't have a good feeling when I notice that Grayson is sitting on the corner of the black lacquer desk. We've been friends since grade school, and we've worked together since we were old enough to work. I move farther into the room, and Loco stops right next to him.

"What's up? You guys haven't come at me like this since I went on that binge."

Grayson crosses his arms over his chest. "Heard

9

through the grapevine that a certain someone is back in town."

It takes a minute, and then the brunette with eyes like mine flashes through my mind. The last time I saw her, her hair had been pulled back in a severe ponytail. She'd had pale skin and was painfully thin with tears running down her face, but her face held no expression. It was like she'd been fucking dead, and I wish she would've been.

"So." I try to sound flippant.

"So?" Grayson sighs. "What are you going to do if you see her? You can't touch her."

I feel my lip twitch, wanting to snarl at Grayson. "Don't you think I fucking know that? I'd give anything to destroy that bitch, but I can't leave my ma. She just better hope I don't see her."

Loco moves to stand in front of me. I don't want to hear the words that are sure to come out of his mouth.

"You have got to let that anger go. Your mom's forgiven her, why can't you?" He places his hands on my shoulders. "I know you hate her, but that hate is going to eat you alive."

"She ruined everything. That fucking bitch destroyed my family." My ears are ringing—I'm so pissed.

Loco speaks slowly, quietly. "Chase, it was an accident."

"I don't want to fucking hear it." I turn and stomp out of Loco's office, not stopping until I reach the bar. I spot the girl from earlier and motion her over with my head. The bleach blonde comes over, her hips swaying as she moves toward me.

"Hey Chase," she purrs as she wraps her arms around my waist.

I grab her and throw her over my shoulder, ignoring her squeals, and carry her into the back. I let us into my room that I keep at the clubhouse, and it's really convenient for times like this. I throw her down on the bed. I watch her bounce up and down on the black comforter before I follow her down. Ripping her shirt up and off, watching her big, fake tits bounce, I feel my dick start to get hard. In seconds, I'll proceed to bury my dick in this random fucking pussy and forget everything.

———

The power sander in my hand moves slowly over the fender of the bike I'm rebuilding. This is the third bike I've rebuilt and sold for a huge profit. I've always been good at fixing and building bikes, so it was just natural for me to work on them professionally. Loco paid for me to go to school for motorcycle technician training.

I did the two-year program, and I swear to God I was smarter than the teachers I had. Of course I aced everything and found myself bored, but I still did my best. The teachers fucking hated when I corrected them for something fucking wrong and stupid that they tried to teach. I focus back on the fenders in front of me.

It's been four days since I learned that Brylee was home, and I haven't seen her. Oh, a couple of times I've really wanted to search for her, but I've refrained. Loco's words have kept running through my mind, and every time I shut them out.

I'm afraid of what I'll do if I see her. It's quite possible I'd kill her. For years I've played that exact scenario in my head, and every time I watch myself snap her neck. Do I feel good when I wake up? No, not at all.

I focus back on the fenders, and once I'm done, I prime them and leave them sitting in my garage to dry. I'll paint them when I've got the frame ready to paint as well. Putting everything away, I sweep the mess on the floor and dispose of it in the trash. Once I'm happy with how it all looks, I head inside.

On the way to my bathroom, I strip out of my clothes and climb into the shower. The hot water washes over my sore, aching muscles, and it feels fucking amazing. I grab my bar of Irish Spring and scrub the sweat and grime from my body—washing my hair and my beard before rinsing off and climbing out.

Wrapping a towel around my hips, I move to stand in front of the mirror. I scratch at my unruly beard. With scissors in my hand, I begin to trim the longer pieces until it hangs just a little bit longer than my chin. I grab my trimmer and clean up around my mouth, cheeks, and neck. Quickly I brush my teeth and then walk across the hall to my room. It's a sad sight to see, that's for sure.

My furniture doesn't match, my mattress and box spring are on the floor, and I don't have blinds or curtains in here, so I have a blanket hanging in front of the window, but what the fuck do I care? I don't bring anyone here, and if I do, they don't go anywhere but the living room and maybe the bathroom.

Not bothering with clothes, I collapse on top of my blankets and pass right out.

———

I wave to Mom as I pull out of the driveway. For the past five years, she's lived in this little two-bedroom bunga-low. It's not in the best shape; the siding is old, the steps need to be fixed, and the yard is overrun by creeping Charlie. Even with all that, Mom's brightened up the front with vibrantly colored flowers.

Earlier I had come over to "celebrate" my brother's birthday. Ma made lasagna with garlic bread and her famous chocolate cake with vanilla frosting. She had all of his school pictures out on every visible surface.

It always started the same way. I'd come over, and while we waited for the lasagna to cook, she'd make me share my favorite memories of Kyle. I'd hate every minute of it, but for her, I'd do anything.

Dad didn't show up, but I'm not surprised. Every year when he did show up for Kyle's birthday, he would sit with tears in his eyes and his face drawn. It was torture, but he loved my ma and would sit through it for her. Maybe he'd finally had enough. He couldn't keep up the charade that we were a normal family celebrating a loved one's birthday.

We'd eat, and she'd ask me about the shop, about the club, and if I was dating anyone. Why she's desperate for me to get married and have kids is beyond me. Maybe she thinks it'll fill some void inside of her or me. I just don't have the heart to tell her that the idea of procreating makes me ill. Never would I bring a child into this fucked-up world.

When it was time for birthday cake and ice cream, I listened to Ma brokenly sing "Happy Birthday." It was the same every year—I have to turn my head away so she can't see my eyes turn glassy. I rapidly blinked back the tears that still threatened to fall even ten years later.

I never stay long after that. Usually I head to the clubhouse, get drunk, and either fight or fuck. My brothers all know to steer clear of me when it's Kyle's birthday—well, everyone but Grayson and Loco. Over the years they've learned how to deal with me.

Ma sends me home with most of the lasagna, garlic bread, and cake. That's perfect, now I won't have to worry about groceries. When I went to take my leave, she walked me to the door. She cupped my cheek. "When did you get to be so handsome? I love you, Chase. Know that."

"I know, Ma. I love you too."

I stepped outside and climbed into my truck, which brings me to now. I stop by my house and throw my leftovers in the refrigerator, grabbing my cut and slipping it on. Grabbing my keys from the counter, I head into the garage to get my bike. I slip my helmet on my head and back out of the driveway.

I take the long way to the clubhouse so it'll give me a chance to clear my head. We're set up on the edge of town. When we party, we tend to get loud and rowdy. It's your typical clubhouse: an old factory that was converted. We have the tall chain-link fence that surrounds the property. The Jackals are a legit club and have been for over twenty years.

Loco's dad used to be the president back in the sixties until the eighties, when he handed over the club to Loco. They used to peddle pussy and weed. Now we've got the garage, and we offer protection if needed. Pretty much no one messes with us, and we don't mess with them. Occasionally we'll do runs, but not enough to worry about getting on someone's radar.

We're a brotherhood first and foremost. We love to ride and have each other's backs. That's why these guys are the only ones that I could stand to be around on a day like today. Pulling into the lot, I back my bike into my spot and push down the kickstand.

We have prospects, and they're usually relatives of other members. They're usually the gophers that do all of our running and clean the clubhouse after a party. Loco's youngest son, Zeke, is eighteen and is already prospecting. He has always felt like my little brother. With a smirk on his face, he comes over to me. "What's up, Chase?"

"Not a fucking thing. Where's your dad?"

"He's inside playing cards. He sent me out to keep an eye on the bikes." I nod and make my way inside. They've had to beef up security after one of our members' bikes was stolen. In all the years the Jackals have been here, this has never happened. Loco's convinced it was an isolated incident and just some jackass, but I guess we'll see.

I pull out a cigarette, sticking it between my lips and lighting it before making my way toward the bar. I ask for a beer and a double of Jack. The prospect grabs me both, setting them down in front of me. I take the shot and signal for another and do that one as well. Standing up, I pick up my beer and take a drag of my smoke.

Loco and some of the old-timers are in the back corner playing poker. I sit down at a table off to the side of the poker table. They're in the middle of a hand, so I just quietly drink my beer and smoke my cigarette.

When the hand is over, Loco turns to me. "How's your ma?"

"Same as always." I don't need to explain any further because he knows.

"You going to be fighting or fucking tonight?" He looks at me with a raised brow. Last year I was ready to

EVAN GRACE

fight everyone so they had to "babysit" me while I tied one on.

I take a drag of my cigarette. "Honestly, I feel like going home and going to bed."

It's not hard to see the look of surprise on all of their faces. Normally I'd either already be tying one on or scoping out a bitch to spend the night with. "Do you need a ride home?"

"Nah...I'm good. Thanks." I finish my beer and tell everyone bye. A couple of the girls give me pouty faces, but I just give them a chin lift and head out.

Grayson pulls into the lot as I climb on my bike. He gets off his bike and comes toward me. "Where are you going?"

"I'm heading home. It was a long fucking day."

He nods in understanding. Grayson has been to my ma's for Kyle's birthday celebration, and it's always been a huge support for me. He's always had my back, and I've always had his.

"How's your ma? I thought tomorrow I'd take her some flowers."

I roll my eyes and shake my head. "You're always kissing her ass. You are such a suck-up."

"Whatever, asshole. We still going out tomorrow?"

A new strip joint opened in the next town over, so a bunch of us are going to check it out. "Yeah, that sounds good."

I take off toward home. I'm two blocks away when I see a woman jogging down the street. She's tall and thin with decent tits, but my body locks up when I see who it is...Brylee fucking Whitmore.

Rage fills me, and I want more than anything to turn my bike around and approach her, but I don't. I get home

16

and park my bike on the street and jump into my truck. It carries me in the direction that she went. My eyes scan side streets and alleys, but I don't see her anywhere.

The extreme glee I feel knowing that I'm finally going to get to say everything I've dreamed of saying to her for the past ten years any minute now scares me. I want to make her crumble. I want to make her pay. I want her to remember every word that comes out of my mouth. The words etched into her brain forever.

I spot her up ahead, and she's running into the side entrance. "It's her," I whisper to myself. Pulling over to the side of the road, I watch her disappear down the lane that leads to Kyle's grave. Slowly I pull out and turn down the lane and spot her up ahead standing in front of my forever thirteen-year-old brother.

My mom picked this spot because it was secluded and provided Kyle with some peace and quiet.

I pull my truck to the side, and as I climb out, I look around and don't see anyone. The main entrance is on the other side of the cemetery so they won't see or hear anything. I don't have any clue what I'm going to do, but I've got to do something.

THREE
BRYLEE

After lacing up my tennis shoes, I jot down a quick note to my parents letting them know I'm out for a run. Earlier, Dad had an appointment with his cardiologist, and then they were going out to dinner.

"You should get out of the house," Mom said, lifting a hand to caress my face, but I moved away before she made contact. Hurt colored her gaze, and as much as it killed me to shut her out, I didn't try to bridge the gap between us.

"I'm kinda tired, but you two enjoy the town." The smile plastered on my face was a lie, but as long as they couldn't see through it…

"If you change your mind, call us, sweetheart." They left shortly afterward.

I haven't left the house much since I've been home. Maybe it was the fear of running into someone I used to know.

Only being home a few days, and I already can't wait to go back to seclusion. Yesterday, Mom asked if I had started looking at schools near or in Chicago—they've been on me for a while about going to college. Nothing interests me.

My sophomore year I dropped out of high school and got my GED. When my life spiraled downward, I didn't think I had a future. Why plan for a career I'd never have, right? So I started working as a waitress in my twenties. I'm pretty good at it too. The well-known Italian restaurant is an easy way to make good tips, and it's easy to fake a smile or pretend to be someone else— someone who has a life and their shit together.

Outside, the air is hot and humid, making my clothes stick to my sweat-covered body. I stretch my arms over my head then bend down, leaning side to side, stretching my legs. Turning on my phone, I open my music app and pull up my running playlist. Sticking my earbuds in, I trek out.

Over the years, along with prescribed medication, jogging became my antidepressant. Whenever my thoughts turn dark and when the past weasels into my mind, I throw on my running shoes and jog.

I've got no real destination in mind; I just listen to my music and let my feet carry me where they want to go. I don't really pay attention to my surroundings, which is so stupid and dangerous.

Slowing my speed, I see the sign up ahead: *Cross Creek Cemetery*. Every instinct I have tells me to run right past it.

Is that what I do? No, instead I jog in the side entrance, and I wind my way toward the back—where memories assault me and nausea pools in my belly.

"Brylee, could you come out here?" Dad hollers from outside. I slip on my shoes before flying down the stairs and out the front door. Mom and Dad stand by a red four-

door car. *"What do you think? It's in good shape. Has some miles on it, but it'll get you to school, work, and out with your friends, at least for the next few years."*

I wouldn't care at all if it was old and covered in rust. It's so cool to have my own car now.

"I love it," I say reverently. *"It's perfect! Thank you so much."* I hug them both, even though I just get an arm squeeze before taking the keys from my dad and climbing inside. The inside is tan, and the seats are covered in fabric.

The radio has a touchscreen and a CD player. I turn it on as Dad opens the passenger side door and climbs in. *"It's a Honda Civic. I got the plates and the insurance taken care of. You've got a full tank of gas. You really like it?"*

I rub my hand back and forth on the steering wheel. *"I do. It's so great. Can I take it for a spin?"*

"It's your car. Just go grab your driver's license."

Nodding, I climb out of the car and bolt into the house, grabbing my purse off the counter. I head back outside, and my parents are standing at the bottom of the stairs. I hug my dad and then my mom. Ugh, why do they get so weird when I hug them?

"Be careful. Call us if you stop anywhere."

"I will. Promise." I climb into my car, buckling my seat belt. I wave goodbye to them as they watch me pull out of the driveway.

First I stop by Kaylee's. As soon as I pull into her driveway, she comes running out. *"Oh my god! This is so awesome. It's so cute. I'm going to go ask my mom if I can go for a drive with you."* My bestie disappears into her house and moments later comes running back out and climbs into the passenger side.

Once she's buckled in, I pull out of the driveway, and we drive around town listening to music and talking. She turns toward me. "I have got some news for you. Okay, so Megan Daniels's brother, Grayson, is best friends with Chase, and...apparently he asked Grayson to ask his sister about you. He's interested in asking you out."

I don't say anything at first. My heart is beating rapidly in my chest. That fluttery feeling begins in my stomach.

"Bry? Are you okay?"

Pulling onto a residential street, I throw my car into park. "Are you messing with me?"

"God, no. Megan knows you've been crushing on him, and she couldn't wait to tell you, but she didn't have your number. If he calls you, are you going to go out with him?"

I take a deep breath and then turn toward Kaylee. "I...I want to, but I'm a virgin, and he's been with lots of girls. What if all he wants from me is sex? I don't think I'm ready for that yet."

"I don't think that's it. Megan told me that Grayson told her that he's never seen Chase this interested in someone. He says you have the prettiest eyes." She squeals, clapping her hands together excitedly.

"Really?" I whisper breathily. "Okay, yes, if he calls me, then I will definitely say yes to going out with him."

"Crap, can you take me home? I have to work on my algebra homework."

I drop her off and then decide to drive around a little bit longer. When I'm ready to head back home, I turn by the park, and my purse falls to the floor. I turn my head quickly to grab it, and that's when the sickening sound of something hitting my car and then the windshield has me slamming on the brakes as a scream rips from my lips.

I stop in front of the headstone, and tears silently run down my face. I read the name over and over: *Kyle Jason Foster. The* boy died two days later from brain trauma. He was only thirteen when I killed him. He'd been skateboarding but hadn't worn a helmet. I didn't see him when he crossed the street because I hadn't been looking. The screeching of rubber against the asphalt and the smell of burned tires fill my mind. The memory is as fresh as the day it happened.

"No, don't go there." Music continues to blare in my ears. I hug myself tightly, standing there, but the wetness won't stop running down my cheeks. A heaviness I haven't felt in so long pours in. I never knew Kyle, but when I saw his picture attached to his obituary, an ache so deep and guttural stabbed at my chest. He was a cute kid with dirty blond hair and ice-blue eyes.

I read the article and cried silent tears, I was the cause of so much devastation. Then I found the portion talking about who he was survived by: Chase, my school crush, was his older brother. I threw up.

My vision blurs as Weezer's "Feels Like Summer" replays in my mind. I need to get out of here, but my legs feel like they're full of lead. The hairs on the back of my neck stand up, and I go to turn and leave, but an arm wraps around my chest while a hand covers my mouth, muffling my scream.

The scent of motor oil and stale cigarette smoke fills my nostrils as a calloused hand scrapes against my dry lips. The urge to vomit comes over me, and I swallow it down.

The earbuds fall from my ears. The attacker doesn't

say anything as they drag me backward. Adrenaline spikes, and I fight. A grunt of pain escapes the person as I connect my palm with his bearded face. His grip loosens, and I kick him in the leg, freeing myself.

I run. My heart beats at an erratic pace.

Heavy footfalls pound behind me. *Oh god!* I pick up the pace. In my mind I scream, but my mouth won't actually open and release any sound. All I think is *run, run, run!*

He grunts behind me, and I'm about to sprint harder when arms slink around my waist and he tugs. Our momentum is too fast, and I stumble forward. Kyle's tombstone comes into view. A blinding pain knocks at the side of my head.

Then nothing but darkness takes over.

———

When my eyes flutter open, I wince. My head throbs. Looking down, I find my hands are tied to a chair. My heart races and I try to push myself up from the chair, but my ankles are restrained, too. Another rope secures my chest to the chair so I'm upright.

"Hello!" It sounds more like "lo" because a gag is shoved in my mouth. My breathing speeds up. I struggle against my bindings and attempt to scream around the gag.

My head throbs more, and bile crawls up my throat, but I try to swallow it down. Glancing around, I appear to be in a dingy basement. A single light shines near a set of stairs. The musty scent burns my nose; the air is heavy, and I blink tears away.

Is this where I'm going to die? What'll happen to my

parents? Who would miss me? Sadness fills me because, besides my parents, no one would care if I was gone.

I resume my efforts trying to get loose, but the knots are too tight.

A door nearby creaks open. I pant around the gag and through my nose. My pulse is as frantic as I am as a dark figure moves down the stairs. All I want to do is cower, but I can't.

The man grabs a bucket, moving it until he's in front of me, then flips it upside down and sits on it. The dim lighting prevents me from seeing him clearly, but I can feel his eyes on me. A cold shiver runs down my spine. If I weren't so scared, I'd be embarrassed that I've wet myself.

Why isn't he doing or saying anything? How's he going to kill me? Is he going to rape me first? Is he going to cut me into little pieces? Every terrible idea after another runs through my mind. I should've stayed out of the cemetery. Should've just kept running. I could be home right now, safe and secure.

My body trembles, and my teeth chatter around the gag. My body jerks and twitches. It's like my body is trying to escape, but I'm strapped to the chair. He moves, and I can't help the whimper that slips past my lips.

He lights a cigarette. The flame is too small to make out his features. I hear him inhale, then smoke blows right in my face.

I cough around the cloth in my mouth, but he does it again. This time I hold my breath until the acrid smoke clears.

He puts out his cigarette right on the floor, stands up, and disappears upstairs, stomping with each step he takes. I hear his footsteps moving around, and an occasional drawer slams upstairs. I try wiggling my hands to get the ropes to loosen, but they won't budge, and it hurts my wrist. Moving my feet, I try to free those ropes, but again I can't get them to budge.

My head painfully aches, and all I want to do is lie down. Instead, I close my eyes, bending my head forward. It's uncomfortable, but I'm so sleepy I don't care.

———

Something hits my foot, and I jerk awake to find my captor standing in front of me. It's still dark, so I can't see him. I can only hear his breathing. My heart beats a rapid rhythm, and tears leak from my eyes. My wrists ache from trying to get loose earlier. *Is this the end?* I shut my eyes, squeezing them tight.

"I brought you some water. I'll take your gag out for you to drink, but if you scream, I'll put the gag back in, and you'll get nothing. Do you understand me?"

I open my eyes to see a bottle of water in front of me with a straw sticking out of it. My cottonmouth waters at the prospect of a drink. Do I trust that it's not poisoned? Who am I kidding? I'm probably dead already. I nod.

He sets the water down and grabs my gag from both sides and pulls it out of my mouth so it rests around my neck.

My captor picks up the water and holds the straw to my lips. I take a slow sip, waiting for it to burn my throat or something, but instead, it's cold and delicious as it runs down, easing the ache in my throat. Greedily I suck at the straw, getting as much as I can before he takes it away. He pulls it away from my lips and I whimper.

"Open your mouth. Take these for your head." He holds two white pills, and when I open my mouth, he slips them between my lips and then the straw to them. I swallow the pills down and drink and drink until there is nothing left. "I'll bring you something to eat later." He slips the gag between my lips again and tightens the knot in the back.

I watch his dark figure disappear up the stairs, then the door shuts. What is he waiting for? If he's going to kill me, I wish he'd do it already. I can't stand the wait, it's making me crazy.

I sit quietly and listen. A radio turns on, rock music blares, then a loud noise that sounds like a drill or something rumbles.

My eyes start to grow heavy, and the pain in my head dulls. I fight sleep for as long as possible, but they're as heavy as bricks. Again, I fade into nothing.

FOUR
CHASE

In my garage, I turn on my radio and the belt sander as I kick and throw shit. What was I thinking? I fucking kidnapped her. Brylee is in my motherfucking basement tied to a chair. Grabbing her had been an impulsive thought. My plan had been to tell her off, but I heard her soft cries, and something in me snapped.

Fuck, she fought me, and I felt myself get a little hard when she bucked against me. When she slipped away from me and took off running, I didn't think. I just ran after her. I had done a flying tackle, and I can't forget the sound of her head hitting the tombstone. For a second, I was worried I'd killed her, but she groaned when I lifted myself off of her. I carried her to my truck, laying her down on the bench seat.

From the look of her head, she just grazed it, but fuck, it was loud. When we got back to my place, I pulled into the garage and closed it. It was a tight fit and was going to be hard getting her in the house, but I'd manage somehow.

Once I had her down in the basement, I had to decide

EVAN GRACE

what to do. I ended up dragging a chair from the kitchen downstairs and found some nylon rope in my garage. First I had tied her feet together, and then I hoisted her up into the chair, tying her wrists to the armrests and then tying the rope around her chest to help hold her up.

I grabbed a red bandana from upstairs and used it to gag her. When I stepped back, I looked her over. Her face was pale, scratches covered her knees, and her hair was a rat's nest, but she was still the most beautiful woman I'd ever seen, and that made me hate her even more.

When Kyle's accident had happened, I had been working at an auto parts store across town. I'd been your typical high school bad boy, I guess. I didn't get into trouble, or at least not too much. I had decent grades, and I played baseball and football. Girls flocked to me, and I had no trouble sweet-talking them into bed. I was just a typical rowdy, horny high schooler.

I'm just finishing restocking the shelves and getting ready to take my break when Grayson comes rushing into the store. The look on his face causes an ache in the pit of my stomach to form.

"Gray, what's up?"

"Your brother's been in an accident. You need to get to St. Peter's Hospital."

My boss, Tom, is standing nearby. "Get out of here, son."

I follow Grayson out to his car and climb in. "Dude, what the fuck happened to Kyle? Is he okay?"

He shakes his head. "I don't know, man. The car hit him while he was crossing the street on his skateboard. Jake and Pete were with him and saw the whole thing. It was a girl who did it. She didn't have time to stop. I don't know if she didn't see him or he didn't see her, it happened so fast. The girl managed to call 911 and get the ambulance there."

We're quiet the rest of the ride there. As soon as he pulls up in front of the emergency room doors, I jump out of the car and run inside, finding my parents sitting in the waiting room. My mom jumps up and runs to me.

"Your brother's in surgery, they said he's got brain trauma. They're trying to alleviate the pressure. They don't know if he's going to make it."

I wrap my arms around my mom as she cries gut-wrenching sobs. My dad's head is hanging low, and he's got his face buried in his hands. "It's going to be okay, Mom."

I'm not sure how long we sit waiting to hear how he's doing, but we know nothing, and it's killing me. Grayson's been by my side the whole time I've been waiting. Kyle's two buddies that were with him sit in the corner with their parents.

My dad steps outside—I'm sure it's to smoke. My mom grabs my hand between both of hers, squeezing them tight. My dad comes back a moment later and sits next to my mom, rubbing her back. I lean back in my chair, my head resting against the wall. I've never been the praying type, but I figure it doesn't hurt to give it a shot now.

I'm not sure how to do it, but I just start talking, in my head, of course. "God, whatever I have to do for you to save my brother, I'll do it. I'll go to college, I won't sleep around anymore, I'll be nicer to him. Please save him...please."

After four long hours, the doctor finally comes out. We all stand up as he comes over. "I'm Dr. Marx, and I've been taking care of Kyle. Your son suffered massive trauma to the brain. It's swelling too much, so we did a bone flap removal. Our hope is that it relieves the pressure. For now, we've got him in a medically induced coma.

"We're giving him diuretics to hopefully help with the swelling. Anticonvulsants have been started because, due to the nature of his injuries, he could begin having seizures, and we want to make sure that doesn't happen. He's in critical condition, and the next twenty-four hours are crucial. As soon as we get him settled in the ICU, we'll come get you."

It takes two hours before we're escorted down to the ICU. They will only let two at a time go in, so my parents go first. I watch them disappear behind sliding doors.

I pace back and forth while I wait for my turn to see my brother. Everyone that kept vigil in the ER waiting room headed home a while ago—some promising to return the next day and check on him.

It feels like forever when my parents finally come out. My mom comes toward me and cups my face in her hands. "Be prepared, honey. He looks a little swollen, and the top of his head is completely covered in bandages. They said we should talk to him, that he can hear us."

I step through the doors, and the nurse points me to his room. She warns me that he's got lots of tubes coming out of him, but Kyle isn't in any pain.

The rhythmic beep greets me as I step into the room. My brother looks so small in the hospital bed. His face is black and blue, and he's got a tube in his mouth helping him breathe. I sit in the chair next to the bed and grab my brother's hand.

"Hey, you little shit. I know you love attention, but

this is the worst way to go about it. You're going to be fine, you hear me? When I find out who did this to you, I'm going to make them pay."

Shaking my head, I clear it of the thoughts of the past. I had been stunned that it had been Brylee who hit Kyle. We learned who it was the day after he died, and we heard that they arrested her. She was charged with involuntary manslaughter. I guess against the advice of her family and lawyer, she pleaded guilty.

I heard my mom telling my dad that she had gone to see Brylee and spoke to her and that she forgave Brylee for what happened. My mom sounded so sad when she told Dad that it was like Brylee wasn't even there. She was borderline catatonic.

At her sentencing, I watched them bring her in. She had been ghostly white, her hair limp, and her already thin frame was practically skeletal. One part of me took such joy out of the fact that she looked like death warmed over, but a teeny tiny part wanted to hold her and tell her it was going to be okay.

I grab a beer and the joint I had rolled earlier. Stepping through the back door, I sit on the folding chair on my shitty little deck. Placing the joint between my lips, I light and inhale the familiar smoke, holding it in my lungs and then slowly blowing it out. I hit it a few more times before taking a drink of my beer.

By the time I finish it, I'm good and stoned. Slouching down in my chair, I close my eyes. I try to clear my head of any thoughts of my brother, Brylee, or the fact that she's fucking tied up in my basement. What am I going to do with her? This is something I certainly should've thought out, but no, I saw her and on impulse I grabbed her.

A foot kicking my chair has me jerking awake. Flying out of my chair, I find Grayson laughing his ass off. "You're a fucking dick," I growl. "Today is not the day to fuck with me."

"Fuck, I wasn't thinking. You don't seem fucked up. What's up with that? I figured you'd be passed out from drinking or somewhere having a fuck fest." He pulls up a chair and sits across from me.

"I don't know, I just didn't feel like it."

"Where's your truck? I almost didn't stop, but all of the lights are on."

My eyes widen because it hits me that I have Brylee tied up in my basement. How could I forget? How long have I been out here? Fuck, she hasn't eaten, and I gave her those pills hours ago. I have to get rid of Grayson.

"It's in the garage. I was working on it earlier." I fake a big yawn. "I'm beat."

"Okay, I get the hint. I'll see you tomorrow. Call me if you need me."

I walk with him around the side of my house to the front. "I will, brother. I appreciate you coming to check on me."

"Anytime—I'll talk to you tomorrow."

I watch him walk to his bike, climb on, and then drive away.

Running back around to the back, I bolt inside the house and down the stairs. I find Brylee with her head tilted forward and her soft snores filling the room. Sniffing the air, the scent of urine hits me, and nausea pools in my belly. I look down, and it's obvious her shorts are soaked and the ground is wet around her. I back away from her slowly because I'm not going to let myself feel bad about it, even though part of me wants to get her cleaned up.

Upstairs I make her a quick sandwich and cut it into small squares and grab a water. I move down the stairs and stand right in front of her. Kicking her foot hard enough for her to feel it, I watch as her head flies back, a muffled whimper escapes her lips and tears fall from her eyes, but it doesn't matter because I won't be swayed by her tears. She has no clue who I am or why she's here, but I'm not ready to tell her yet because—fuck, I don't know what I'm going to do.

"I'm taking the gag out. Remember, if you scream, I'll stick it back in and never take it out. Understand?"

Nodding her head slowly, I reach out, pulling it from her mouth and letting it hang from her neck. "I made you a sandwich. It's bologna, that's all I had." I keep my voice low. I'm not sure if she'd recognize it. That's why only the light from the stairs is lit. I can keep to the shadows and keep myself hidden until just the right moment. What will I do with that moment, I don't know, but I want her to hurt.

I grab a piece of the sandwich and hold it to her lips. At first, she doesn't open, so I grab her chin, squeezing it until she opens. "You need to fucking eat. Now open up or I'll force this sandwich down your motherfucking throat." A whimper slips past her lips, but she slowly parts her lips, watching as she bites into the sandwich. She swallows, and then I give her another bite.

Once she's finished half of the sandwich, I hold the water with a straw in it to her lips. She greedily sucks down half of it. Pulling it away, I feed her the rest of her sandwich and the last of the water.

"How's your head?" She dips her head down, refusing to look at me.

Grabbing her chin again, I lift her face. A lone tear slips from her eye and leaves a silvery trail running down her cheek. My fingers twitch—aching to wipe it away, instead, I curl my lip into a snarl and push her head away.

Moving my face down inches from hers, I whisper, "I'm not going to ask you again. How is your head?"

"I-it h-h-hurts," she stutters out. Shame fills me, but I ignore it. She brought it on herself.

I stand up and back away from her. "You fucking smell." Fresh tears leak from her eyes. I can barely see them as they drip from her chin. "Pissing all over yourself like a child."

Her body jerks as if I've hit her. In a way, I guess I have, but with words.

"What did you expect? I've been tied to a chair for who knows how long. I was gagged. I couldn't call for you." Her voice is so soft and lyrical, but with a hint of attitude.

"That's true, isn't it? I suppose I could take you to the bathroom and maybe give you some clean clothes."

"Just let me go. I p-promise I w-won't tell anyone that you took me."

She probably wouldn't, but I can't let her go yet. "Oh, I'm sure you wouldn't, but I can't let you go. Not yet."

"Why? W-What did I d-d-do?"

Pacing back and forth in front of her, the truth about who I am threatens to spill from my lips, but it's not time. I charge at her, grabbing her arms. She shakes violently as she tries to shrink into herself. If it's possi-ble, I can smell the fear coming off of her. The cloying scent burns my nose and leaves a bad taste in my mouth.

I let go as if I was burned. Without a word, I go upstairs and grab my hidden bottle of Jack out of the cupboard. The sound of the cap being unscrewed echoes in the kitchen. Tipping the bottle back, I let it run down my throat, welcoming the burn. I carry the bottle to my couch and plop down on it.

Again I tip the bottle back, chugging down as much as I can before I start to cough with spit flying everywhere. I set the bottle on the TV tray sitting next to the couch. Getting up, I move through my house and go out into the garage. Grabbing a pack of cigarettes, I pull one out, sticking it between my lips.

After I light it, I take a deep drag, the smoke travels down into my lungs, and I blow it out slowly. The effect of the alcohol hits me, and I sway a little before righting myself. Leaning against my truck, I stare at the wall.

I've never seen someone that fearful before. I need to tell her who I am so she understands what all of this is about. That it wasn't some random kidnapping. She needs to know I'm going to punish her for what she did.

I finish my cigarette and put it out. Stumbling back into the house, I strip off my clothes on the way to my room, and when I hit my bed, I fall on it, passing out immediately.

———

Bam. Bam. Bam. Bam. Bam.

I peel my eyes open and see the sun is peeking around the edges of the blanket.

Bam. Bam. Bam. Bam.

"What the fuck?" I mutter as I push myself up in bed before crawling off of it. I grab my jeans off the floor and hop from one leg to the other as I pull them on. I look out the front window and see it's Loco.

Pulling it open, I can tell he's pissed. "What's up, brother?"

He pushes his way in, storming past me into my living room. "Do you know what time it is?"

"Fuck, I don't know. I may have had a little too much to drink last night." I scratch at the back of my head. A nervous habit I've had since I was a kid.

"Chase, it's eleven thirty."

Shit, I was supposed to be to work at nine. *Fuck*, Brylee's been down there by herself since last night. I've got to get rid of Loco. "Shit, I passed out before I could set my alarm."

Quirking an eyebrow at me, I don't turn away, he'd know I was lying. "You look like hell." He leans toward me and sniffs. "You smell like Jack."

"I tapped into my emergency bottle."

Loco just shakes his head. He places his hand on my shoulder. "Are you sure you're okay? I know his birthday is always a tough time for you, but I can't watch you go down the self-destructive path again."

"Seriously, I'm fine. Yes, it's hard and it fucking blows, but I can't change any of that. I'm not going down that path again. I haven't touched any blow or heroin since I got out of rehab, you know that." I've been clean of the shit for just shy of three years. I won't fuck up like that again.

Loco tugs on his braid and then walks to the door. "Take today off. Get your head straight and get some sleep. Grayson said you guys are going to that new strip club tonight. Go get your dick wet, and tomorrow you'll be good as new."

I nod and don't tell him that I won't be going anywhere because I have the girl who killed my brother tied up in my basement. I could tell him what I've done, and he'd probably help me deal with her, but instead, I keep my mouth shut.

"Call me if you need me."

"I will, thanks."

Loco steps out of the front door. I stand in the doorway watching him until he's on his bike and rides away.

With quick feet, I run through the house. Flying down the stairs, I'm hit with a smell that makes me gag. Brylee's soft cries have me moving toward her. Her body jerks in the chair, and her cries turn painful-sounding. "What's wrong?"

"I SHIT MYSELF, ASSHOLE! Just kill me and get it over with." She screams at me, but when she tells me to kill her, there's a finality to her voice, like she's come to the conclusion sometime in the night that she's going to die, and she's made peace with it.

I know what I need to do. I'm not that cruel that I'd make her sit in her mess, would I? No, I can't do it. "Give me a few minutes, and I'll take you up to shower. You're gonna have to do it with me in there with you. We'll throw those clothes out, and you can wear something of mine." I back away from her. "I'll be right back."

As I move up the stairs, her cries follow me. I don't like the feeling in my gut, but for now, I ignore it. In my room, I grab an old T-shirt of mine and a pair of my boxer briefs. I take them into the bathroom and lay them on the counter and then go into the kitchen to grab a knife to cut her ropes and a garbage bag for her clothes. She might as well pitch them. I grab the only other towel I have and set it with her clothes. At least it's fucking clean.

I turn on the overhead vent and grab some incense I have to help mask the smell when she's up here. I light it before I move through the house. I haven't decided what I'll do with her once she's done, but I'm sure I'll figure it out. I've got plenty of rope.

I run down the stairs to the basement. I realize there is a good chance that when she sees me she'll recognize me, but I'll just have to make sure she doesn't look at me. "I'm going to cut you free, but do not try anything or I'll make you sorry. Do you understand me?"

She nods her head and keeps it down. Good.

First I cut the rope around her ankles, then I get behind her and cut the ropes around her chest, and finally I cut the rope around her wrists. I grab an old blanket and wrap it around her waist when she stands up. Grabbing her hands one by one, I have her take over holding the blanket.

I grab her around her biceps and lead her to the stairs. "Keep your head down and don't look at me." She nods her head and walks in front of me with slow, jerky steps. We reach the bathroom and I turn the light off so she can't see me.

"Just get in the shower, shut the curtain, and put everything into this trash bag." She takes it from me and climbs inside the shower, pulling the curtain behind her. The water kicks on, and I hear the rustling of the bag while I plug my nose so I don't smell anything.

It's a good five minutes before she finally sticks her

arm out with the garbage bag in her hand. I take it from her. "I t-tied it u-up." I double knot it while she showers.

I hear my cell phone ring in the other room, but I don't dare leave her alone. It's not like she can go anywhere, but I'm not taking any chances. I'm sure it's just Grayson and I'll have to tell him I'm not going to the club with him.

The water shuts off, and silence fills the bathroom. That's when it hits me she probably needs a towel. I grab it from the sink. "Here's a towel for you to dry off."

"Thank you." She takes it from me.

After she's dried off and dressed, she opens the curtain and steps out. I hand her the only comb I have and watch as she quickly combs out the tangles. Her hair hangs down to the middle of her back, and I forgot that it had a soft wave to it. My dick starts getting hard as I let my eyes rake over her body. I know I shouldn't look, but I can't help it. She's fucking beautiful, and even thinking that, I want to scream because she's evil, she took my baby brother from me. I need to remember that.

I lead her into the kitchen and have her sit at the table. She doesn't fight me when I wrap the rope around her arms and chest before tying her feet together again. I grab her hands, making sure she can reach the top of the table. With quick hands, I make her a sandwich, grab a bottle of water, and set them both in front of her.

"I'm going downstairs to clean up. Eat, and I'll be back shortly."

FIVE
BRYLEE

I watch his retreating back and the sound of his footsteps on the stairs. My stomach rumbles and has me reaching for part of the bologna sandwich. I hate it, but I'm so hungry I don't care. Before I even know what's happening, the sandwich is gone, and I'm sucking down the last of my water.

This morning I was mortified when I had my accident. I had tried to hold it because my stomach started cramping, and I couldn't stop it from happening. I cried the whole time, but nothing but silence had surrounded me, and I knew my captor was either asleep or gone. When the knocking started at the door, I had thought I was saved, but I quickly realized it wasn't going to happen.

I tried to listen to what they were saying, but my cries made it impossible to hear. He's going to kill me today, I just know it. I've made peace with it. My parents will no longer have to worry about me. I don't know if I believe in heaven or hell, but I know I'm going to the latter for what I've done.

Pain hits me in my chest when I think about all of the things I'll never do. I'll never fall in love, I'll never kiss a man, and I'll never experience the touch of one. When I was younger, I wanted lots of babies. I wanted to be a mom who had lots of kids that had me running all over, but our home would be so filled with love that I wouldn't care. I'd have a husband who loved me completely and spent his days trying to make me happy while I did the same for him.

Life had other plans for me, I guess. I've spent the last ten years merely existing. It's been a lonely existence but I don't and would never let anyone close to me. I'd only hurt them, and as soon as they learned I was a murderer, they'd leave me anyway.

I hate myself. Every morning, I wake up thinking why couldn't I have just fallen asleep and not woken up. I know it's wrong, and the meds help drive those thoughts away, but sometimes they creep in. I can barely look at myself in the mirror most days, hating the person staring back at me.

Kyle's mom came to see me right before I got sent to juvie. I remember her being there, sitting in front of me. Her lips moved, but I couldn't hear what she was saying. I felt like I was underwater. She tried to reach for me, I remember that, but the guard must've told her no because she shrank away, leaving shortly after that.

She tried to see me in the hospital, but I had refused to leave my room and see her. Once I was released, I moved away, and I haven't been back until now. Heck, they probably moved away. I wouldn't want to stay in the town where my child died.

The sound of footsteps on the stairs has my heart beginning to race again. My sandwich threatens to come up, but I swallow it back down and close my eyes when I hear his footsteps on the linoleum.

He stops next to me—I can feel his body heat and smell the light scent of sweat and lemon cleanser. Shame fills me because I'm the reason why he smells like cleanser, but then anger fills me because I wouldn't have made a mess had I not been tied up in his basement.

"You ate."

I nod my head yes.

"Are you still hungry? I'll make you another sandwich if you want one." His voice is deep and gruff.

"Y-yes, I'm s-still hungry."

He walks away, and my eyes drift to his back. A black tribal design covers a majority of his back, it's lots of swirls and patterns. His disheveled hair is dishwater blond and curls behind his ears.

At the counter, he starts putting together my sandwich. He told me not to look at him, but I catch sight of his profile. Why does it look familiar? I feel sick at the thought that it's someone who knows me.

He turns with the sandwich in his hands, and his face comes into view. I would know those eyes anywhere. I feel the blood drain from my face. Flashes of the past hit me in rapid succession. The first time I saw Chase, he was running off of the football field. Then the day I swear he was going to talk to me, then Kaylee telling me that he wanted to call me, and then when I had been sentenced. He had looked at me with such disgust and hatred.

Tears begin to cloud my vision, nausea pools in my belly, and my body starts to shake. He freezes, eyes widening, and rushes toward me. My mouth opens, but he covers it with the palm of his hand, muffling my scream.

My pulse pounds, and I pant against his hand. He curses under his breath and looks at me closely. "If I remove my hand, do you promise not to scream?"

I nod immediately. I'm not stupid, I won't try anything. As soon as he removes his hand, I take a deep shuddering breath. My head dips down and I stare blankly at my lap. I can hear his heavy breathing and then his footsteps and then the unmistakable flicking sound of a lighter. The scent of smoke burns my nose, and out of the corner of my eye, I see him take a drag of his cigarette and then blow it out.

"You know who I am."

"Y-you're Ch-Chase F-Foster." I hate that I sound weak right now, stuttering like a fool, but I'm so freaking scared right now. He's Kyle's big brother. This has got to be his chance for payback. I should've been expecting something like this to happen sooner or later. Karma was going to come for me, it was only a matter of time.

He smokes his cigarette and just stares at me. I can't tell what's going on in his head, but it can't be good. He kidnapped me—he's kept me tied up in his basement. Chase left me to sit in my own filth. Every time I think about it, humiliation fills me, but that's probably what he wanted. Is he going to beat me down until I'm nothing before he kills me?

After he puts his cigarette out, he comes walking toward me. That's when I notice he's got the name Kyle tattooed on his chest.

Lowering my head again, shame fills me. What do I do? What do I say to him?

He gets down on his haunches next to me, and my

body begins shaking uncontrollably again. My heart is beating so hard I swear he can hear it. A thin sheen of sweat covers my body as I watch him with weary eyes. I should try to be prepared for whatever it is he plans on doing. How does one plan for their own death? If I ask, will he let me write my parents a goodbye letter?

Turning to look at him, he's still the most beautiful man I've ever seen. His hair is short but long enough to curl around his ears. It's messy like he just crawled out of bed. Chase's face is covered in a dark-blond beard that frames those full lips I used to fantasize about kissing.

"I-I'm s-sorry about Kyl—"

He startles me by standing quickly.

"Don't you say his fucking name! You fucking killed him!" he roars in my face.

I begin to openly sob and can only nod my head because it's the truth. My heart is completely shattered, and I feel myself die a little inside.

"Shut up! Stop crying!" He grabs my chair by the back and drags me through the kitchen. I cry out as we hit the stairs. My body jerks as it hits each step. This is it —I close my eyes and pray that he kills me quickly. I'm afraid that he may want to torture me first to punish me.

We reach the bottom, and he drags me to where I sat before. He ties my wrists to the arms of the chair, and without a word, he's up the stairs, and the door slams closed. I hear water turn on—it must be the shower because it runs for a while. It finally shuts off, and I hear footsteps move around. They stop, and then I hear rustling around and then a couple of stomps.

Water runs again for about a minute before turning off again. Then more moving around until a door slams. In the distance, I hear a motorcycle start, is he leaving?

Maybe he's sending someone else to do it. My thoughts race as silence fills the space around me. Both wrists begin to itch, and I begin to lightly rub them on the arms of the chair.

The first time I cut my wrists was six months into my year sentence in juvie. My roommate found me before I bled out. I spent two weeks in the hospital and convinced them I wasn't going to try and hurt myself again.

After about a month they quit watching me like a hawk and I tried it again. The second time I had lost so much blood that I coded twice on the way to the hospital and they thought I wasn't going to make it. It was then the courts decided that I was not fit to go back to juvie. I spent six months in a mental hospital, the first three I was on suicide watch. I couldn't even use the bathroom alone. I always had to have a chaperone. I was diagnosed with PTSD, severe depression, and anxiety.

My meds and running have helped, although the meds make me feel like a zombie most days, but I guess it's better than being sad and crying all of the time. I've been off my meds for two days now, and I doubt it'll make a difference and I'll probably be dead before I begin to go through withdrawal.

I close my eyes and let myself drift away to that place in my mind where nothing matters and I no longer hurt.

———

CHASE

The stripper with her ass in my lap has been trying to get my dick hard for the past ten minutes. She keeps grinding against me, but I can't focus. I wasn't going to come tonight, but after I blew up, I had to get out of there because I knew I would hurt her if I didn't.

Everyone keeps looking at me, and I'm not sure what they're seeing except maybe someone who just doesn't want to be here. Everyone else around me is having a good time. Grayson's getting his dick sucked by a curvy redhead, and the other guys have strippers on their laps with tits in their faces.

I grab the blonde on my lap by the waist. "Get off me, sweetheart."

She pouts as she climbs off of me, but one of the other guys grabs her, and she eagerly climbs on his lap. I shake my head and make my way outside to have a smoke. Taking a drag, I lean against the building, blowing it out slowly. The look on Brylee's face when she realized who I was hit me right in the gut, and her cries after I screamed at her still echo in my ears.

What am I going to do with her? For so long all I've thought about is finally being face-to-face with her, and then I saw her and something just snapped inside me and then I snatched her. Now she's in my basement, she knows who I am—should I kill her? Should I let her go? I honestly don't think she'd rat me out. Fuck, maybe she'd go back to wherever it is she came back from.

I snuff out my cigarette, walk over, climb on my bike, and ride home.

When I pull up in front of my house, I take a deep breath. I step inside and quiet greets me. I toss my keys on the table and walk through the kitchen to the basement stairs. Slowly I walk down the stairs, and at the bottom I see that Brylee's asleep. She looks uncomfortable as fuck, but I don't do anything about it and head back upstairs.

In my bedroom, I lay down on my bed, staring up at the ceiling. Before I fall asleep, I come to the conclusion that when I wake up, I need to make a decision about what to do with Brylee and I need to make it quickly.

GRAYSON

"Where the fuck is Chase?" Loco pushes himself out from under the car he's working on and looks at me.

"He called out sick. Did you two tie one on last night at the strip club? Fuck, maybe he found himself some pussy and stayed with them all night."

Shit, maybe he was right, maybe Chase did go home with someone. I worry about my brother, he's always fucked up around his brother's birthday, but this year he's different. It's almost like he's distracted, but I don't know with what. I hope he's not using again. Sure, we all fucking dabble a little bit in coke and shit, but for a while there he was so bad I thought for sure I was going to find him dead from an OD, but luckily he got his shit together.

"I don't know. All I know is he just fucking disappeared last night. I thought he went out to smoke, but he never came back."

Loco stands up and walks over to me. "How about at lunch we can run over to his place to see if he's there? We'll make sure he's okay."

He returns to the car he was working on, and I go into the storeroom to take inventory to see what parts I need to order. While I deal with that, I can't help but worry about Chase. He's my best friend and has been forever.

I've always had his back, and he's always had mine. Losing Kyle had almost killed Chase. He loved his little brother so much. Even with five years between them, they were close.

Kyle, from the time he could crawl, would follow his brother around and Chase never cared, at least not most of the time. He was never too busy for his baby brother. When Kyle died, Chase and I had been there visiting, and he coded. They worked on him for a long time before they called it. My best friend collapsed on his brother's body while he sobbed so hard it made me start to cry too.

Even after their parents came in, no one moved Chase away from his brother, letting him get his grief out. He never cried again after that.

Things spiraled out of control pretty fast from there. We both liked to party, but he quickly took it to a whole other level. He'd disappear for days at a time, and when he showed up he always looked strung out.

I'd been so relieved when we got him to agree to treatment. I know he still smokes weed and likes his whiskey, but he doesn't touch the hard drugs anymore, or at least I hope he hasn't. Two days of odd behavior doesn't mean he's fallen off the wagon, but something is up with him.

Getting back out front, I'm just finishing up with a customer when a woman walks in with a paper clutched to her chest.

"Can I help you?"

She looks around and then back at me. "I'm looking for Chase Foster. I heard he works here."

"He's not in yet. Is there something I can help you with?"

The woman holds out the paper to me. "My daughter

Brylee is missing. I was wondering if maybe he had seen her."

I turn the paper around and stare at the picture of Brylee Whitmore, the girl who hit Kyle with her car. In high school, Chase had a thing for Brylee, but she was younger and inexperienced and he always thought she was too good for him, even though that girl watched him wherever he went. I always figured it was only a matter of time back then before the two of them got together, but fate was a cruel bitch and had other plans.

"Ma'am, I don't mean to be rude, but do you really think he's seen her?"

Her eyes fill with tears. "No, I suppose you're right. She was never the same after that day," she says almost to herself.

"When he comes in later, I'll ask him and have him call you."

She gives me a hopeful smile. "That would be wonderful. Thank you."

I have her write her number down on the back of the paper, and I wait until she's gone before I rush out to Loco.

"Loco, I think we have a problem."

SIX
CHASE

I felt bad calling out this morning, but as long as Brylee is in my basement, I can't go to work. Hopefully, they buy that I'm sick. In the kitchen, I get a pot of coffee brewing and jump in the shower. Once I'm done, I make some eggs and toast, carrying them and a cup of coffee downstairs for her.

As soon as I hit the bottom of the stairs, I immediately sense something's wrong. I turn on the overhead light and I see that she's awake, but she's staring at the wall and not moving a muscle. Squatting down in front of her, she doesn't look at or acknowledge that I'm there. "Brylee?"

She doesn't answer me, and her eyes do this weird slow blink. I reach for her wrist to check her pulse when I feel a weird ridge on her skin. Flipping it over, I see two whitish-pink vertical lines. I check the other wrist and find the same thing. My thumb strokes over the skin, and my gut clenches. The scars are old, but how old?

"Brylee, look at me." She slowly turns her head and looks at me. It's like the lights are on, but nobody's home. I snap my fingers in front of her face, and she barely acknowledges it. I grab her face and pull her toward me. "Hey, I need you to answer me."

A single tear falls, and I brush it away. She was fine before—what happened that would make her act like this?

I hear pounding on my front door. "Who the fuck is that?" I ask myself before running up the stairs. Throwing open the front door, I find Loco and Grayson standing there. They don't even say anything, Loco just pushes past me, followed by Grayson.

"What are you doing?"

Loco grabs me by the back of the neck. "What did you do with her?"

"What are you talking about? What did I do with who?" *Fuck, do they know?*

"Where the fuck is Brylee, Chase? Her mom came into the shop today looking for you. Wanting to know if you've seen her." Loco turns away and then comes back at me, pinning me to the wall. "Where the fuck is she?" he roars.

It's no use lying. I might as well tell them the truth. "She's tied up in the basement."

Grayson, followed by Loco and me, takes off toward my basement stairs. He flies down them, cursing when he hits the bottom. Loco moves toward Brylee until he and Grayson stand in front of her. "What's wrong with her?"

She doesn't even react to two strangers standing in front of her.

Grayson gets down on his haunches. "Hey, Brylee. Do you remember me? I'm Grayson, you went to school with me and my sister, Megan. She used to hang with you and Kaylee. Do you remember?"

Brylee does that slow blink and then looks at Grayson and then looks at Loco. "I'm ready." It sounds so quiet I almost missed it.

Loco leans down. "You're ready for what, sweetheart?"

Slowly turning her head, she looks at all three of us and then lowers her head. "I'm ready to die."

"We'll be right back, sweetheart," Loco says while stroking a hand down her hair in a comforting gesture. Why does a part of me want to hit him for touching her? He signals for us to follow him up the stairs.

As soon as we step into the kitchen, Loco's hand wraps around my throat, and he shoves me hard against my refrigerator. "What the fuck did you do to her? She's in your clothes, did you hurt her?"

"Fuck no, I didn't touch her. She'd messed herself and needed fresh clothes so I gave her some of mine. I don't know what's wrong with her. She was okay yesterday." I close my eyes as flashes of the day before hit me. I'd screamed at her and told her she killed my brother. "Shit, yesterday she told me she was sorry about Kyle and I told her to never say his name and that she fucking killed him." Of course it comes out as a wheeze.

Loco lets go of me and my body sags against the refrigerator. Silence surrounds us, and Grayson and Loco stare at me with the same expression—like they don't fucking know me at all. Like I'm a stranger and I fucking hate it.

Loco turns away from me. "Grayson, go untie her and carry her up here." Pointing at me, he barks, "You don't touch her. We have to figure out how to fix this without hurting that girl who has already been hurt enough. She paid for what she did. I know what she's been through. Your mother worried about her and asked me to keep tabs." Leaning in close, he whispers, "She suffers from severe depression and PTSD. All she does is work. She has no life, no friends. Don't you think she's paid enough?"

Before I can ask why he never told me any of this, Grayson steps into the living room with Brylee in his arms. I don't know whether I want to strangle her or knock him out and take her from his arm, holding her in mine.

"Sit her on the couch." Loco gets down on his haunches in front of her. Her body immediately begins to tremble. What the fuck have I done? "Brylee, my name's Loco." He laughs softly. "I know, it's a terrible name. I'm not crazy, I promise."

My stomach clenches as I watch her scratch at the scars on her wrist. Grabbing her and hurting her was supposed to be satisfying, but it's not. In fact, it's the complete fucking opposite. I move into the kitchen. Grabbing a cigarette, I place it between my lips and light it—inhaling deeply and exhaling slowly, the taste of the tobacco thick on my tongue.

Finishing my cigarette, I snuff it out, and back in the living room I find Loco still down in front of her. "Please talk to me. Sweetheart, come back to us. Chase didn't mean what he said. He was just being a dick."

She starts shaking her head wildly back and forth. "I-it's m-m-my f-fault. I-I-I k-killed h-him." Brylee pulls her knees up and hugs them to her chest. She buries her head in her knees. I can hear her whispering, but I don't know what she's saying. Loco signals Grayson over to him and whispers something in his ear.

Grayson glances at me before heading out the door. I chase after him. "Where are you going?"

He turns on me so fast, shoving me and knocking me down. "You've gone too fucking far, Chase. I love you like a brother, but this is so fucking wrong. If your purpose was to destroy her, then congratulations, because you fucking did it."

Grayson jogs to Loco's truck, climbs in, and then drives away.

Getting up off the ground, I head into the house. Loco's sitting on the other end of the couch watching Brylee. She's back to staring at nothing.

Silence fills the room as I continue to stare at her. What's going on with her? What's going on in her head right now? This is falling apart faster than I could imagine. I've always had a quick temper and make rash decisions.

Grayson returns not too long later. He walks past me and into the kitchen, returning with a bottle of water. He gets down in front of her, and that fucking trembling starts again. I stand up, but Loco shoots me a look that has me sitting back down.

"Brylee, no one is going to hurt you. I promise."

"I-I h-have to g-go to the b-bathroom." Her eyes are glassy, but she won't look any of us in the eye.

"I'll take her." I stand up and move toward her. Loco shoots up from his spot on the couch. "What?"

"Son, you're not taking her. Let Grayson do it." He looks at Brylee. "Sweetheart? He's only going with you to make sure you're safe. I'm worried about you."

She looks at the hand Grayson is holding out, then at me and then Loco. He nods at her before she grabs my brother's hand and he helps her off the couch. Stepping back to make room for them to pass by, she pauses in front of me for the briefest second. Her eyes meet mine, and all I see is pain and anguish. I do a full-body flinch and watch her walk woodenly down the hallway toward the bathroom.

I run a hand through my hair before grabbing the joint I had rolled the day before. Placing it between my lips and with a flick of my thumb, it's lit. The sweet familiar taste of my OG Kush hits my lungs. The familiar earthy, lemony scent hits my senses as I hit it again.

"Let me hit that." Loco grabs the joint from me. He blows out the smoke before hitting it again. "You always have the best weed. I wish you'd give me the fucking name of your dealer. You selfish asshole."

As I'm taking the joint from him, Grayson enters the kitchen with Brylee next to him, her arms hugging herself tight. My friend signals for me to hand it over, and I do.

"Brylee, I want you to hit this, okay? Just a couple of puffs, and then you can lie down." Grayson sounds like he's talking to a child, but at least she's acknowledging him. He sticks it between her lips, and she sucks on it until she starts to cough. I move toward her, but Loco stops me with a hand on my shoulder. Grayson puts it between her lips one more time.

It's the same thing again, She takes a huge drag of it and coughs. I watch her, and the moment it kicks in, I can tell because her eyes become heavy-lidded and she looks at us with a dopey look and half-grin that, if I wasn't so freaked out, I might find it endearing.

Grayson hands Loco the joint and starts leading her out of the kitchen. Following close behind them, he tells her he's putting her to bed. My stomach clenches at her whispered words.

"If-if you're going to rape me, I-I'm a v-virgin."

Grayson's body locks up tight. He turns her to face him and leans down in her face. "No one is going to touch you."

Brylee tilts her head to the side and stares at him before turning and looking at me. "It's okay. I'm ready to die. I promise not to fight you."

I'm frozen as she turns back and follows Grayson into my room.

"You need to fix this before you return her to her home. That girl is one step away from finishing what she started all those years ago. If you can't fix it, then I will." His grip is punishing on the back of my neck.

I want to shove him off of me, but I don't dare. He's showing a softer side of himself with Brylee, but I know he can be a mean motherfucker in the blink of an eye.

"I'll make it right, I promise." I mean it. This was a mistake—I should've never followed her that day. *Her phone.* "She had a phone with her the day I grabbed her. It'll be by Kyle's headstone."

"Jesus fucking Christ! I'll go and bring it back here. You text her parents and make up some lie about her. We don't need them calling the police, or fuck, maybe they already have. If we have to have her call them, we will. I love you like a son, but I want to strangle you right now. You need to get your shit together."

I watch his retreating back as he disappears down the hall into my bedroom. Following behind, I stand outside the door listening to Loco talking to Brylee. "Did you take the pill Grayson gave you?"

"Y-yes." Her voice is sleepy and sluggish.

"Good. That's gonna help you relax and get some sleep. Don't worry, you're safe, okay?" His voice is paternal-sounding, firm, but soft and soothing. "Either Grayson or I will be here. He's not going to hurt you."

"B-but I-I deserve i-it. I'm a h-horrible p-person." I listen as she begins to cry, my heart breaking for her.

Where is all the hate I feel for her? It has to still be there. Nothing has changed since I grabbed her. Kyle is dead because she hit him with her car. *It was an accident*, my mom's voice echoes in my head. *She was just an innocent sixteen-year-old who made a mistake that she'll have to live with for the rest of her life.*

Up until now, I've never asked my mom why she forgave Brylee, but maybe I ought to now. Loco and Grayson step out of the room, and the three of us make our way toward the living room.

"She's asleep, and when I say asleep, I mean you could scream into her ear and she probably wouldn't budge. Grayson is going to stay with her. I'll drop her phone off if I find it before heading back to the shop. Chase, I want you at work within the hour." He stomps out of the house, and I follow him out.

"What do you mean you want me to go to work? Shouldn't I stay here and help fix things?"

Freezing, he turns around and moves toward me. "She needs sleep, and since Grayson is here, I'm a man down at the shop. Plus, you need to remove yourself from this place while you think about what you've done and how you're going to make that right."

Loco hops in his truck and leaves, and I head inside to shower and apparently get ready for work. After I hop out, I step into my bedroom, followed by Grayson, so I can get my clothes. Brylee is fast asleep on my mattress, her soft snores filling my room. I watch her and wonder if I could ever forgive her, and the answer is that I don't know if I can.

I look at my brother, my best friend. "I'm not going to hurt her."

"Yeah, well, excuse me for having a hard time believing you. You know, seeing as you kidnapped her and all." You're not friends with someone for twenty years without fighting every so often, but he's super fucking pissed right now.

"I told you that I fucking regret it. What else do you want me to do?"

"I want you to fucking fix this because I'm afraid to leave this poor girl alone. Yes, she's the reason Kyle isn't here anymore, but it was an accident—"

I get in his face. "Shut the fuck up, Grayson. I said I would fix it and I meant it." I storm past him and am putting my boots on when Loco comes in.

"I found her phone, it was lying face down next to Kyle's tombstone. It's dead, but her phone is like yours, so we can plug it in and charge it." I follow him into my kitchen, and he plugs it in before turning it on. I expect him to say it's locked so we can't get into it, but it's not. "She's got a ton of missed calls and texts from her mom and dad."

Loco tells Grayson that he'll text him later with what to say to her parents via text message, and then he leaves.

"I'll be back later. Call me if you need me," I tell Grayson, but all he does is shoot me a pissed-off look. *Whatever*, I don't have time to deal with this shit.

SEVEN
BRYLEE

My eyes flicker open. Where am I? Lifting my head off the pillow, I look around and see I'm in a bedroom. I'm in Chase's bedroom, and the past few days come back to me, and my stomach turns and I curl in on myself. It appears to be dark, maybe nighttime or early morning, but silence fills the house.

Whatever they had given me knocked me out, but I was thankful for it because then I couldn't think of what was going to happen to me.

I hug the pillow to my chest. The day before, or whenever it was, I could hear them talking about me. They wanted Chase to fix whatever was wrong with me.

Don't they know that there is nothing left to fix? Oh well, he can try, and I know it's only because he feels guilty and not because he really wants to.

I have to pee, but I can't seem to make myself get up. My body feels like it's full of lead. Rolling to my back, I stare at the ceiling. My whole body hurts, but sometimes that happens, and I'm sure spending two days tied to a chair didn't help either.

It takes all of my might to push myself into a sitting position. Once the cobwebs clear, at least enough to get up, I push myself onto all fours and slowly crawl off the mattress. I move into the hallway and see the flicker of the TV coming from the living room. On wobbly legs, I make my way into the bathroom. After using the toilet, I wash my hands and then splash cold water on my face.

Back in the hallway, I slowly make my way toward the living room. Grayson is asleep on the floor and Chase is on the couch. His eyes open as I step into the room. My whole body locks up tight, and my heart beats wildly in my chest. He slowly gets up from the couch and moves toward me with his hands up in a surrendering motion.

"I'm not going to hurt you."

Oh, but little does he know that I'm perfectly capable of hurting myself so much worse than he ever could. If he'd just kill me, he'd be doing me a favor. He could end my pain, and then I wouldn't have to do it myself.

He takes small, careful steps toward me. My mind is screaming at me to run, but I'm frozen. Once he's right in front of me, my eyes flutter closed, then open. He's just as beautiful now as he was back in high school. The signs of age or stress look really good on him. His eyes are as hypnotizing as they used to be. Chase smells like motor oil, or what I suspect motor oil smells like.

"Are you hungry? You've been asleep for a day and a half."

My stomach growls loudly, and he chuckles softly but quickly covers it up with a cough. "Come on, I'll make you a sandwich." He has me walk with him into the kitchen and makes me another bologna sandwich.

I take a bite and have to choke it down. I'm hungry,

but I can't taste it, and it feels like sandpaper going down my throat. I can only manage one more bite, it hurts too much.

"You need to eat." He pushes the sandwich back toward me.

Shaking my head, I whisper, "I can't."

He sighs. "Fine. Do you need anything?"

"Why do y-you care? T-this is what you wanted, right?" I wrap my arms around myself. "Can I go lay back down now?"

I don't wait for him to answer. I just turn around and walk back to his room, shut the door, and collapse on his bed.

I try closing my eyes and clearing my head, but every time I close my eyes I can see Kyle slamming into the windshield and Chase's words screaming in my ear, but not because they were mean but because they were true.

Tears begin to roll down my cheeks, and I place my hands over my ears, praying for Chase's words to stop replaying in my head. Over and over they taunt me, and each time they break my heart. Hell, I don't think I have much of a heart left to break as it is.

"Please stop. I'm so sorry," I whisper quietly as I cry.

I'm not sure how long I cry for, but when I seem to run out of tears, I wipe my face off and come to a decision and a plan that I should have executed a long time ago. Easing off the mattress, I move to his dresser and can barely see, but I feel around until I find what I'm looking for.

On silent feet, I make my way toward his closet. Easing it open, I grab onto the closet rod and pull on it. It seems sturdy enough, and hopefully, it'll support my weight. I loop the belt around it, and I move to stick my head through the hole I made when the light flips on, causing me to stumble and fall into the closet.

I look up, and Chase and Grayson are staring at me. I can't help it when I begin to sob, and we're not talking about quiet little sobs, we're talking loud and ugly sobs. My body shakes violently as I curl up in the bottom of his closet. "Just let me die. That's what you want." My voice cracks. "It should've been me!" I ball my fingers into fists, my nails biting into the flesh. "It hurts every day. I'm alive and he's not."

I feel myself being lifted into strong arms. I begin kicking, slapping, and thrashing about, and it doesn't last long because I'm just too fucking tired to fight anymore. Something is pushed between my lips, and then water is poured into my mouth. I swallow but then sputter and cough, spraying water everywhere.

A hand strokes my hair as my sobs turn to cries. In no time, my head starts to feel heavy and like it's full of cotton. My eyelids feel heavy, and then my limbs feel like lead. Sleep is coming, and I welcome it.

CHASE

The moment Brylee falls asleep, I let out a heavy breath. Earlier I had sat outside my room and listened to her as she cried. I've never been more conflicted in my life. I had to stop myself from going to her and telling her it was going to be okay. When her cries stopped, I had thought she'd fallen asleep until I heard her moving around.

Grayson joined me as we stood outside my closed

door and listened to the unmistakable sound of my closet being opened and then the sound of a belt jingling. I looked at Grayson, and with a sigh, I opened the door and threw the light on and watched as she tumbled into the closet. We moved into the open door. She looked up at us and began to cry and they sounded painful.

"Grab her, and I'll get her another pill." Grayson steps back as I maneuver picking her up and carrying her in my arms to the living room.

With her in my arms, I sit down on the couch. She continues to cry even when Grayson sticks a pill between her lips. We manage to get some water in her mouth to swallow it, but then she starts coughing and spitting water everywhere.

My hand strokes her hair in slow caresses. It doesn't take long before her cries finally quiet, and I know the exact moment that she falls asleep because her body goes limp in my arms.

"I think she's finally out."

He looks at her. "Yeah, I thought so. Fuck, man, she was really going to do it. Seriously, Chase, what the fuck happened?"

"I told you. I know I've fucked up. I'm going to fix this, I promise. She's tried to kill herself before." I tilt my head toward her arms, and he moves close, grabbing her hands. "Flip them over."

Grayson looks at them and then back at me. "Fuck, man, she tried twice." I watch his thumbs stroke over the scars.

There is a tiny part of me that really wants to punch him for touching Brylee so intimately. I don't understand the feeling that swirls around in my belly. I try to ignore it, but instead, I hold her more tightly to my body. Her breath hits my neck in heated puffs of air. Slowly I rock her back and forth after she curls up tighter against me.

Why does holding her feel right? No, fuck no, it doesn't feel right.

"Take her from me," I bark loudly. Standing up with her in my arms, I pass her over to Grayson and storm out of my house, climb on my bike, and ride.

I ride and ride until I reach country roads and hit the throttle. The sun isn't rising yet, but in the distance, the black night is turning a deep purple hue. It won't be long before the sun rises on the horizon. I can't believe I fucking comforted her, that I tried to make her feel better. Pulling over to the side of the road, I tip my head back and let out a primal scream. "Fuck you, Brylee!"

Climbing off my bike, I grab rocks off the side of the road and start hurling them. I do it in no particular direction, I just throw them, one after the other. "Fucking bitch! I fucking hate you!" Why was she making me feel anything but hate for her? She ruined my life, she fucking destroyed my family.

You know that's not true, my sweet boy—it was an accident. My mom's voice sounds in my head. Covering my ears, I scream, "I don't want to hear it."

I cup my hands on the back of my neck and walk down the road and then back. We should've let her finish hanging herself in my closet. She could've ended all of our pain.

No, I don't fucking mean it. Why? She's got my head all fucked up. I know what I need—I need to go talk to my mom. Pulling my cell phone from my pocket, I look at the time. It's only five in the morning, but she's an early riser. I'll grab some donuts or muffins on my way. I turn my bike around and head back into town.

———

Climbing off my bike in front of my mom's, I grab the pastry bag out of my storage compartment under my seat. I make my way up the walk, and before I can ring the bell, she opens it, smiling widely. "Well, if this isn't the best surprise. Come on in, baby boy, the coffee is brewing."

I follow her into the house and into the kitchen. She takes the bag from me and places it on the counter. While she places muffins on a plate, I grab a couple of mugs and fill them with coffee. We sit at the table, and I can't get anything past my mom.

"You look tired, baby. What's going on?"

"Why did you forgive Brylee?"

She freezes with her cup halfway to her mouth. Setting her cup down she looks closely at me. What can she see?

"Are you the reason her parents have been looking for her? Please tell me you didn't hurt her." Her eyes are glassy, and I know she's ready to cry.

Holding my hands up, I shake my head. "Please, you need to listen to me, okay?" She nods. "The day of Kyle's birthday I had been at the clubhouse, but I wasn't feeling it, so I decided to just go home. Well, I was driving along the road when I saw a girl running, and I saw it was her. I ended up turning around and following her. She ran into the cemetery, and I knew where she was going. She was standing in front of his tombstone and she was crying. I had only meant to tell her off, to finally say all of the things I wanted to.

"Instead, I grabbed her, but she fought me and got away. I tackled her, and she hit her head. I threw her into my truck and took her home. I tied her up in the basement and left her there in the dark. I never touched her, I promise. The day before yesterday I helped her get cleaned up, and then she finally realized who I was and she freaked out. She became hysterical, and when she tried to tell me she was sorry, I screamed at her and told her she killed my brother—"

"Oh, Chase, I-I can't listen to any more of this. Where is she now?"

I hang my head in shame because my mom looks so hurt and so unhappy with me. "She's probably sleeping in my room. Grayson is there watching over her. He gave her something that would make her sleepy."

She stands up. "I want to see her. I'm going to see for myself that she's there and that she's okay." I stand up too, and she comes around to stand right in front of me, cupping my cheek with her palm. "I know you think you were doing the right thing, but my sweet boy, what you've done is so wrong. If the police find out, you will go to jail for kidnapping. Ugh…I want to hug you, but I want to smack you upside the head too."

Letting me go, she grabs her purse and her keys. I follow her outside and watch as she climbs into her car and then backs out of her driveway. Following behind her, I have no idea what to expect when we reach my place.

Jumping off my bike, I meet her at the front door. Before I can open the door, Grayson throws it open and gives me a dirty look before looking at my mom with a wide-eyed expression. "Hey, Ma. What're you doing here?"

She pushes past him and disappears down the hall.

He turns back to me. "What the fuck?" he whispers harshly.

"I went to talk to her this morning, and she knew something was up. You know her, we've never been able to get anything past her. She wanted to see for herself that Brylee was okay. Is she still sleeping?"

"Yeah, I sat in the corner of your room and kept an eye on her. She was sleeping deeply, so hopefully, she's still asleep. I sent her parents a text this morning basically saying that she was having a rough time and was sorry that she hadn't texted them sooner because she knew she worried them. She said that she'd call them later. Hopefully they fucking bought it."

"Listen, I'm sorry I left like I did, but she's got my head all screwed up. All I've wanted was to have some payback, but now that she's here—fuck, man, I just don't know anymore."

I sit down on the couch, blowing out a breath. My eyes stay locked on the hallway as I wait for my mom to reemerge.

Grayson sits down on the other end. "Loco says he'll be over this afternoon. If she's up, he wants to talk to her."

"Why?"

"I don't know. My guess is he wants to know where her head's at and if she plans on going to the police. I think he wants to be prepared for whatever happens when we let her go."

All I can do is nod. Fuck, I don't want to go back to jail. When I was at my lowest, I'd gotten busted with blow. Luckily it was a small amount or I would've been locked up longer. It was after Loco bailed me out that I worked on getting clean, or getting off the hard stuff, I should say.

We both sit in silence as we wait for my ma to come out of my bedroom. I don't want to go back to jail, but if that's my fate, then I'll accept it.

My bedroom door opens, and my mom comes out into the hall. She doesn't come to us. Instead, she leans against the wall and stares at the ground. *Fuck*, I hate when my ma gets all silent and contemplative. She was like that a lot after Kyle died and then again when my dad split. Ma shakes off whatever has her quiet and comes out into the living room.

"Chase, I swear to God if you don't fix this, I will kick your ass! All I had to do was step in your room and could feel her sadness thick in the air. You will fix this, you will fix her, and I don't care how you do it. You've got to let that anger go, son. You asked me how I could forgive her. I forgave her because the day I went to see her, I was unsure of how I felt, but then I got a real good look at her and I realized that whatever punishment they gave her—whatever hurtful words I could spew—well, it wasn't nearly as bad as whatever was going through that poor girl's head.

"It was a terrible mistake, honey. A mistake she's going to live with for the rest of her life. Isn't that punishment enough? We can't change what happened, and no amount of hate or payback is going to bring Kyle back to us. I know it's not healthy that I make you cele-brate his birthday every year, but it's more to keep his memory alive because I don't want to forget a moment of joy that he brought into our lives. If you can open your heart and forgive her, then maybe she'll start to forgive herself."

She hugs Grayson and then me before leaving.

"Your ma is a smart woman," Grayson says, and I nod because it's true. "You didn't sleep much last night. Why don't you take a nap? I'll stay until Loco gets here or you get up."

Moving to the recliner, I flop down and then pull on the lever until the footrest comes up. I push back on it until I'm lying down and promptly shut my eyes.

EIGHT
BRYLEE

My eyes open slowly, but slowly because they feel like they weigh a hundred pounds. My mind is foggy, and it takes a second to clear the cobwebs. Kidnapped, Kyle, Chase, tied up. It all comes back to me—even whichever day it was that they caught me trying to hang myself in his closet.

I don't understand why Chase tried to stop me because isn't this what he wanted—me dead and gone as payback for his brother? Curling into a ball, I feel whatever energy I had when I opened my eyes deplete, and it's not long before I fall back to sleep.

"Brylee? Wake up, darlin'." My eyes fly open, and the huge Native American man is standing in the doorway. I sit up and shrink against the wall. "Hey, no reason to be scared, I'm just here to check on you, and I wanted to have the chance to talk. I promise that's all we're doing."

There is something about those dark, piercing eyes of his that makes me believe what he's saying. Nodding my head slowly, I grab the blanket and pull it up and over my body. My mind is still fuzzy, but it'll clear eventually.

"Can I bring you something to eat, something to drink? You've slept a lot the last couple of days."

"I-I'm not hungry, but I'd love some coffee." Maybe once he's out of the room, I can climb out the window.

"Okay, come with me, and I'll make some." There's a twinkle in his eyes, almost like he is fully aware that I was going to make a run for it.

Crawling off the bed, I stand up on wobbly legs and slowly follow him out of the room. "I have to go to the bathroom." He nods and leads me to the bathroom. I close the door behind me, and after I pee, I wash my hands. When I look at myself in the mirror, I can't help but cringe. The ever-present dark circles are super dark, which tends to happen if I sleep a lot. I grab Chase's comb and work it through my brown rat's nest.

When I'm finished, I rub some of his toothpaste on my teeth and my tongue before rinsing my mouth. I reach for the doorknob and open the door. I believe his name is Loco—he's typing away on his cell phone, but he stops when I step into the hall. Following him down the hallway, I see that the back of his T-shirt says Jackals Motorcycle Club Est. 1968. *We live to ride and ride to live.*

They're bikers—does that mean they're dangerous? Does that mean for sure I'm going to die? I just don't want it to hurt. Maybe they'll make it quick and painless. I don't understand why they haven't done anything yet. I keep waiting and waiting, but nothing. I'm ready for it to end, though—ready for all the pain I feel to end. My parents will be okay, I've been almost nonexistent to them for a long time now.

Do they know I'm missing? Are the police looking

for me? I'm pulled from my thoughts when I reach the living room and find both Chase and Grayson standing there, watching me closely. My eyes shift to stare at the floor, avoiding eye contact with them. What do they see when they look at me? A murderer, because that's all I see.

I hustle until I'm standing next to Loco, putting him in between Chase and me.

"No one is going to hurt you."

His words cause me to jump.

He curses under his breath. "Come sit."

A minute later a cup of coffee is set in front of me. Reaching out to grab it, my arm feels like it's filled with lead. I bring the cup to my nose and breathe in that familiar scent. Taking a tiny sip, the strong nutty flavor hits my tongue. I swallow it down and it hits my stomach like a handful of nails. Ignoring the pain, I take another sip. I can hear them talking quietly in the living room. Chase's voice can be heard saying, "killed herself. I don't know."

I haven't had my meds since the day Chase grabbed me. Between whatever they gave me and the lack of my meds, I feel heaviness in my body. I pick my feet up until they're resting on my seat. Wrapping my arms around my legs, I rest my forehead on my knees. I should never have come home. What am I saying? This hasn't been home in a long time.

In Chicago, it's easy to blend in and fade into the background. At work I pretend I'm normal, smiling and talking to the customers and then going home where I can be alone. My coworkers used to try to get me to go out with them, but you can only tell people no for so long before they stop asking you to go out and eventually stop talking to you at all. I've heard them talk about me. Saying I was weird and I probably had an apartment full of cats.

No, I'm not the cat lady. That would require taking care of something, and I can barely take care of myself. Oh, I'm not incompetent or anything. I mean, I go to the doctor and take my meds as prescribed, but I can't let myself feel any sort of joy. That's why I have no friends, and anyone I was friends with when I was younger is ancient history. Most of them scattered in the wind after I killed Kyle.

My stomach knots up, and I feel like I have a lump in my chest, which is normal when I think about that day and everything that happened that first year. Kaylee tried to reach out after the second time I tried to kill myself, but I wouldn't take her calls and sent her letters back. She eventually gave up, and a part of my heart shriveled up and died.

Last I heard, she was married and pregnant with her first baby. My eyes burn, but I blink it away. When we were younger, we made grand plans to be each other's maids of honor—to be godmothers and official aunties to each other's babies. Instead, I'll die a lonely sad sack.

Lifting my head, I grab the coffee mug, bringing it to my lips. It's a little bit cooler now, and I swallow several large gulps. At least it's warming the chill that seems to always be there right under the surface of my skin.

I hear footsteps, several of them, as they enter the kitchen. Setting the cup down again, I wrap my arms around my legs, burying my face in my knees. The sound of chairs scraping the floor signals that they're sitting down. Why?

"Brylee, look at me." It's Chase who's speaking. "Please."

Why does that one word make me lift my head and look at him? It hurts to look at him, knowing what I ripped away from him. My eyes begin to burn, but I rapidly blink until it stops. For a moment, I swear his eyes soften, but I know I was just seeing things because it's not there now. More than likely I was just imagining it.

"I know what I did was wrong, and I'm sorry. When we take you back to your parents' house, are you going to call the cops and turn me in? Nothing will happen to you, no matter what the answer is. I just want to be prepared if the cops show up and arrest me." He leans on his forearms on the beat-up table.

I shake my head. There's no way I'd turn him in, this is entirely my fault. If I hadn't hit his brother, he wouldn't be filled with grief and pushed to do something so tragic. "I won't say anything." My voice is muffled by my knees.

"If we take you back to your parents, you're not going to try and hurt yourself, are you?" Loco says.

My eyes drift to his face. He looks like he's maybe forty. Crow's feet line his eyes, giving him a harder look. He reaches out, grabbing my hand, and flips it over. His thumb strokes the scars on my wrist. I try to yank it away from him, but his grip is strong. "Please let me go."

"Why did you do it?" he asks. I hear Chase tell Loco to stop. Tears well up in my eyes. "Why, sweetheart?"

Something snaps in my brain. I yank my hand out of his grip, and in the process fly up from my chair, knocking it to the ground. "You want to know? I'll fucking tell you!

Every day and every night I fell asleep and woke up to the sound of Kyle hitting my windshield. Every time I closed my eyes, I saw them load his broken body onto that ambulance. I just wanted it to stop. I wanted to die. They should've locked me up and thrown away the key."

They're all standing up looking at me with the same look on their faces. I look at Chase. "If I could've swapped places with him, I would've. Every day I prayed that God would take me and bring Kyle back to you—I did." My voice cracks. "I just want to go back to Chicago, back to my boring, lonely life because that is my punishment for what I did." Grayson and Loco approach me from opposite sides.

I grab the chair, holding it up so the legs are facing out. My heart beats rapidly in my chest as tears drip from my chin. "Sweetheart, put the chair down."

"No! You don't get to tell me what to do." I look at Chase. "You should've killed me," I cry and throw the chair at Loco as he comes after me. On quick feet, I turn and run into the living room. Arms band around me, lifting me off the ground. "No!" I kick, flail, and fight violently, but whoever is holding me is too strong. I keep swinging my arms and kicking my legs. Throwing my head back, I try to hit them, but don't.

My energy seems to deplete quickly, probably because I've hardly eaten. I'm not sure how much time passes, but I finally collapse in the arms of who I'm assuming is Grayson. A whimper slips past my lips when I feel myself being transferred to someone else's arms. I try to fight, but all the fight in me is gone.

I'm laid down on the mattress, but this time someone follows me down—pulling me into their arms. An earthy, woodsy scent surrounds me. and a hand strokes my hair until I feel my eyes drift shut.

———

CHASE

I feel it the moment she falls asleep. Her body is wrapped around mine like a spider monkey, and her weight settles on me. Puffs of her breath hit me in the neck—it smells like coffee and sadness.

Brylee completely shattered in front of us earlier, and I should've been happy. I should've enjoyed every second of her pain, but instead, it created an ache in my chest. The loneliness, despair, and guilt came off of her in waves, and the whole time I kept waiting for the joy to come, but instead, I had to keep my legs locked to keep from going to her.

For ten years she's literally tortured herself because of what happened. I'm surprised she didn't try to kill herself again before now—before I brought all the pain back to her and threw what happened into her face.

I've been a shitty person over the years—I've hurt people intentionally. I've used people and discarded them like they were trash, but this is by far the worst thing I've ever done. What's sad is over the years I couldn't wait for the moment to come to destroy Brylee, for destroying my family, but my ma is right. It was an accident—a terrible fucking accident, and she's punished herself enough for a lifetime.

I untangle myself from her when I find Loco standing in the doorway. As soon as I stand up and turn, looking back at her, she immediately curls into a small ball, hugging her knees to her chest. Keeping my eyes on her, I slowly back out of my room.

Loco stands in front of me with his arms crossed over his chest. I've always loved and respected him, but I'm fucking pissed. I shove him hard against the wall. "What the fuck was that? Why would you make her talk about it?"

His hand wraps around my throat, pulling me until our bodies are almost touching. "I'm gonna let that slide because these past few days haven't been fucking easy on you, but this is not on me. You're the motherfucker who kidnapped her and kept her in your basement for two fucking days tied to a chair. I'm sorry that she got upset, but I wanted you to hear it from her lips. Don't you see? Don't you get it? That girl might as well be a ghost. What kind of life do you think she has?"

I don't answer him. I just stomp down the hall and into the kitchen. I grab Brylee's cell phone and turn it on. There's a text from her mom.

Mom

I'm sorry you're having a rough time, but to disappear like this is unacceptable. We thought something happened to you. I even went to see that boy to see if he had seen you. Your father is sick, and he has been so worried about you, and so have I. Sweetheart, what do we have to do to fix you? I know we haven't handled all of this very well, but you used to be so full of life and had a smile for everyone, and now I'm constantly terrified that you're going to leave us forever. Tell me how to help you—tell us what to do. Please let me know you're okay.

Something hits the back of my hand, and I realize it's a tear. Fuck, why does this make me so sad? Forever, all I've felt is hate toward her and now…and now I don't know what I feel. It's similar to what I felt when I saw her for the first time. I'd been a junior and she was a freshman.

"Chase!"

I turn as my best friend Grayson comes jogging down the hall toward me. Today is the first day of our junior year. I'm ready to be done, but I do have it pretty fucking sweet. I'm quarterback for the varsity football team and shortstop for our baseball team. My grades are okay, and thanks to my athletics, I should get into a decent college.

I've had girls hanging off my dick for as long as I can remember. I know I'm good, and I know they love my huge dick and my long tongue, and no I'm not talking Gene Simmons long, but it's long. I see one of my latest hookups, Marley, standing by my locker with her girl posse.

"She is so fucking hot," Grayson says from next to me. He's never had a problem getting the girls either. "Oh, there's my sister and her friends."

I've always looked after Megan for Grayson. She's a good kid, and I help him keep the little shits away from her. Kyle's always had a little crush on her. I scan her friends when a pair of ice-blue eyes meets mine. My eyes rake over her, she's got her brown hair pulled back into a low ponytail and no makeup on her face.

Her cheeks turn the most adorable shade of pink, but before I move toward her, I remind myself that if she's with Megan and her posse, then she's a freshman, which means she's young…too young for me. I turn away from her and move toward Marley, shoving my tongue down her throat. I feel the mystery girl's eyes on me the whole time, and an ache fills my gut.

It was when my senior and her sophomore year started that I noticed she started doing her hair and wearing makeup, but I still thought she was beautiful without it. Ignoring her my entire junior year had been more difficult than I had imagined. I'd fucked so many girls that year trying to get the willowy freshman off of my mind.

I shake these thoughts away and read her mom's text again.

> **Brylee**
> I'm okay. I promise.

I tap the message out and hit send and set her phone back down.

"Did her mom text her back?" I turn to Grayson and nod. I hand him Brylee's phone, and he looks at it, shaking his head. He hands it back to me. "I've got to get out of here." My best friend in the whole world stomps out of the front door. The sound of his bike starting can be heard through the screen door and slowly disappears as he rides down the street.

Loco crosses his arms over his chest. "Your mom is going to come by later to talk to her before she takes Brylee back to her parents. I don't know if her parents will, but the cops may show up here considering she's got that small cut on her head and rope burn on her wrists. Get rid of all the rope and get that chair out of the basement. If you have any scented candles or spray, you may want to use them downstairs. You don't want any sign that you kept her here against her will."

I nod my head and follow him toward the door. "I'll make sure it's clean." I look down and then at him. "Fuck, man, I'm sorry about earlier. This has me all fucked up. She has me all fucked up."

He grabs me by the shoulder. "Don't worry about it. After she's gone, come to the clubhouse. Tie one on and get your dick wet and just fucking chill tonight. I'll get one of the prospects to keep an eye on her for you. I expect you to be at work tomorrow at noon. Got me?"

"Yeah, I got you."

He gives me a chin lift. "Good. Your ma will be here at four. I expect you at the clubhouse no later than four thirty." Loco pulls me in for a back-slapping hug and then lets me go.

After the man rides away, I close the front door. I grab Brylee's phone off of the counter and sit in my chair. I need to know if she lied about any of the stuff she told us. First I search for any social media apps. I find Facebook, and when I open it, I see she doesn't have a profile picture, any info, or any friends. The search icon on the top beckons me. I see she's searched for her best friend from school, Kaylee, and Grayson's sister, Megan.

She also happened to search for me...interesting. Next, I click on the picture icon, and there are none, no pictures, no screenshots...nothing. Pulling up her contacts, she's only got three: her mom, dad, and someone named Roberta.

Brylee wasn't lying, she has no one. In high school, anytime I saw her, she was always surrounded by friends. Her smile could thaw the coldest heart, but I refused to go there and pursue her until she was at least sixteen, for obvious reasons that never happened.

My ma arrives right at four o'clock. She doesn't bother knocking, she just walks right in. "Hey, Ma."

"Hey, honey. I stopped and picked up a couple of things for Brylee. It's just a pair of jogging shorts and a tank top. There is also a pair of flip-flops too." She holds up a plastic bag with the familiar red bull's-eye on it. "Is she up?"

"I don't know." My mom disappears down the hallway and steps into my room.

On silent feet, I move down the hall and toward my room. In the doorway, I stand watching the scene in front of me. Brylee has her head buried in my pillow, but the way her body moves and jerks, I know she's crying. My mom is rubbing small circles on her back, talking to her in hushed tones. She turns and looks at me—her eyes filled with unshed tears. Ma turns back to Brylee and continues rubbing her back.

In the kitchen, I grab my hitter and my weed and take it out back. I load it and bring it to my lips, lighting then inhaling the sweet, smoky flavor and then slowly blowing it out. Loading another I light and inhale it before slowly blowing out. This stuff gives me a helluva body buzz and makes me feel completely chill, even if on the inside I don't really feel that way.

I head back inside and back down the hall, but I can't see what's going on since the door is shut. In the bathroom, I brush my teeth and splash cold water on my face. After slapping on some deodorant, I head back out to the living room.

It feels like forever before the door opens, and then my ma and Brylee enter the living room. I don't want to admit that my body reacts to seeing her in the tiny pair of shorts, tank top that shows off her small, pert tits, and flip-flops. Fuck, her legs are long, and images assail me of those very legs wrapped around me while I pounded into her relentlessly. I shake off the thoughts running through my head.

My ma has her arm wrapped around Brylee's waist. "I'm going to take Miss Brylee home." Brylee's eyes meet mine—there's a hollowness in them that leaves me feeling uneasy. She's slightly pale, causing the dark circles under her eyes to stand out in a stark contrast. Her brown hair is in a loose braid that hangs over her shoulder, and again my body reacts.

She breaks eye contact first, staring down at the floor. Brylee is tall, at least five foot nine, but next to my mom, who is a shorty, she seems so small. "Yeah, okay." My mom nods before leading her outside.

In the doorway I watch her as she gently helps Brylee into the car, even buckling her in and then getting in on her side. My ma backs out of the driveway, and just like that she's gone.

NINE
CHASE

My eyes open, and a groan slips past my dry lips. I push myself up and look around. Apparently, last night I passed out on the sofa in the middle of the clubhouse. I'm alone and fully clothed, thank God. I know Loco wanted me to get my dick wet, but the thought of fucking some random bitch didn't sound appealing at all.

Stumbling down the hall, I make it to the bathroom to take a piss and splash cold water on my face. That helps the cobwebs start to clear.

When I got to the clubhouse, the party was already in full swing. Loco was in his usual spot in the corner, running a poker game, and his girl Tiffany was perched in his lap. They've been together twenty-two years, and he's actually happy with her. Even with all the pussy thrown in his face, he never partakes. Well, I won't say never—Tiffany swings both ways, and sometimes she brings a third to their bed, but it's mostly for her, not Loco.

His oldest son, Elan, isn't a member of the club, but when he's home from California, where he lives and works, his dad gets his old bike out and he'll ride with us. He was there along with his baby brother Zeke. Drinks had been flowing, and everyone was having a good time.

A couple of girls made it known that they were up for some play with me, but I just ignored them and sat hanging with my brothers. I needed it more than they could've possibly known. I'm not sure if Grayson or Loco told them what I did, but if they had, no one treated me any different. We're a brotherhood first and foremost, and I know they'd have my back always, just like I'd always have theirs.

The last thing I remember is playing a fucking game of quarters like a bunch of high schoolers. Obviously I fucking lost.

Back in the hall, I make my way back to the main part of the clubhouse and start a pot of coffee. While that's brewing, I quickly roll myself a joint and light it. Nothing cures a hangover faster than a little wake-and-bake and coffee.

I'm just pouring a cup when the front door bangs open and Loco, Tiffany, and Zeke come in carrying boxes, which I can only hope are donuts.

Tiffany drops hers right in front of me. "We got your favorite." I open the lid to see a dozen glazed donuts.

Standing up, I wrap my arms around her. "I'm stealing you away from this asshole." I look right at Loco, who just shakes his head.

"Oh, honey, you couldn't handle all this." She kisses my cheek and then takes the rest of the donuts, setting them up on the counter. Her asshole old man laughs before pulling her into his arms.

You'd never know that they aren't married, but their relationship works. In the beginning, Loco was kind of a prick and screwed around on her. Tiffany had gotten fed up and took Elan and split, moving in with her sister. That was the wake-up call he needed because after that he went after them and didn't come back until they were with him. They've been inseparable ever since, and if he cheated now, she'd rip his balls off.

After my fourth donut and second cup of coffee, I feel semi-normal. Grayson came stumbling out a little while ago with a sexy little redhead who didn't even acknowledge him as she walked by us and out the door. I vaguely remember her from last night. She'd come with one of the hangarounds. She had seemed uncomfortable at first—I'll have to get that story from Grayson when he doesn't look like he's going to bite someone's head off.

I'm climbing on my bike to leave when I hear Loco holler my name. "What's up?"

"I had Zeke and Kev keep an eye on Brylee last night. Zeke said that he could see her through the window and that she was lying on the couch with her head on her mom's lap most of the night."

I can only nod because what else can I say except, "Thanks."

Taking the long way home, I let the wind blow through my hair. I ride and ride and ride until I feel myself completely relax. Parking my bike in the drive-way, I step inside and make my way into my bedroom and collapse on my bed.

Burying my nose in my pillow, I can smell her all over it. My dick gets hard, and this time I don't stop myself from doing anything about it. I pull off my T-shirt, unbutton my jeans, and pull them off. I wrap my hand around my cock, stroking it as I imagine sliding into

Brylee's tight, virgin pussy. I don't know for sure if she's a virgin, even though she told Grayson she was.

It doesn't take long before that familiar tingle starts at the base of my spine. I close my eyes and imagine what she'd look like when she comes, and I explode all over my hand and my stomach. As I clean myself off, I get disgusted with myself. I had no business jerking off thinking about her.

Needing to clear my head, I decide to go out to the garage and work on the bike I started rebuilding a few weeks ago. I throw on my goggles and start sanding down the frame so I can get it ready for painting. I've decided to do the bike in a black matte finish with a red flame design on the front and back fenders and the gas tank.

When I plugged in my design to my computer program when I had the idea, it looked badass and almost sinister. This will definitely get me some ka-ching when I sell it. Loco wants me to do this full time, but this is my hobby, my passion—I'm afraid that if I did it full time, I'd start to hate it or dread it.

Shit, sometimes I won't work on a bike for over a month, and sometimes I'll rebuild two at a time.

Once I'm done sanding it, I wipe it down and then apply a thin layer of body filler. I leave it to dry and head inside to shower. When I step out of the shower, I step into my room, throwing on a pair of old basketball shorts and a sleeveless T-shirt. In the back of my closet, I pull out my old, beat-up pair of tennis shoes.

I slip a baseball cap on my head backward and start to run. Fuck, I haven't run in years—not since high school. My shoes slap against the pavement, and the smell of fresh-cut grass hits me as I hit the end of my street. Up ahead, I see the side entrance to the cemetery. God, how long ago was it that I saw Brylee run in there?

I look both ways before crossing the street. Jogging down the road that leads to the back of the cemetery, I spot Kyle's tombstone up ahead and make my way toward it. At first, I stand in front of it just staring at it. Then I move to the side and sit down.

"Hey, you little shit." I pause, waiting and praying for him to answer me. "I miss you. I miss you every fucking day, and don't give me shit about cussing either." My brother was the sweetest, most loving kid in the whole world. He was never bad, never annoying. I should've found it irritating that he was the good kid, but I loved him too much.

I took him everywhere with me. It never bothered any of my friends. He was the surrogate baby brother to our group.

"I screwed up—I screwed up bad. I don't know why I grabbed her. I mean, I know why I did it, but when I actually had Brylee, I couldn't do anything." I close my eyes. "Remember when I took you to get ice cream and you knew right away that I was staring at her? You asked me who that babe was, and I told you that one day she was going to be mine. I've ruined that. I've never watched someone mentally break before, but that's what I've done—I've broken her, and I'm afraid of what she might do because of me.

"You and I both know I've always been kind of a dick." I let out a humorless laugh. "For so long, I thought I hated her for taking you away from us, but she hates herself enough. She's tried to end her life three times because of guilt. Why does the thought of her not being around anymore fucking hurt? Kyle, she's got my head all screwed up. She's making me feel things I don't want to feel—at least not with her.

"It feels like a betrayal to you. I did something stupid today thinking about her. What's wrong with me? I feel like I'm losing it. Do I forgive her? Mom has, hell, you would've forgiven her yourself if you could. What should I do?" I close my eyes. "Please, Kyle, give me some sort of sign."

A stick snapping behind me has me lifting my head and turning. Brylee is the last person I expected to see here. She stares at me wide-eyed and slowly starts to back away. "I-I'm sorry. I'll g-go."

She turns and starts to walk away, but I run after her. "Brylee, wait, please." She stops but doesn't turn around. I move toward her and stop when I'm maybe a foot away. The scent of peaches hit me as the wind blows her hair.

Is this my sign, you little shit? I ask my brother.

"You shouldn't be out here by yourself. You never know when some creep might grab you." How fucking lame am I?

At first, she just stares at me, but then her mouth twitches slightly. It was such a small movement that had I not been looking directly at her, I might've missed it.

"What are you doing here?" She shrugs her shoulders and looks at the ground, kicking at a pebble with her foot. "Brylee, answer me." It seems that the more forcefully I talk to her, the more she listens or responds.

"I don't know. I went for a walk and just ended up here. I'll leave you alone." She starts walking down the road, and at first, I just watch her walk away, but something nudges me to go after her.

I stare up at the trees. "Subtle, bro, subtle."

Jogging to catch up with her, we walk side by side as

we make our way toward the exit. She turns in the direction of her parents' house, so I follow along. "Why don't you drive?" She starts walking faster—her long legs eating up the pavement. "Why don't you drive, Brylee?"

I grab her arm, turning her toward me, but she yanks it away. "Why do you think?"

"That was ten years ago. You'll be more careful now."

She turns toward me, her eyes wide. "I tried to, honestly I did, but the thought of getting behind the wheel of a car makes me want to vomit." Brylee again starts making her way down the road.

We walk the rest of the way side by side and in silence. She's leery of me, and rightfully so. She watches me out of the corner of her eye, and I don't know if it's because she's waiting for me to hurt her or grab her. I can't say I don't blame her.

Once we reach her house, I notice that Brylee's mom is watching us from the porch, wringing her hands together nervously. I watch as she walks to her mom, and the woman holds on to her daughter so tight that from where I'm standing, I can see her knuckles are white. She leads her daughter inside as the scent of her mom's roses hits me.

Her mom glances at me with curious eyes just before the door closes. I'm not really sure what to do, so I lift my chin and then walk away. On my way home, I think about Brylee, I think about Kyle, and my head is more fucked up than ever. Beginning to jog again, I head back toward my place.

After a shower and a sandwich, I lock up my house. In my room, I climb into my bed and promptly fall asleep.

TEN
BRYLEE

"Honey, you need to eat more."

I look up from my plate at my dad, who smiles at me encouragingly.

I force a smile. "I will, Dad." I take a bite of my potato that tastes like dry paste in my mouth. Grabbing my glass of water, I take a large swallow and force it down.

It's been two days since I found Chase talking to himself at the cemetery. I'm not sure if I should be sad or grateful for it. That day he walked me home, my mom had questioned me about it—wanting to know why he was walking me home and why we were talking at all. I didn't have to lie to her because the truth was I didn't know why, and that's what I told her.

Since then I haven't been able to stop thinking about him. My emotions have been all over the place as well, and I know it's just from being home and everything that's happened to me since I've been home. Luckily, we were able to start my meds back up before I began to start having symptoms of withdrawal.

It's been exhausting pretending to be okay. Inside I feel like I'm dying, my body feels like it weighs five hundred pounds, and every muscle aches from forcing them to move. At night and in the morning I still hear the sound of Kyle hitting my windshield. I always cry quietly as I replay the accident again and again, but this time Chase is there, screaming and crying for his brother, and I fall apart. Last night in my dream he actually wrapped his hands around my throat, squeezing it until I woke up coughing and wheezing.

I finally finish eating and feel my dad squeeze my shoulders and kiss the back of my head. "Thank you, honey."

Guilt fills me because he shouldn't be worrying about me. He just had a heart attack. I surprise us both by wrapping my arms around his waist. "I love you, Dad."

It's sad that I can't really remember the last time I told him that. My parents haven't ever been overly affectionate people, but these past couple of days they haven't stopped hugging or touching me. I'm confused by it, but I like it. He squeezes me. "I love you too, honey." His voice is thick with unshed tears.

Standing up, I wrap my arms around him again, hugging him tightly. We finally let go, and I grab my e-reader and go out the front door, sitting on the steps while I read my favorite book in the whole wide world, *Rock Chick Regret* by Kristen Ashley.

This story breaks my heart, makes me swoon, and makes me laugh. Since I discovered this series, Sadie and Hector have been my favorite couple. Sometimes I feel like Sadie, like I don't know who the real me is. I didn't go through what she did, but I live with a different kind of pain.

The sound of approaching motorcycles has me looking up. Two, what look like teenagers, stop in front of my parents' house. The one with raven hair and lightly tanned skin climbs off his bike. "What's up, Brylee? I'm Zeke, Loco's boy. He wanted me to stop by and bring you this stuff." I walk slowly toward him, unsure if this is some sort of trick or what.

He gives me a cocky grin and holds out the bag. I take it from him and see that there are books, coloring books for adults, and a journal inside. I don't know why that makes me tear up, but it does, and I do. "P-please tell him I said thank you." I keep my head down as I say it, not wanting him to see the tears.

"I will. Damn girl, you're fucking hot but too skinny. You need some meat on your bones."

My head jerks up, and he gives me a smirk that I'm sure all the girls love, climbs on his bike, and rides away, followed closely by his friend. I see on the back of their vests that they're prospects for the Jackals MC. Loco is the boss, or whatever they're called…I think.

In my room, I set the bag on my bed and pull the three books out. The first is *Ugly Love* by Colleen Hoover, then *Mack Daddy* by Penelope Ward, and last is *Me Before You* by Jojo Moyes. I haven't read any of these, but I've wanted to. After reading the blurbs of each book, I set them on my nightstand and grab the journal out of the bag.

If I had to guess, Loco didn't pick this stuff out. The books are all romance, and the journal has watercolor butterflies all over it. I flip through the blank pages and have nothing that I want to say. My thoughts are all over the place, and I don't know if I could get them down if I tried. Setting it on my nightstand, I slide down my bed until I'm lying on my side with my hands tucked under my chin.

My phone beeps, and it startles me. I grab it and see I have a text message. It's from an unknown number.

Unknown number: Everything okay?

What do I do? I don't know who this is. Maybe it's the wrong number.

Brylee: I think you have the wrong number.

It doesn't take long before I get a response back.

Unknown number: Brylee, it's Chase.

What is he doing texting me? No one texts me ever. Is this so he can mess with me? Is this all it is to him, a game? A way to get back at me for Kyle?

Brylee: Oh, hey, Chase. I haven't changed my mind if that's what you're wondering. I won't go to the police. My parents believed the story you told them, and I confirmed it when I came home.

I don't get a response, so I set my phone back down, curl up on my bed, and close my eyes.

———

My mom went back to work this morning—she's the secretary at the local junior high. She left me with a list of my dad's meds and what he can have to eat, and she left my meds out on the counter too. I've been taking this combination for the last five years, and I don't really want to feel like I did before. There's no way I'd stop taking them. Especially after everything that's happened recently and all the feelings it brought up again.

My dad sits in his recliner and watches *The Today Show* while I make his oatmeal and dry toast. It all looks gross to me. I grab a banana and eat that while the oatmeal cooks. When his food is done, I carry it out to him. "Do you need any fruit for your oatmeal?"

"Do we have blueberries?"

"I'll go check." In the refrigerator, I grab the container of blueberries and carry them out to the living room. I dump them in his bowl until he tells me to stop. "Will you be okay if I go for a walk?"

He grabs my hand. "I'll be fine. Go enjoy your walk. If I need you, I'll call."

I force my lips to tip up into a smile and then walk back to my room, grabbing my new tennis shoes and slipping them on.

I grab my phone and ear buds—I had been surprised that they were able to find them both at the cemetery and they still worked. Reaching up, I touch the lump and scab on the side of my head, and I'm thankful that my hair covers it because it would be completely noticeable. In the entryway I say goodbye to my dad and that I'll be home in a little bit.

Sticking my earbuds in, I make my way down the steps to the sidewalk and start walking. The music plays in my ear, and I know I should turn it down for obvious safety reasons, but really, who cares? If something happens, it happens.

The smell of wet grass hits me as I walk along the park. My eyes drift to kids running around with smiles on their faces and waving to their moms or babysitters who stand off to the side. A burning sensation starts in my eyes as I watch two toddlers chase each other in circles. It sucks knowing that I'll never have children of my own. Oh, I could have them if I wanted them, as far as I know, everything works, but I just can't do it.

A part of me is fearful that if I had children that they

would be taken from me. Of course, I would deserve it, or at least that's what I've convinced myself of. I shake off the melancholy and continue walking.

Up ahead I spot a coffee shop but realize I don't have any money. I walk past and can smell the fresh coffee beans. As I walk past the front door, it opens. Kaylee stands in front of me with a huge pregnant belly.

"Brylee?"

I take my earbuds out. Everyone used to tease us because our names rhymed and we'd tell people it was because we were sisters. If they didn't know us, we really played it up, but of course we looked nothing alike.

"Oh my god, it's really you. How are you?"

"I-I'm good. You look beautiful." Her honey-blonde hair is up in a knot on her head, and the maxi dress she's wearing highlights her adorable baby belly.

Kaylee's sea green eyes glisten like she's going to cry. "Thank you. I feel great." She grabs me and pulls me into her arms, hugging me tightly. At first, I hold myself stiff, but then images assault me. We met in kindergarten. We had been on the playground playing, and she marched right up to me and told me I was pretty and that she and I were going to be best friends forever.

I had asked her why she thought that and she said that she could feel it down into her bones. We were insepa- rable after that, well, until the accident, and then I pushed her away or at least ignored her until she gave up and walked away.

"T-that's really—that's really great." An awkward silence greets us. What can I say to her? *Sorry I ignored you and stopped being your friend. Sorry I was too trau- matized and hated myself so much that I couldn't face my soul sister?*

95

Kaylee reaches out, tucking a loose strand of hair behind my ear. "Honey, what happened to you? You just —you just disappeared. I'd heard you were in a hospital, I heard you'd moved across the country, and shit, I heard you were dead."

I lower my head, looking at my shoes. "I couldn't f-face y-you after what I did."

"Bry, it was an accident. No matter what, I loved you. I would've had your back, I would've been there for you. It was like you gave up."

I can't hear anymore of this right now. It hurts too much. "Um, I have to go so I can get back to my d-dad. It was great seeing you. Congratulations again on the baby. It's lucky to have you as his or her mommy."

Before she can say anything, I walk away from her, leaving her as she calls out my name. It's not until I'm halfway down the street that I wipe away the lone tear sliding down my cheek. Again, this just solidifies that I shouldn't have come home. Too many memories, too many people that are better off without me here.

Sighing with relief, I make my way up the walkway to the front door of my parents' home. I step inside and find my dad snoring while asleep in his recliner. I grab his dirty dishes and take them into the kitchen. Loading the dishwasher, I add soap and then turn it on. My eyes drift to the butcher block on the counter, and slowly I pull out one of the knives. I stare at it as it taunts me. It would be so easy to drag the blade across my skin. I've done it before, and I could easily do it again, but I can't—I can't do that to my parents.

In my room, I lie down and thankfully feel myself start to fall asleep. *Thump, thump.*

———

Carrying the bowl of broccoli to the table, I set it down in front of my dad, who curls his lip at it. "Your mother is trying to kill me," he whispers with a gleam in his eye.

"No, she's not. She loves you, I love you, and we want you healthy." I move to go back into the kitchen, but he stops me with his hand on my arm. "Is everything okay?" I ask.

"We want the same for you." His words cause me to freeze. "You're my only child, and I feel like I've failed you." I don't miss the tear that slides down his cheek.

A knot forms in my chest, and I hate that he thinks that he failed me. Maybe they weren't overly affection- ate, but they still loved me and took care of me. "Dad, you didn't fail me." He stands up, and I wrap my arms around him. "You didn't." He pulls away and then cups my face in both hands. Tears immediately fill my eyes because I've missed this—loving, human contact. I can't remember the last time I willingly touched someone affectionately.

My mom enters the dining room and looks at the two of us. "Everything okay?"

I turn my head while I wipe my eyes. "Yeah, Mom, everything is fine. Sit, and I'll bring the rest of dinner out."

She doesn't take her eyes off me as I walk by her and into the kitchen, grabbing the platter of baked chicken off of the stove. My mom and dad both watch as I sit down in my chair. I place a chicken breast on my dad's plate and one on my own before handing it to my mom.

Conversation is stalled as we begin to eat, or at least

I'm pretending to. "How was your first day back at work?" I ask my mom.

"It was good, honey, thanks. Did you two have a good day?" She looks between the two of us.

"We did. Your daughter's oatmeal is almost as good as yours. We both took a big nap too." My dad smiles at me and then my mom.

The doorbell rings and startles us all. I push back from the table. "I'll get it." Walking through the living room, I reach the front door. Pulling it open, I'm shocked to see Chase standing on the other side. "H-hey," I say through the screen door.

"Sorry to just drop by like this, but I wanted to see if you wanted to go for a run." That's when I notice he's in another sleeveless T-shirt, basketball shorts, and a bandana wrapped around his head. I don't want to admit that even after what he did to me I still get a tingle when I look at him.

Do I want to go with him? A part of me does, but then a part of me is nervous and scared to be alone with him. "Um, yes, sure. Can you give me a few minutes to change?" He nods his head. "Would you like to come in and wait?"

"I'll just wait out here for you if that's okay." He turns and sits down on the top step.

In the dining room, I find my parents talking softly. "Who was that?" Mom looks at me with a raised brow.

"C-Chase is here. H-he wants me to go for a run with him."

"Oh, well I didn't realize you were friends."

With a shake of my head, I say, "We're not. I'm not sure why he wants me to go, but I want to." I'm not sure why that is either. When I look at him, all I see is this pain—this beautiful pain. I can't explain what that even means, but it makes me want to wrap my arms around him, holding him until the pain is gone. Of course I wouldn't because I'm the reason he's even in pain. It's all my fault, and that's why I'm not sure why he even wants to hang out with me.

I kiss them both before grabbing my tennis shoes. Stepping out onto the front stoop, I sit down next to Chase, the smell of oil and gasoline tickling my nose. "D-did you w-work today?" I slip my shoes on.

"Yeah, I smell, don't I?" Out of the corner of my eye, I watch him sniff himself. He crinkles his nose, and I don't want to admit I find it hot.

"Just like oil and gasoline, but it's not bad, I kind of like it." I feel my cheeks heat up. I feel his eyes on me, but I stand up quickly and begin to stretch.

He joins me, and then we begin to jog. I love and hate running. I love it because I'm able to clear my head and not think about anything. I hate it because I burn so many calories I can barely eat enough as it is. That's why I'm too skinny, and I can't remember the last time I had a period. Vitamins are a part of my daily routine to keep my hair from falling out.

We run in silence—only the sound of our panting breaths can be heard. I'm lost in thought when I realize that Chase is no longer next to me. I stop, turning around to see him hunched over with his hands resting on his thighs.

"Are you okay?" I hesitantly reach out, touching his back when I reach him. As soon as my hand makes contact with his back, he jerks away like my touch hurt him. My stomach pitches and my heart sinks. He can't stand me touching him, so why in the hell did he invite me here? "I'm going home."

With those parting words, I turn around and start running as hard as I can. What hurts is that he doesn't call after me or try to follow. I run as fast as I can, not stopping until I reach my parents' house. I step inside and walk directly to the kitchen, snagging a bottle of water out of the refrigerator. Gulping it down, I spy my parents through the kitchen window sitting on the back deck.

After jumping in the shower, I slip on a pair of shorts and a camisole with a built-in bra. I brush out my hair before throwing it into a knot on top of my head. Grabbing my e-reader, I head out back and sit with my mom and dad while we all read. A long-forgotten feeling comes over me...contentment.

ELEVEN
CHASE

I should've gone after her, explained my reaction to her touch. It had been unexpected, but not unwanted, because her touch was soft, gentle. I can't remember the last time someone touched me like that—well, other than my mom.

Pulling my bike into the parking lot of the clubhouse, I back up into my spot and give Zeke a chin lift as he comes sauntering over, a cigarette hanging from his lips. "You know those are bad for you."

"Says the prick who gave me my first smoke." Okay, so I may not be the best influence to some of these younger guys, or at least I wasn't a good influence before. I shake my head as I walk past him and head into the clubhouse.

It's midday, and the clubhouse is virtually empty. Most of the guys are at the shop, and the others are at their regular jobs they have. The retirees sit at the bar, drinking coffee and shooting the shit until we all start making our way back there toward the end of the day.

At least twice a week, the old ladies make a huge

dinner and we all eat together. Loco has always been about family, and that's what we always were to each other. Those who know about Brylee and what I did have had my back, whether they agreed with what I did or not.

I pull up a stool next to Murph. He's one of the originals, but unfortunately, arthritis keeps him from being able to ride anymore, so he mainly hangs out at the clubhouse offering words of wisdom to us younger guys. He pours me a cup of coffee and slides it to me. "Thanks, Murph. You keeping an eye on things around here?"

"Someone needs to keep an eye on you punks. How's your ma doing?"

I take a sip of the bitter black brew. "She's doing great, better than me these days." Shouldn't that tell me how forgiveness is such a good thing? My mom has obviously opened her heart when she forgave Brylee, so why can't I?

"You know I ran into your ma shortly after you hit your rock bottom. I bought her a coffee, and we sat and talked for three hours...three. She's got a big heart with a capacity for love that knows no bounds. Before that day I never understood why she forgave that girl for Kyle or forgave your dad for splitting when you guys needed him, but she said something that stuck with me for a long time.

"She looked right at me. 'If I don't forgive them and continue to live with that hate in my heart, I'd be setting myself up for a lonely, sad existence. Never forgiving them isn't going to bring Kyle back.'" He leans into me, dropping his voice to barely a whisper. "I know what happened with that girl." My eyes widen. "Don't worry, I would never say anything to anyone. I just wanted to say you have an opportunity here—an opportunity to free yourself of those invisible chains. It's just up to you if you're man enough to break them."

Murph gets up and slaps me on the back a couple of times before walking away, leaving me to ponder his words. After finishing my coffee, I head out. The brothers are all starting to show up, and to be honest, I need some time alone, some time to think about what I should do. Climbing on my bike, I head toward home.

I'm sure the boys will give me shit for not partying like I used to, or partying like I was up until the Brylee incident, but they know I've always done what I wanted —never caring what they thought. Well, maybe that isn't too accurate. I've always cared what my ma, Loco, and Grayson thought the most out of everyone. On my way home, I stop in front of Brylee's parents' place and shut off my bike. I'm not sure what I'm doing here, but I can't seem to stay away.

I head to the door, and before I can even knock, the door opens and Brylee is standing in the doorway.

"What are you doing here?" She steps out onto the stoop and lets the screen door bang shut behind her. Brylee crosses her arms defensively across her chest.

"I don't know, I just wanted to check on you. Do you want to go get a coffee?"

She tucks her hair behind her ear. I don't miss the way her hand trembles. "I-I could go f-for a coffee. Let me go get my shoes." I watch her disappear inside, and my eyes didn't miss how long and gorgeous her legs are. I've never seen a longer pair of legs on a woman before.

Fuck, my dick is starting to get hard just thinking about those legs wrapped around me. What is my problem? I turn my back to the house and adjust myself as I think of anything but sex, and sex with Brylee.

Dammit, I shouldn't be here. This was a mistake, and I'm a fucking coward. Moving down the sidewalk, I hop on my bike and take off. I make the mistake of looking in my rearview mirror because I spot Brylee standing on the sidewalk looking at my retreating form, and I don't miss her hurt expression before she turns around and heads back into her house.

I drive around for an hour before pulling up in front of my mom's place. Climbing off my bike, I head to her front door, knocking. A moment later she opens it with a surprised smile.

"Hi, my baby boy. What a nice surprise." She pushes the screen door open. "Come in. I was just getting ready to have a bowl of ice cream."

Following her into the kitchen, I sit at the table while she dishes some out in two bowls. I'm not a big sweets eater, but for her, I'd do anything.

She hands me my bowl. "Why aren't you partying with your club tonight?" My mom may not know what goes on there, and luckily she never gives me shit, but she lets me live my life.

I shrug. "I don't know. I may head back over there. I asked Brylee out for coffee today."

Her lips tip up into a smile. "That's wonderful. How did it go?"

"She said yes, but when she went inside to get her shoes, I took off." The look of disapproval is all over her face. Her brow is furrowed, and her lips are in a flat line. "I know, I know. I'm not sure why I left, and she looked hurt when I did."

"Okay, well, what happened right before you left?"

Do I tell her? Do I tell my mom that I was thinking about Brylee sexually? I've always told my mom almost everything, but how can I admit that? How can I admit that I'm attracted to the girl that killed my brother? "I watched her walk back into her house and I noticed that...you know, those are things I'd rather not share."

My ma reaches out and grabs my hand. "Oh, honey. It's okay to have those kinds of thoughts. She's a beautiful woman, and you're a healthy male." Oh, for fuck's sake. This woman is crazy, but then the seriousness sets in...again.

"But what about Kyle?"

"Honey, what about him? Do you really think he'd have a problem with you spending time with her?"

Shaking my head, I know the answer. My brother may have only been alive for thirteen years, but he was an old soul. Sure, he'd like to go hang with his friends, but he loved helping others. He was unique, good, and pure.

It's like she can read my mind.

"You always put your little brother on this huge pedestal. Yes, he was a good boy and loved to help, but you're forgetting he learned a lot of that from you. When you were a teenager, you were girl crazy, and I swear I kept waiting for some girl to show up claiming to be pregnant by you, but you were truly a good kid. Your dad and I were lucky because of both of you. Don't ever think that we thought he was better than you. We loved you and love you the same."

"I always just thought of Kyle as this perfect kid who did no wrong."

"That's because you only have good memories of him, which is great. You don't remember when he used to follow you around repeating everything you said until you got so pissed at him you called him a little asshat. Or when you'd come in past curfew and he always busted you for it and then told us."

I laugh because she's right. He always got me in trouble. How come I forgot that?

We finished our ice cream, and I left a short time after that. Now in my kitchen, I roll a joint and take it out back and light it. After hitting it a few times, I pick up my cell phone.

> **Chase**
> I'm sorry about earlier. That was a shitty thing to do.

I have smoked half my joint before my phone dings, signaling I've got a text.

> **Brylee**
> It's okay. I figured it was a mistake.

Staring at her words, a sinking feeling fills my gut. She thinks it was all a mistake, but of course, why wouldn't she? I invited her out for coffee, and then while she was getting her shoes, I left without a word.

> **Chase**
> No, that's not it. I just had a stupid male moment. Would you like to meet for lunch tomorrow? Let me make it up to you.

> **Brylee**
> I don't know if that's a good idea.

I play it cool because I don't want her thinking anything bad or that I'm going to ditch her again.

Chase

Sure it is. I get to apologize for tonight, and you get free food. It's a win-win for both of us.

Brylee

Okay. What time and where?

I text her to meet me at the little diner down the street from the shop, and thankfully she agrees. I snuff out my joint and carry it into the house, setting it on the counter. I grab a beer out of the refrigerator, twisting off the cap and taking a swig.

After I finish it, I lock up and head into the bathroom to shower and brush my teeth. When I collapse on my bed, I can still smell her. I should've washed them, washed away her scent, but I just couldn't, and I have no clue as to why. Rolling over, I bury my face in my pillow, and as I take in her scent, I feel myself drift off.

———

"You didn't stay long at the club yesterday. Murph said you were kind of quiet, and he got kind of deep with you. What'd you do after you left?" Loco says as he helps me work on the radiator we're fixing.

"Went and saw Ma, then went home." Do I tell him about lunch today? No, he would try to come with me— probably to make sure I don't hurt her, which I don't plan on doing. "Is that a suitable answer for you?"

"No need to be a smartass. I worry about you—you and Grayson are like my sons. Both of my boys look up to you and respect you two."

I look at him from across the engine. Is he sick? Is

something more going on that he hasn't told us? "Why are you getting deep? You okay?"

Loco's a lot more laid back than he used to be. I've seen him beat the shit out of multiple people before, and back in his wild days he was always in and out of jail for assault. He's definitely mellowed out, but he's still a bad motherfucker, and I wouldn't mess with him. Back when I hit rock bottom, I tried to fight him after he'd taken my hidden stash, and I was too fucked up to realize that it was a big mistake. He didn't hit me, but he body slammed my ass…hard.

"I'm fine. I'm just worried about you. I know you still drink and smoke weed, but that other shit and everything that's been going on here recently had me worried that you might dip into the stronger stuff." His dark eyes bore into mine.

"I swear to you that I won't. To be honest, the thought of using that shit hasn't even crossed my mind. I've started running again." Loco doesn't hide the surprised look from his face. "Yeah, I know. It's fucking tough too. I gotta quit smoking—I can barely run a mile without having to stop and catch my breath. I ran the other day with Brylee." I don't know why I just told him that.

He freezes. "Really?"

"Yep. We didn't really talk. It was going fine, and then it wasn't, and it was totally my fault. I had my hands on my thighs, bent over trying to catch my breath, and she touched my back and I flinched. It hurt her feelings because she took off running back to her parents." I don't tell him about asking her to have coffee and then leaving, nor am I going to tell him about lunch.

"Just tread carefully with her. She's very fragile right now."

"Don't you think I know that? I watched something break in her eyes, and it's because of me. I'm just trying to make things right. It's the least I can fucking do." I bend back down, finishing the job, because then I need to get cleaned up before I meet Brylee for lunch.

We work silently, *thank God*, before we're finally finished. I head into the locker room and scrub my hands with the soap that helps get the grease off of them. Using the little brush, I get under my nails. They're good, not great, but I don't have time to dick around. I know if I'm not there by noon, she'll leave. I splash cold water on my face and then run my hands through my hair.

I quickly take my coveralls off, stick them in my locker, and throw on my cut. After sticking my wallet in my back pocket, I head out the back door and head around the side of the building. I approach Whistler's Diner and head inside, grabbing a booth by the door so I can spot her when she comes in.

"Hey, Chase. Can I get you something to drink?" Marilyn, who's been working here since they probably opened, asked with her grandmotherly smile.

"I'll take water for now. I'm waiting for someone."

Her gray eyes twinkle with mischief. "A lady friend?"

Shaking my head, I nod. "Yeah, I am, but it's not what you think." She winks and then walks away. I shred the napkin in front of me as I watch the front door, waiting.

It's now five after twelve, and I think she's standing me up until the bell over the door rings, signaling someone is either walking in or leaving. When I look at the door, my heart starts beating a rapid rhythm in my chest. Brylee's hair is down and hanging over her shoulder. She's wearing jean shorts that showcase her long, slender legs and a royal-blue short-sleeved cardigan over a blank tank top.

I stand up as she approaches our booth. She looks nervous, which I hate because I'm the cause for her nervousness. "Hey, Brylee. How are you?"

"Um…I'm good. How are you?" She sits down across from me, and I follow suit.

"I'm good. It's been a busy day so far. How's your dad?"

Marilyn interrupts us. "Hey there, honey, can I get you something to drink?" She looks at Brylee closely. "Do I know you, sweetheart? You look familiar."

"I'll just take water, and I used to come here with my folks a long time ago." She doesn't elaborate further and looks uncomfortable.

Marilyn, being the sweetheart she is, nods and excuses herself to get Brylee's drink. Since her hair is down today and she's got it hanging around her face like a shield, is she worried people will recognize her, or is it being seen in public with me? Nah, that's not it. She's too shy and awkward for that.

When Marilyn comes back with Brylee's water, I order a double cheeseburger and fries, and she tries to order a side salad and a cup of fruit. Normally on a date, although this is not a date, I wouldn't care because then I was getting off cheap, but this girl is too damn skinny, and I'm making it my mission for her to put some weight on.

"No, Marilyn, get her what I'm having." Brylee looks at me with wide eyes from across the table. "You're too thin. Fuck, you need to take better care of yourself."

Brylee sucks her bottom lip between her teeth and looks down at her lap. We sit in an awkward silence until our food is delivered. I thank Marilyn, and she gives me a small smile before disappearing.

I pick up my burger, taking a huge bite. As I chew, I watch her look at me, then back down at her burger, and then back at me. "Eat." My mom would slap the shit out of me if she heard me talk with my mouth full.

Brylee grabs her burger and takes a huge bite. She crosses her arms across her chest as she chews the wad of burger in her mouth. Well, if forcing her to eat is what I've got to do, then so be it. I grab some fries and swipe them through the ketchup and shove them in my mouth. I know I look like a pig right now, but for every bite of food I take, Brylee takes one too.

I'm pleased when I take my last bite to see that she's eaten almost half of her food. She shoves her plate away. "There, are you happy?"

I can't help it and throw my head back and laugh. She's acting like a petulant child. "Yes, I'm very happy, thank you. Do you want dessert?"

"No, thank you. I'm seriously full. What do you care if I eat anyway?"

A sigh slips past my lips. "Because I do, and just leave it at that."

After paying the check and ignoring Brylee when she tried to hand me money, with a hand on her lower back, I lead her outside. "T-thank you for lunch." She starts walking down the street.

"Hey!" I hurry after her. "Brylee, wait."

"What do you want, Chase? Why do you insist on us spending time together? You hate me, remember?"

"I don't know what I'm doing, Brylee, but I can't

stand seeing you so fucking sad. Especially since I know I'm the cause."

Her eyes glisten as she stares at me. "You're not the c-cause. I am. I j-just can't stop thinking about it. Did you know that I had the biggest crush on you in high school?"

I nod because I had asked about her when I first really noticed her and began asking about her. The accident happened before I ever had the chance to ask her out.

"I had a thing for you too."

She nods because I know Megan had told her I was asking about her back then.

Another one of those awkward silences surrounds us as we stand outside the restaurant. "Do you have plans tomorrow?"

"No."

"There's a party at the clubhouse tomorrow night. Why don't you come? I could pick you up."

Her ice-blue eyes widen in surprise. I'm surprised myself because I can't see her at the clubhouse hanging out with my brothers, the old ladies, and any other hangarounds that frequent our place. Parties can get pretty wild at times, and a lot of the women that hang out there wear little clothing and have no problem fucking or being fucked in front of anyone.

"Come on, it'll be fun."

She chews on her lower lip. "O-okay, sure."

"Okay. I'll text you with the time I plan on picking you up."

"Thank you for lunch." I watch as she walks away. She really needs to get over her aversion to driving because her parents' house is at least ten minutes driving from here, and it'll take her at least an hour, if not more, to get home. Maybe I can help her with that before she goes back to Chicago.

The idea of her going back to Chicago, where she'll be all alone, makes something hurt inside of me. I don't know why, and I don't have time to analyze it because I have to get back to the shop.

Slipping in the back, I take my cut off and hang it up in my locker and throw my coveralls back on. I pop a piece of gum in my mouth before heading out into the garage.

"Get in here." I hear Loco call after me when I walk past his office.

"What's up?" I say as I stand in front of his desk.

He looks at me closely. What does he see? "Nothing, just wanted to see how you were doing/ Have you seen or talked to Brylee? Zeke just called and said he saw her walking down the street." He looks at me pointedly.

"We met for lunch."

"Why, and why didn't you tell me?"

He's really pissing me off. "I don't know why it's any of your fucking business, and I told you I was going to make things right with her."

Loco slams his fists on the top of his desk, and he shoves his ass out of the chair. "It's my fucking business because your little stunt made me an accessory to kidnapping, and I'd prefer not to go to fucking jail."

I scrub a hand over the top of my head. "Sorry," I mutter. He's right, and if she were to ever go to the cops, not only would I be busted, but so would Loco, Grayson, and my ma. She won't, though, I know it.

He sits back down in his chair. "How was she?"

I shrug. "She doesn't talk a whole lot. I did get her to eat half a burger and some fries."

Loco nods. "That's good. She needs to put on some weight."

"I'm bringing her to the clubhouse tomorrow for the cookout."

"Are you sure that's a good idea? She's extremely skittish—the clubhouse might be too much for her. Although Tiff will be there to help keep an eye on her—fuck, maybe it's a good idea. I've never seen someone so lonely." He sighs. "Get the hell out of here."

That's exactly what I do.

TWELVE
BRYLEE

Staring at myself in the mirror, I place a hand on my stomach to quell the butterflies that have been flitting around all day. Chase should be here any minute to take me to his clubhouse for a party. I'm not sure if it's like the clubhouses I've seen on TV, but hopefully, he's not going to leave me by myself.

Earlier today I had Googled *Sons of Anarchy* to look at the women and what they wore. I walked to the mall and bought a pair of faded, ripped, denim jeggings and a red fitted T-shirt with a faded American flag on it.

While I was at the mall, I stopped into a salon and got six inches cut off my hair and some subtle layers added around my face. Now it hangs to just above my bra strap. It helped me not look so gaunt. I even stopped at the food court and grabbed a piece of pizza. I was only able to eat half of it, but that was something.

Back in Chicago, it wasn't unusual for me to go long periods without eating anything. Between my medications and the bouts of depression, my appetite would be nil. I'm not sure what's changed, but I guess I'll take it.

I'm certain this isn't a date, so I only put on a little bit of makeup and swipe my ChapStick across my lips.

A knock sounds at my door. "Brylee?"

"Hey, Mom. What's up?"

"Um…Chase Foster is here." She steps further into my room, shutting the door behind her. "What are you doing with that boy?"

"What do you mean?"

She moves until she's standing right in front of me. "Honey, you share a history with him. How are you supposed to get better if you're around a reminder of what happened?"

"I don't know, I just like spending time with him, and it's just kind of nice to get out and do something."

My mom steps closer and cups my face with her hands. I don't miss the soft look on her face as she looks me over closely. "You look beautiful. I love the haircut, it suits you."

"T-thank you."

She steps back but keeps her hands on my face. "A part of me doesn't want you going anywhere with Chase, but then another part of me wants to push you out the door." She gives me a smile that warms me to my soul. "You better get going; you don't want to keep him waiting. Will you be coming home tonight?"

I'm sure my face turns beet red. "Of course I am. It's not a date, it's just a friend thing, or not even a friend thing…I don't know what it is, but it's definitely not a date."

"Well, have a good time." She surprises me when she leans up and kisses my cheek.

Taking a deep breath, I grab my purse and head

downstairs. I don't see Chase, but then I hear my dad talking to him outside. Oh god, my dad's treating this like a date, and he's probably going to have Chase running for the hills again. I step outside, and I don't miss the double take I get from Chase. I know it's just my hair, but it feels nice to have someone look at me like that—like I'm desirable.

"Hey." I'm trying to sound casual when I feel anything but. I hug my dad. "Bye, Dad."

"Son, I expect you to be careful with her on the back of that." That's when I realize that his motorcycle is parked on the street.

I hear him say something to my dad without really hearing what he said. Finally, Chase is next to me, and silently we walk side by side to his bike. We reach it, and he pulls up his seat and grabs a helmet out of it and a pair of what look like sunglasses with clear lenses. He sticks the helmet on my head and adjusts the strap until it's snug under my chin.

"I really like your hair." He surprises me by fingering the end of the strands. "It looks healthier." My stomach pitches because it wasn't because he's attracted to me, it's because it no longer looks limp and lifeless.

He slips the glasses on my face and then climbs on the bike. I stand on the curb, and I'm not sure how I'm going to get on the bike. "Take my hand." Placing mine in his, I ignore the way my hand feels in his. "Just throw one leg over and put your feet on those pegs." He points to the tiny silver bars sticking out below. I do what he says and get on slowly and carefully. Chase reaches behind him and grabs my arms and wraps them around his waist. "Hold tight, and when we turn, lean with me."

"O-okay."

He starts the bike, and the vibrations make their way through my body. Once he takes off, a squeal slips past my lips. It feels like we're going faster than I'm sure we are. The scenery flies by, and I notice we're heading toward the edge of town. Up ahead, I see one of the old factories that are surrounded by a huge chain-link fence.

There are bikes, cars, and people everywhere. The butterflies begin to take flight in my stomach again, and I have to tell myself not to chicken out.

Chase pulls into the parking area, shuts off his bike, and backs into a spot in between two other bikes. "Hop off."

Chase holds out his hand, and I grab onto it before swinging my leg over and off. I glance around and see men and women, some of whom are scantily clad, everywhere.

After he climbs off his bike, Chase rests his hand on my lower back and leads me toward the door. The smell of marijuana hits me when we step inside. There are people everywhere, and rock music plays quietly in the background. Girls all holler after Chase, flashing him brilliantly white smiles and flashing so much cleavage I don't know why they're even bothering wearing shirts. I feel out of place, and it's obvious I'm no competition with these women.

We head toward a group in the back, and I immediately recognize Loco and Grayson. Loco has a beautiful blonde woman on his lap. They spot us, and all three of them stand up and walk toward us.

"Hey, Brylee."

"H-hi, Grayson." He gives me a warm smile and then slaps Chase on the back. Loco has his arm wrapped around the blonde that was on his lap. I try to summon up a relaxed smile, but I'm afraid that it looks like I'm in pain.

"Hi, Brylee. You look beautiful, that haircut suits you." He flashes me a smile before taking a swig of his beer. "This is my old lady, Tiffany. You've met our boy Zeke, he's around here somewhere."

Tiffany pulls me into a hug. "It's so nice to meet you," the buxom blonde says.

"It's nice to meet you too." She loops her arm through mine and leads me toward the bar.

"What would you like to drink? We have pretty much every hard liquor and beer."

I'm not really supposed to drink on my meds, but I'm so out of place here I need something. Otherwise, I'm going to get awkward and uncomfortable. "I'm not much of a drinker. What do you recommend?"

She ends up grabbing me a spiced rum and Diet Coke and grabs a pitcher of beer for the guys. I follow her back to the table and take a sip of my drink. Chase pulls out the chair next to him, and I sit down. Tiffany resumes her spot on Loco's lap. I sip my beverage while I watch them all interact with each other. It must be nice to have so many friends.

While I sip my drink, people stop by the table to shake Loco's hand and slap the other men on the back. It's not lost on me that lots of scantily clad girls come over to talk to Chase, totally ignoring me, but I guess that's okay because we're not even together. He's just being nice, and he probably is kissing up to me to make sure I never go to the police, which I have no intentions of ever doing.

When it's time to eat, Tiffany brings me a fresh drink

and leads me out back and introduces me to some of the other old ladies. They're actually a lot more welcoming than most of the girls inside. I offer to help, them but they wave me off.

"Are you having a good time?" I turn to find a man with long blonde hair and a scruffy beard with the most beautiful mossy green eyes I've ever seen.

"I am, thank you. I'm Brylee." Like the nerd I am, I hold my hand out.

He flashes me a smile that I'm sure makes it easy for him to get the ladies before slipping his hand in mine. "I'm Jackson. Have you gotten anything to eat yet?" I shake my head. "Well, let's get you fed." Jackson leads me over to the table and hands me a plate. I take a little bit of everything and get a cheeseburger from the man manning the huge grill.

I look around trying to find Chase—I got separated from him, and it's been a few minutes since I've seen him. On our way to some picnic tables, I spot him, and my stomach sinks. He's leaning against the wall and a girl in teeny tiny shorts has her arms wrapped around his waist, smiling widely up at him.

"Are you and Chase together?" Jackson asks as we sit down on the end, facing each other.

"What? No, not at all. We're just friends. How long have you been part of the club?"

He takes a drink of his beer, washing down the bite of his brat he just took. "For about five years. I moved here about six years ago and met Loco when I brought my bike into his shop. He introduced me to the boys, and we all just clicked. I like being part of the brotherhood—they have my back, and I have theirs."

120

"That's great. What do you do for a living? Do you work at the shop?"

He flashes me the most adorable smile. "Believe it or not, I'm an English teacher at the high school."

"Really?" He laughs and nods. "Sorry, I shouldn't have reacted like that. You just don't look like a teacher."

"Yeah, I know. Of course, when I'm teaching, I pull my hair back in one of those douchey man buns."

I laugh and it feels good.

————

CHASE

Jessica grabs onto the front of my cut and tries to pull me down to kiss me, but I pull away. I can't do that to Brylee. Speaking of Brylee, she disappeared on me outside with Tiffany, and when I came out, Jessica latched onto me. I glance around, and when I finally spot her, I freeze. She's sitting across from Jackson, and I know that look on my brother's face. He's flirting with her, and if I'm being honest, I don't fucking like it.

Moving toward their table, I notice something that makes me pause. The smile on her lips is the same sweet smile that drew me to her back in high school. My heart starts racing, and then I get mad because, for some ungodly reason, I want to be the reason she smiles like that. Jackson's a good guy and I respect the hell out of him, but right now I want to throttle him.

Sliding into the spot next to her, I don't miss the way her face shuts down, and Jackson doesn't miss it either because his eyebrow is raised as he looks between the two of us. "Thanks for keeping her company." I give him a chin lift.

Without thinking, I reach out, tucking a strand of her hair behind her ear—she freezes as I do. What did I just do? I don't want to give her the wrong idea about this. I only brought her so she could get out and be around people. "I'm gonna grab some grub." I get up and get in line for the food.

My eyes keep drifting to Brylee and Jackson, and I don't like her sitting with him, but I can't do anything about it—I won't. While standing in line, I feel arms wrap around my waist. Looking behind me, I find Kelly smiling up at me. "What's up, sugar?" She's got the mouth of a Hoover.

"Nothing, I just saw you standing here by your lonesome." I turn around and don't miss the fact that her tits are on full display for me. I should just fuck her, and then I can stop thinking about Brylee. Speaking of Brylee, I turn my head just a tiny bit, and out of my peripheral, I see that she's looking at us.

I grab Kelly's face and kiss her—tongues dueling, stomach turning because I know this is going to hurt Brylee. Finally pulling back, I slap Kelly on her ass and send her on her way with the promise of us hooking up later.

"What's up, bro?" Grayson slaps me on the back. "You gonna hit the Hoover tonight? She's got a pussy that is so fucking hot."

"Fuck, I don't know, maybe. Maybe I'll just let her blow me." With his mouth and hand, he makes the signal for a blow job. Giving him a shove, he laughs as he walks over to the picnic table where Brylee, Jackson, and now Loco, Tiffany, and Sherry, our VP Nash's old lady, are sitting. He's in jail for ninety days for assaulting a preppy asshole who was hitting on Sherry at a concert.

I sit at the picnic table after filling my plate with food, and while I eat, I stew in silence.

BRYLEE

I knew this wasn't a date, but watching him kiss that girl made nausea pool in my belly. Why did he bring me here if all he was going to do was hang on other women and leave me alone with people I don't know? Jackson is really nice and cute, but what if he knows about what I did and this is some elaborate plan to humiliate me? No, I promised myself I wouldn't let my thoughts go there.

After finishing my spiced rum and diet, Jackson offers to take me inside to grab another. His hand is resting on my lower back as we make our way inside. "Are you having a good time?" he asks as we lean against the bar waiting for our drinks.

One thing I notice is that girls may look at him, but his attention is only on me. "Y-yeah, everyone's been cool so far." I take a big drink to quell my nerves.

"You have feelings for him, don't you?"

I stare at him and feel my cheeks heat up, and I shake my head. "I don't know what I feel."

It's true, I don't. All I know is that I don't like seeing Chase with other girls, and I don't have the right to feel that way. Jackson orders a couple of shots, shots I really shouldn't do, but I don't care right now. Doing one after the other, I let the alcohol warm me.

He orders me another drink and leans in. "I don't

smoke, but if you want some weed I bet I can find you some."

I can't help it and giggle—me giggling. Because let's be honest, I'd have a better chance finding weed than I would anything else in this place, the sweet, skunky smell is thick in the air. "I'm sure you wouldn't."

He grabs my hand. "Come on."

We make our way through the crowd, and I wish I felt something with my hand in his, but instead I feel nothing, and that makes me pissed. He introduces me to his friends like I came here with him. Everybody is sort of nice but leery, and again it makes me wonder if people know about me, about what I've done.

The "old ladies" are nice to me, but the skanky girls, or "club whores," as Jackson called them, looked at me with calculating eyes, and several tried to get Jackson to go off with them, but he paid them no attention.

We sit with Grayson and another guy with a shaved head and a half-naked girl on his lap. Grayson holds a joint out to me, and I take it, hitting it twice before handing it back to him. "You having a good time, Bry?"

I nod. Between the drinks and the weed, I'm feeling no pain, and it feels good. My body is loose and my mind fuzzy. I could get used to this. "I am, t-thanks," I say, tucking my hair behind my ear.

"What's going on over here?" I freeze and look up. Chase is standing next to me.

"I think your girl is fucked up." Grayson lifts his chin in my direction.

Standing up, I excuse myself to go to the bathroom, but Chase stops me. "Do you need me to go with you?"

I can tell he's just been kissed because his lips are red and swollen, and it makes my heart hurt. Shaking my head, I walk past him and make my way through the crowded room. In the hallway to the bathroom, a couple is practically having sex against the wall. I slip into the bathroom and am happy to see stalls. Slipping inside one, I do my business when the door opens.

"I'm gonna fuck Chase so good tonight," a high-pitched voice says.

"What about that girl he brought?" the other voice asks.

I hear laughter and feel my stomach turn. "You mean Skeletor? That girl looks anorexic, and from what I hear, she's the bitch that killed Chase's little brother a long time ago. When I was talking to him earlier, he made it sound like he just felt sorry for her. She sticks out like a sore thumb."

"Jackson seems to like her," the other voice says.

I hear a snort and then another. "Whatever. He's probably keeping her busy so Chase doesn't have to deal with her, and then he can spend time with me."

I hear a couple more snorts, and then the door opens and closes. Stepping out of the stall, I move to stand in front of the mirror. Tears run silently down my face. How could I have been so stupid? This was just some elaborate ruse to make me feel stupid, and it worked. They must all be laughing behind my back.

On the back of the sink, I see a little mirror with a few lines of white powder on it. I pick it up, place my nose against it, and snort the whole trail of the bitter powder. Plugging my other nostril, I snort the second line. When the mirror is empty, I squeeze it in my hand until drops of blood drip from it. I throw it against the wall, and it shatters into little pieces.

I'm not sure if it was meth or coke that I just

ingested, but all of a sudden I feel twitchy and not so drunk anymore. Looking at myself in the mirror, I wipe the powder from my nose with the back of my hand.

My heart is pounding in my chest. I feel the blood dripping from my hand, but I do nothing to stop it. I feel humiliated, sad, and so wired right now that my mind is racing.

My hand shakes as I reach for the door, and I make my way down the hall toward the crowded room.

THIRTEEN
CHASE

My eyes keep drifting toward the hallway where the bathrooms are. Brylee disappeared a while ago, and I haven't seen her since. I should've gone with her. Instead, I left her to fend for herself. Jackson keeps looking in that direction too.

"Are you going to flip your shit if I ask Brylee out?"

He'd honestly be good for her. He's truly one of the good ones, but I'm a selfish asshole and don't want her with anyone even though I won't make a move on her myself. "No, I guess not," I lie.

"Good, because I kind of like her."

A commotion and shouting have us standing up. It's not unusual for a fight or two to break out.

I see Loco with Tiffany in tow moving through the crowd, and then he turns to me with worried eyes, and I know right away it's Brylee. I pick up the pace, shoving and moving people out of my way. I find her standing next to the bar. She's got a straw up her nose and snorts two lines and then takes two shots. I notice she's got blood all over her, and some people cheer her on and some look at her nervously.

She lifts her head and looks at me with sad eyes, and my heart squeezes in my chest. Brylee runs a hand nervously through her hair as her eyes dart around the room. She's so fucked up right now, and I fucking hate myself because I brought her here and then left her to herself and let her see any of the club whores touch me.

I move toward her, but her eyes get wild, and she starts to slowly back away from me with her hands up in a defensive manner, and that's when I see the cut on her palm. "S-stay a-away from me. Y-you w-win."

I don't know what that even means, but I keep moving toward her, and her back hits the wall. "Brylee, come here. I need to see your hand." I remember that when I'm forceful with her, she actually listens. "Brylee, come here, or I will come get you."

Brylee's spine stiffens. "I'd like to see you try," she shouts.

I move toward her quickly, bending to put my shoulder in her stomach and fling her over my shoulder. She begins screeching and hollering, punching my ass with her small fists. I give her a firm slap, and she freezes.

"What was that?" she screeches.

I carry her through the crowd, and people are clapping and cheering me on. We reach the hallway that leads to our rooms and head to mine, pulling the keys out of my pocket. Once we're inside, I toss her on the bed and lock the door. In my little bathroom, I grab a washcloth and get it wet. Back in my room, I see she's on my bed fuming. Her arms are crossed across her chest.

"Hold out your arm," I command, and reluctantly she

does it. Her lower lip is out in an adorable pout that makes me want to bite it, but then I remember I'm a little pissed off right now. It takes one look to realize the cut isn't that bad. After I get it all cleaned up, I dress it and then sit down next to her.

"I-I'm sorry," she whispers. She sounds defeated and embarrassed. "I've n-never done cocaine before. I don't drink either."

"Why did you do it then?" I stare at the ceiling because I know why she did. "Baby, you're freaking out right now. I can see it in your eyes. I want to help you come down, okay?"

She pulls her feet up and sticks them on top of my mattress and wraps her arms around her knees. When she nods her head, I let out a relieved breath. I pull out my phone and send Loco a quick text.

> **Chase**
> Brylee's freaking a little bit. I'm gonna help her come down. Can you send Zeke to get her some hot chocolate?

> **Loco**
> We already have some here. Tiffany's getting it ready now, and she'll bring it back. Tiff has her car here, and it's parked by the back door if you need to get her out of here.

> **Chase**
> Thanks, man, I appreciate it.

> **Loco**
> You bet. She can't come back again if she's gonna do that shit, though.

He's right. If she were to lose her shit and had to go

to the hospital, the cops would definitely come snooping around. We may not be criminals, but we're not choirboys either. Staying under their radar is important to us.

While I wait for Tiff to show up, I start the small shower in my bathroom and let it get warm. Back in my room, I grab a rubber band out of my nightstand, and I take Brylee's hair and put it up into a bun on top of her head.

A knock sounds at the door, and I open it to find Tiffany. "Here's her hot chocolate." She hands me a CD. "Play this. It used to help bring you down." I look at *Fleetwood Mac Greatest Hits* and remember plenty of times lying in this bed trying to get my mind and heart to stop racing.

I kiss her cheek before closing the door and locking it. Moving to Brylee, I help her stand and lead her into the bathroom. "Let me help you." I take off her shoes and socks and then remove her shirt and pants. Leaving her in just her bra and panties. I try to avoid looking at her body, but I'm only human.

Even though she's painfully thin right now, she still has a pretty banging body. It reminds me of a Victoria's Secret Angels' body, except with smaller tits. "Just step inside for a few minutes. Let the warm water run down your back and your chest." I grab her face with both hands before she steps in the shower. "When you get out, I want to know what it was that pushed you to do that shit."

Her cheeks turn red and she nods.

While Brylee stands under the spray, I stare at nothing—or at least anything but her. When the water shuts off, I wrap a towel around her and lead her back into my room. I throw one of my T-shirts on her and hand her the hot chocolate. "Climb into bed and get comfort-able." Thankfully my sheets are clean. I'd hate for her to smell another girl on them.

I stick the CD in my player, and Stevie Nicks's smooth voice comes over the speakers. Kicking off my shoes, I climb into the bed next to her, wrapping my arm around her. Her body vibrates with nervous energy, so I stroke her arm up and down, up and down. "Tell me what happened."

She sighs. "I was in the bathroom, and a couple of girls came in. One said she was going to f-fuck y-you. The other girl mentioned me and she said I looked anorexic and that you brought me because you felt sorry for me. Then she said that Jackson was spending time with me to keep m-me out of y-your hair so you could fuck that girl. She said she heard that I was the one that killed your brother." The last part comes out as a pained whisper.

I rest my cheek on the top of her head, kissing her forehead. Her flowery scent wraps around me. "I'm so fucking sorry. I can't seem to say that enough to you." I hug her to my chest as she starts to cry. "I'm sorry I kissed Kelly and that I did it in front of you."

"T-then why did you?"

Do I tell her the truth? Yes, I owe her at least that.

"Because, Brylee. Because you have me all tied up in knots. For so long I thought I hated you, but then things changed, and then I saw you with Jackson and thought he'd be the type of guy you need because he is a good guy...the best, and I'm just not. I thought if I kissed her and you saw, you'd maybe make a move on Jackson or let him make a move on you."

She pulls back so she can look in my eyes, and I see

that her pupils are dilated. My stomach rolls when she sniffs repeatedly. I grab her face and pull it close, kissing her forehead. Her eyes clench closed, and I use my thumbs to wipe away the tears that slide down her cheeks. "I d-don't want Jackson."

I realize that she's straddling my lap, and I have to fight my dick getting hard because it wants to more than anything. I need to move her before my hormones try to take over.

Lifting her up, I set her back on the mattress next to me but put my arm back around her. She grabs the cocoa and gulps it down. When she sets the mug down, she snuggles against my chest with her arm across my stomach.

Neither of us speak, we just listen to Stevie sing about landslides. I can no longer feel her heart beating rapidly against my arm, and soon her breathing slows down. Tomorrow she's going to feel like shit, but I'll take care of her.

Between her soft breathing and Fleetwood Mac playing softly in the background, I feel myself nod off.

The sound of retching wakes me, and it takes a second for the cobwebs to clear, and I remember that Brylee's here. I fly out of bed and run into my bathroom, where I find her with her head in my toilet. Thank God Tiffany pays a couple of the old ladies to clean the clubhouse, including the bathrooms in our rooms.

I grab a washcloth and get it wet, placing it on the back of her neck. I squat down next to her and rub my hand up and down her back. This goes on for a while until she rests her head on the toilet seat. When she looks up at me, I can see her eyes are bloodshot. I grab the washcloth from her neck and run it under the water again, but this time I use it to wipe off her face.

After I throw the washcloth in the sink, I bend down and scoop her up in my arms. I carry her into my room and lay her down, crawling in behind her. Her back is firmly against my chest, and I wrap my arm around her and feel her fall back to sleep, and then I do the same.

My eyes flutter open, and the sun is shining too fucking bright in my window. In front of me, Brylee groans and buries her head under my pillow. "What happened to me last night?"

I rub a hand over her back. "What's the last thing you remember?"

She rolls to her side and faces me. Bags stand out under her eyes, and she's got that morning-after-a-bender look. I hate seeing it on her like that. My hand reaches out and strokes her cheek. Brylee closes her eyes and rubs against my hand. "I remember everything," she groans. "I'm so embarrassed. I've never done cocaine before. I've never drank that much before. I'm never drinking again."

I can't help but chuckle a little bit. "I've said that a time or two in my day. I hate to break it to you, but the next couple of days are going to suck. I want you to come stay with me. Let me take care of you. Will you?"

"I don't know why you want to take care of me." She eyes me skeptically.

"I promise there are no ulterior motives. I owe it to you." I scrub my hand over my hair. "I hurt you. I'm the one who brought you here. I fucked you over and left you to fend for yourself. Let me do this for you." I can see the war waging inside of her. Understandably so, but I need her to let me do this.

"Do you promise this isn't some ploy to hurt me more? Of course, you could say it's not just to get me where you want me."

"I promise you that this isn't some evil plan to hurt you," I plead to her. "Let me take care of you."

At least five minutes pass before Brylee slowly nods her head before grabbing it in both hands and moaning. "Ugh...I think I'm dying." She looks up at me with those sad eyes of hers. "Please don't hurt me." It's barely a whisper, but her words hit me right in the gut.

"I promise I won't intentionally hurt you." Her lips tip up in a tiny smile, and she shakes her head but again grabs it.

Even though she looks like death warmed over and the bun on top of her head is all loose and crazy, she's still adorable. "You can either take a shower here or at my place after we stop at yours to get your meds and stuff."

"I guess at your place."

"Okay, go wash your face and brush your teeth if you want, and then we'll get out of here." She disappears into my bathroom as I put my boots on and tie them. A few minutes later she comes out looking a little better with her hand resting on her stomach. It growls loudly, and I laugh. "Let's also get some good greasy food in you too."

I lead her out to the main area of the clubhouse. The room is empty except for a couple of old-timers sitting at the bar drinking coffee. Loco is leaning against the bar talking to them. They turn our way and I don't miss the way Brylee's steps falter.

"I need to talk to the two of you." We follow him outside, and he hands me a cigarette. "How are you feeling this morning, darlin'?"

"Like death. I'm so sorry. I don't do that stuff, that's not me. Normally I don't drink at all, and what I did was s-stupid."

Loco steps toward her, and she doesn't cower. "That was really stupid. You're a sweet girl and I know things have been crazy since you've been home, but I can't have you in my club if you're going to be reckless and do things that could potentially bring us a whole mess of trouble." Brylee's chin wobbles, but she sucks in a breath and it stops. Fuck, she's stronger than she knows. "Do you understand what I'm saying? I'm giving you one more chance, and if you put yourself at risk again, you won't be coming back."

"I…I understand, sir."

"None of this *sir* shit. It makes me feel old. Now you two get out of here." I tell Loco that she's coming home with me so I can take care of her. "Well, don't be surprised if Tiffany stops by to check on her."

We go to my bike, and I pull it out of my spot. I stick her helmet and sunglasses on and wait for her to climb on.

I drive slowly toward her parents' house. I don't want the vibration causing her to get ill. We pull up in front of her parents' house, and she climbs off. "Do you want to come in?"

"No, I'll wait here. They may not be real happy with me since I kept you out all night."

She nods and then walks up to the door.

While I wait, I search under the seat for a cigarette. I've barely smoked the past couple of days, and I've been dying for one. Of course I don't find one, and whenI look up, I find Brylee's mom. "Hey." I give her a chin lift.

"What are you doing with my daughter? Are your

135

intentions good, or are you setting up to destroy her?" She doesn't hold back, and I can't blame her. "I know what happened is tragic, and I know that girl is going to beat herself up for the rest of her life, but she doesn't deserve to have you play games with her mind and her heart. Nothing you do to her will bring your brother back. I beg of you, if your intentions are anything but friendly, please leave now."

"I don't want to hurt her, I want to help her. That's all I want to do, I swear." Every word I say is true.

"We let Brylee be alone in Chicago for so long, and it did more damage than we realized. It let her erect the wall she had built around herself. How do you help your child heal when all they want is to be alone? She needs to know people care about her and that people want her to get better."

"I know everyone thinks I don't, but I do want her to get better. I want to help her. Mrs. Whitmore, I promise you I only want to help."

She nods and then excuses herself before disappearing back inside the house.

A few minutes later, Brylee comes walking out with a bag over her shoulder. "I saw my mom come out here. What did she say?" She worries her lower lip between her teeth.

I shake my head. "Nothing really, just that I shouldn't let you drink that much." I'm not sure why I lie to her, but I can't go back on it now.

Taking her bag from her, I strap it to the back as she puts her helmet back on. We take off down the street toward my place. When I pull into the driveway, I help her off and carry her bag into the house. She follows me into my bedroom, where I drop her bag.

Brylee's yawn has me looking over at her. "Come get in bed."

She doesn't argue, just crawls on top of the comforter, and her soft snores fill the room seconds later. I kneel down next to her and stroke my hand over her hair. She doesn't even budge. I stand up and head into the kitchen and look through my refrigerator and cupboards and make a list of shit I need to get from the grocery store.

I want to feed her and maybe put a few pounds on her. I'm not much of a fruit and veggie kind of guy, but I'll get that stuff for her. It's supposed to be nice the next couple of days so I'll get stuff to grill.

Once I have my list together, I go in and check on her. She's still sleeping, so I jump in my truck and head to the store. Inside I grab a cart and don't fuck around. I move up and down the aisles until I have a decent amount of food for meals and snacks. I really do hope she likes healthier foods because that's what I plan on feeding her. After getting checked out, I take the groceries outside and load them up into my truck and head home.

I put the food away once I'm home and then throw some chicken breasts into a baking dish and pour some marinade over it, tilting the dish back and forth to make sure every inch is coated. I cover it with foil and throw it into the refrigerator. I wash all of the fruit except for the bananas and put them into a large bowl. It's just straw-berries, raspberries, blackberries, and blueberries.

I head down the hall to my room and check on her. She's fine, so I head out to the living room and lay down on the couch. It doesn't take long before I pass out.

"Chase?"

I hear a whisper, and my eyes flutter open to find Brylee standing over me. Her hair is wet, and she's in different clothes.

"Hey, how'd you sleep?"

"Good, thanks. I took a shower and feel a little bit better."

I sit up and scrub my hands over my face. "I'm going to shower quickly, and then I'll get the grill going. Help yourself to anything in the kitchen."

I make my way down the hall to shower.

FOURTEEN
BRYLEE

I dress and then toss the salad I made and set it aside while Chase checks on the chicken outside. The microwave dings, letting me know the potatoes are done. Carefully pulling them out, I set them on two plates. Chase already told me I had to have some of everything on my plate. I'm not sure when he decided to be my boss, but he sure is bossy all of a sudden, especially when it comes to food and me.

The back door opens, and he comes inside carrying a plate with chicken on it. "I hope this tastes okay." He uses a fork to stab at a chicken breast and then puts it on my plate, and I put salad on them. Following him outside, we sit in a couple of folding chairs that he's got out there and a wrought iron table.

In silence, we eat.

"Oh, I forgot I got you something special to drink that'll help make you feel better." He disappears inside, returning a minute later with a clear plastic bottle. "This is grape Pedialyte. It'll replenish your electrolytes."

"How did you know how to calm me down last night?"

Setting his fork down, he looks up at me. "For about two years, I had a nasty coke habit. I'd been on many benders over that time and needed help coming down. You just remember what works and what doesn't—granted, you may just be more hungover than anything."

"I honestly don't feel that bad. My nose hurts a little bit and my head too."

"I've got a saline solution that you can use to rinse your sinuses."

She looks up from her plate. "I promise I'm never doing that stuff again. I can't thank you enough for everything. You really didn't have to do it."

"Stop thanking me, okay?" She nods. "You know how you can thank me? Eat as much of your food as you can."

I finish most of the food on my plate, and I clean up the dinner dishes and wipe off the counter. The leftovers go into the refrigerator, and I don't miss that he's got lots of healthy food in there, and it makes me smile because he doesn't seem the type to have that kind of stuff stocked, which means he did it for me. Of course, I don't think about it too much because obviously he's not into me.

Last night I thought for sure he was going to kiss me, but instead, he kissed my forehead and then moved me back to sit next to him. I certainly won't be making that mistake again. In the living room, I find Chase reclined in his chair watching a ballgame. I grab my e-reader out of my purse and open the book I've been reading.

Sadie is still trying to find out who the real Sadie is, and Double H (Hispanic Hottie) is being all alpha and swoony with her. These books know how to suck you in and make you lose hours, and this is actually the third time I've read this series. In Chicago, I don't watch a lot of TV, so I listen to a lot of music, read, or listen to audiobooks.

After reading for an hour, I stretch out on the couch and continue reading until I feel my eyes start to drift shut.

I wake to the feel of someone lifting me. "What—"

That's all I get out before Chase shushes me. He lays me down on the bed, and I feel him crawl in beside me, and he wraps his arm around my waist. "Is this okay?"

"Um...yes." I will my body to relax, otherwise I know I'm not going to sleep at all. Closing my eyes, I count backward from one hundred to clear my mind, and slowly it begins to work and I'm able to let my body sink into the mattress.

It feels nice—his body heat warming me.

My eyes open slowly, and I'm so freaking hot. It takes a minute for my wits to return, and I realize there is a large hand cupping my small breast over my T-shirt. Turning my head slowly, I see that Chase is snuggled up behind me. He shifts slightly, and that's when I feel something hard poking me in the butt.

Oh god, he's got an erection. I squeal to myself because this is the closest I've ever been to an erection before. Logically I know it's just a natural reaction and not for me, but for a second I close my eyes and let myself imagine that he's turned on because he is attracted to me.

Rolling over, I look closely at his sleeping face. It's so relaxed, and he looks younger. He's got a scar right above his eyebrow, and my fingers itch to touch it, but instead, I slide off of his bed and stand up and head into the bathroom. I go pee and then wash my hands. After braiding my hair and brushing my teeth, I head out to the kitchen and start a pot of coffee.

I grab the package of bacon and the carton of eggs out of the refrigerator and start making breakfast. I'm just scooping the last of the eggs on a plate when Chase comes out, his hair is all disheveled, scruff covers his face, and he's got sleepy hooded eyes.

"Would you like coffee?" I'm proud of asking with my voice fairly normal-sounding.

He moves behind me and puts his hand on my hip. "I'll grab it, thanks."

I do a whole-body shiver and I hope he didn't feel it —how embarrassing would that be?

My skin still feels warm from where he just touched me. I keep my back to him so he can't see my flushed face and my hardened nipples. Why do I feel so comfortable around him? I shouldn't, after all that has happened, but I just do.

Once I feel myself calm a little, I grab our plates and carry them into the living room. We eat in companionable silence, and once finished, he takes our dishes into the kitchen. "I've got cleanup," he shouts. "Why don't you go get cleaned up or dressed, whatever you need to do? We're heading out in a half hour."

In his bedroom, I throw on some knit shorts and a sleeveless T-shirt and my black Nikes. I move back into the living room as Chase comes out of the kitchen. "I'm going to jump in the shower, and then we'll head out."

I'm incredibly curious about what we're doing.

We've been driving around just listening to the radio for a while. I'm not sure what the whole point is, but I won't complain. It's just nice to be out and about, and I'm not out and about alone. That's one thing over the past few days that really hit me. I. Hate. Being. Alone. Just having someone to hang out with has meant so much more than Chase could ever know.

We start hitting the back country roads on the outskirts of town. He pulls over on the side of the road, throws it into park, and then turns toward me. "It's time you start driving again, and I'm going to help you do it."

I shake my head violently as my stomach starts to hurt. "N—no. I can't do it."

His ice-blue eyes scan my face. "You can do it. We'll take it slow, and I'll be with you every step of the way." Chase hops out of his truck, and I watch him walk around the front of it until he's at my door pulling it open. "Slide over."

With my heart beating in my throat, I slide over until I'm behind the wheel as he climbs in. I'm sweating profusely, and my hands are shaking. "I don't think I can do this," I whisper.

Chase scoots in close, close enough for me to smell the woodsy, earthy scent of him. It's got a calming effect on me, but that still doesn't mean I'm going to do it. He places his hand on my bare leg. "You can totally do this. Do you remember the basics?"

Nodding my head, I sigh. He's not going to let up until I do this. I put my foot on the brake and, with a shaky hand, reach out and grab the gearshift. For a brief second, I close my eyes and take a deep breath.

A shiver slithers down my spine when I hear his

whispered words near my ear. "Brylee, you've got this. Just take it nice and slow."

Opening my eyes, I turn to look at him. We're so close that if one of us leans forward, we'd touch the other person's lips, but instead, we both pull away, and I turn back to the front. My hand shakes as I pull the gearshift down into drive.

Letting my foot off of the brake, the truck starts to inch forward. My heart is pounding, and the blood is rushing in my ears. "Okay, give it a little gas now." Chase sounds like he's in a tunnel, like his voice is muffled.

I do as he says, and we begin to move slowly down the road. My grip is so tight on the steering wheel that my knuckles are surely white, and my fingers begin to tingle. That day comes back to me. Images of Kyle hitting my hood and then windshield rock me. Tears fill my eyes, and I can't breathe.

Slamming on the brakes, I throw the truck into park and am flying out of his truck, running as fast as I can through the open field until my lungs feel like they're going to explode.

"Brylee!" I stop running, bending at the waist while I catch my breath. "What happened back there?"

I find him standing in front of me, and with quick movements, I'm up and shoving him as hard as I can. "Why did you make me do that?" My voice sounds foreign in my own ears, guttural, broken.

Chase grabs my face with both hands—his thumbs brushing the tears away while looking deeply into my eyes. "Brylee, you need to stop being scared to drive. It was an accident." Even though he says the words, they feel hollow. He doesn't believe them when he says them, so why should I?

I pull away from him and start walking back toward his truck. He walks alongside me, neither of us saying anything. Yes, it was an accident, but it still doesn't erase the fact that someone is dead because of me. We reach his truck and both walk to the passenger side. I think he's going to just open the door for me. Instead, he hops in, shuts the door, and locks it.

"Chase!" I knock on the window but he doesn't look at me. "Come on, this isn't funny." At least five minutes go by, and all I've done is continuously knock on the window. I know it's getting to him because I can see his jaw tic, but he won't get out. I stand up on the little step and just stare at him. He just pulls out his phone and starts playing with it.

I can't take his silence anymore, so I hop down and stomp my feet as I make my way around the front end and grab the driver's side door and hop in, slamming the door behind me. "You're being a real asshole," I mutter. His chuckle makes me want to punch him right in his throat.

Closing my eyes, I take a deep breath and then step on the brake while I turn the key in the ignition. His truck rumbles to life, and I put it in drive. Letting off the brake, the truck slowly begins to roll forward. I give it a little gas, and we slowly make our way down the road.

"You're doing great. Loosen your grip on the steering wheel." I shake my head. "Babe, you can do this, you are doing this."

I feel his hand start playing with the ends of my hair as we drive down the empty country road. "You can go a little faster."

I look at the speedometer, and see I'm only going twenty-five miles per hour. Breathing deeply, I give it a little more gas and have it up to thirty. I don't want to admit how exhilarating it is, or how good this feels.

When we get close to town, I pull over and put the truck into park. "Why'd you stop?"

"Um…we're getting close to town. There's going to be traffic and police, and I don't have a driver's license."

"Okay, let's switch places." He slides over, and I lift myself up and feel him slide under me. My body does a full shiver when I feel his chest brush my back. I move to the passenger seat, buckling my seat belt. Chase places his hand on mine, and my eyes drift shut savoring the feeling of his hand on mine. "You did really good today. I'm so fucking proud of you."

Tears fill my eyes. I don't remember the last time someone told me that. Blinking them back, I turn to him. "Y-you don't know how much t-that means to me. Thank you." He squeezes my hand before letting it go. We drive through a fast-food restaurant and grab a couple burgers before heading back to his house.

Once we get back, we sit outside and eat our burgers, and it isn't until I'm crumpling my wrapper that I realize I just ate the entire thing. Closing my eyes, I lean back, letting the sunshine warm my face. The moment a little bit of that heaviness in my heart goes away, I bite my lip hard, keeping the sob that bubbles up from escaping. My throat bobs and aches, but I refuse to cry.

I feel his eyes on me but keep mine closed. I'm afraid to look at him, always afraid that I'll see hate in his eyes as he looks at me. Next weekend I'm supposed to go home, but things are slowly changing. Things have been less strained with my parents, they've been more affectionate, and then Chase has been—has been different.

"I'm going to grab a soda. Do you want one?"

I don't even open my eyes. "Yes, please."

His chair scrapes the cement as he stands up. The back door opens, and then a minute later it closes. I open my eyes and sit up. He lights a joint while I take a sip of my drink. Passing it to me, I hit it twice before blowing out the sweet smoke and handing it back to him.

"Do you want to go see a movie tonight? Maybe go grab some dinner first?"

His questions startle me. Ten years ago I would've given anything to have him ask me out, but now things are so complicated with us, and there is always a tiny part of me that thinks this is all just some elaborate scheme to make a fool of me. Then there's that part of me that still harbors feelings for him and wants this more than anything—even though he had kidnapped me and kept me tied up in his basement.

He's got my mind all screwed up, but not necessarily in a bad way, but right now I don't care. I nod my head. "I'd like that."

"Do you have clothes here to wear out, or do you need me to take you home?"

"I'll go check." I make my way inside and back into Chase's bedroom. In my bag, I find jean shorts and a royal-blue fitted T-shirt that hangs off one shoulder and a black camisole to wear underneath. I pull out my makeup bag and my flat iron and set them on his dresser. I find him in the living room watching baseball. "I have clothes here. I'm going to jump in the shower if that's okay."

"Yeah, go ahead. We've got two choices: action or horror?"

"I like both, so I'm fine with either."

In his bathroom, I pin my hair up since I'm not going to wash it and step in the shower. I shave my legs and my underarms, wash my body, and then get out. I moisturize and then add a little blush to my cheeks, mascara to my eyes, and gloss on my lips. Back in Chase's room, I let my hair down, brush it out, and then straighten it. Finally I get dressed. I notice that my shorts are a little tight around my stomach. That's when I stand in front of the mirror in his room, looking myself over. Do my eyes deceive me? Am I finally putting on some weight? I'm not pale either, and the purplish bags are gone from under my eyes.

I'm beginning to look like a slightly older version of the girl I used to be, but looking down at my wrists, the scars that cover them will be a constant reminder of what a fucking mess I truly am. I shake those thoughts away, not letting myself go there right now. Slipping on my Nikes, I head out into the living room and sit on the couch.

"You look nice. I'm going to go get ready, and then we'll go." He disappears down the hall and into the bathroom, and seconds later, the water kicks on.

I grab my cell phone out of my purse and call my mom to check in.

"Hello?"

"Hey, Mom. I was just checking in. How's Dad?" My dad has been doing really well the past couple of days.

"Your dad is fine, honey, don't worry." I hear rustling around. "Sweetheart, are you okay? How is Chase treating you? Is he—is he your boyfriend?"

I look down the hall, and the bathroom door is still shut and the shower is still on. "He's treating me really well, and no, he's not my boyfriend." Even though a part of me wishes he was. "He's become a good friend, Mom. Guess what?"

"What, sweetheart?" My mom is definitely becoming great at the endearments.

"I drove today. It wasn't very far, and it was on an empty country road, but I did it." Tears fill my eyes.

I hear a sniffle. "That's really great. I'm really proud of you. I know how hard that must've been for you."

The shower shuts off, pulling my attention toward the door. "Thank you. Um...I have to go. Chase and I are going to get something to eat and then going to a movie."

"Okay, honey. Have fun tonight."

"I will, Mom. I-I l-love you."

She's quiet for a minute. "I love you too." We hang up and I stick my phone back in my purse.

A few minutes go by, and the door to Chase's bedroom opens. I try not to stare as he comes down the hall toward me. His dark-blond hair is combed straight back, and he trimmed up his beard. His white T-shirt is tucked into his jeans that mold to his muscular legs. The T-shirt shows off his muscles and his beautiful tattoos.

He slips on his motorcycle boots, slips his wallet into his back pocket, and his phone into his front. Walking past me, his cologne or aftershave hits me, and it smells so good—spicy and a little woodsy. Calling out from the kitchen, he asks, "What sounds good for dinner?"

"I really like Mexican food or pizza. I love pizza."

Chase comes back into the living room. "Pizza it is." He places his hand on my lower back and leads me outside to his truck. Climbing inside, I nervously scratch at my wrist as I watch him walk around the front end and climb in the driver's side.

He climbs in, and his scent wraps around. It's comforting and calming, and I can't figure out why. Especially with everything that's happened between us.

Our history is sad and filled with pain. Logically, I know that we'd never make it as a couple, of course, if that is even what he wants. My head and my heart seem to be on two different wavelengths and constantly at war with each other.

We head across town to Frank's Pizzeria. Pulling into the parking lot, it's packed, and my heart starts to race. What if people recognize me and remember what I did? I don't know if he can sense my internal struggle, but he reaches out and grabs my hand.

"It's going to be okay."

My head bobs up and down, and he gives me a squeeze before letting go and climbing out. I meet him at the front, surprising me, he grabs my hand in his, and hand in hand we walk into Frank's. It's crowded and loud, and I have to tell myself to just breathe.

The hostess looks at Chase like she wants to eat him as we approach the podium. "Hey stranger, how are you?" she chirps happily.

"Hey Lex, looking good." His words are like a stab to the chest. Of course this Lex, or whatever, looks good. She's got huge boobs, curves, and a beautiful face. I don't hold a candle to her. "I need a table for two." The hostess barely spares me a glance before turning back to Chase.

In a quiet voice, she has the nerve to ask him if he wants to get together later. "We could have some fun like we did a few months ago."

I pull my hand from his, and what's sad is he doesn't seem to notice or care. They talk for another minute before the hostess grabs a couple of menus and leads us toward a booth. I sit down across from Chase and grab my menu, flipping through it while Lex flirts with him.

It's like I'm invisible, and all I want to do is punch her in her stupid face.

When she finally walks away, I just keep looking at my menu, avoiding eye contact with Chase, but I can feel his eyes on me. I'm not really even looking at the menu, but where else am I supposed to look? Why does he keep giving me mixed signals?

Suddenly the menu is ripped from my hands, and Chase grabs my hands in his. "I'm sorry about that. I went out with her a few times, but she was super fucking clingy and half crazy. I knew if I blew her off, she'd make a scene, and I didn't want that."

My eyes meet his across the booth, and I believe him. I'm not sure why, I just do, even though he really hasn't given me any reason to trust him at all. "Y-you don't owe me an explanation."

Our waiter comes and takes our drink order. I order a diet soda, and Chase orders a beer. When he walks away, Chase looks over the menu. "Is there anything you won't eat on a pizza?" His eyes lift to mine. What is it about his eyes that just pull me in?

"Um...I don't like anchovies or sauerkraut, but I will eat anything else."

After the waiter returns with our drinks, Chase orders us a large pizza with everything and an order of cheesy bread. I hope he doesn't expect me to eat a lot. Sure over the past couple of days I've eaten more than usual, but for years I ate enough to survive and that's it. I'm sure it'll take a while for my stomach to stretch out.

Chase takes a drink of his beer and then clears his throat. "My mom would like to have you over for lunch this next week. I'll come with you if you want."

The thought of going to his family home makes my

stomach roll. I'm sure there will be reminders of Kyle everywhere, and I don't think I'm ready for that. I don't know why she would even want to see me. Of course, the woman had been relentless when everything first happened. She'd come to see me or try to, but I'd refuse to see her. She wrote me letters I never read, but I saved them. They're in a box in my apartment in Chicago.

"Why?" I choke out. "How c-can she stand the sight of me?" He reaches out and grabs my hands again.

"Okay, no more talking about it. We'll worry about it later." This time he doesn't let go, and the air becomes charged between us. A warmth unlike anything I've ever felt flits through my body as he stares at me. His eyes are bright, and I don't miss the way they drift to my lips. Is this for real or is this an act, something to humiliate me? Why can't I just accept that a part of him may be into me? Maybe because not since high school has anyone been into me. If they were, I never knew or gave them an opening.

"Here you go." Our waiter sets the pizza down as we pull away from each other. A girl sets our cheesy bread and plates down, and they leave us. When he hands me my plate, I notice that he won't look at me. I knew it didn't mean anything. Blowing out a breath, I use the spatula and pick up a piece of pizza and place it on a plate as well as a slice of the bread.

Chase takes the plate from me when I hold it out to him. "Thanks."

After fixing my own plate, we begin to eat in silence. I'm lost in my own thoughts when I feel eyes on me. At first, I ignore it or try to, but I let my eyes drift to the side and find Megan Daniels, Grayson's sister, staring at me and then Chase. She gives me a small wave, and I return it and then look down at my plate.

"What's up, Megan?" Chase calls out.

She comes over and hugs him and kisses his cheek. "Nothing much, I just saw you two sitting over here." Megan turns to me. "It's good to see you, Brylee. Grayson said you were back in town. How's Chicago?"

"I-it's good. It's nice to see you, Megan. You look great." She gives me a kind smile and hugs Chase one more time before heading back to her table where a man about her age and a child no more than two are waiting. "She's married?"

He looks at them and then back at me. "Nope, she's not married. Freddie the prick is Katie's dad. They're not together. It's a long story, and he's only allowed to see Katie in public with Megan there. Grayson's rules, and honestly, it's for the best. The guy played us all and hurt Megan. He's lucky we didn't put him to ground."

I've seen enough television to know what that means. I glance over at their table and get a glimpse at the adorable little girl that looks just like her mom. The guy, Freddie, is blond with dark eyes that are pinned on Megan. He doesn't even look at the child. Of course Megan's attention is completely on her daughter. It makes my stomach hurt to think that maybe he hurt her or the little girl.

"I'll be right back. I'm going to call Grayson and let him know they're here." He gets up from the table, leaving me alone.

Picking up my slice of pizza, I take a bite. I forgot how good Frank's pizza was. I can't remember the last time I ate pizza, or at least good pizza, and by the time I finish my slice and piece of cheesy bread, Chase is sitting back down.

"Is he coming here?"

Shaking his head, he picks up his slice of pizza. "No, he knew about this. He didn't like it, but Megan wants Katie to know her father even if the fucker doesn't deserve to be in the same room as them."

I manage to eat another piece of pizza, and Chase eats three more and drinks another beer before he asks for a box for the rest of our food. Grabbing my wallet, I try to hand him money, but he shakes his head.

After he pays, I grab the box of leftovers, and we walk over to Megan's table. Chase gets down next to the beautiful little girl. "How's my favorite girl?"

She gives him a toothy grin. "Cha Cha!" Katie squeals and he leans forward, kissing her cheek. It makes me feel all gooey to watch him with the little girl, but I bury it away. Sadness washes over me because I know I'll never have that. I'll never be a momma.

Chase stands up. "See you later, Megan." He completely ignores Freddie, who honestly looks like he doesn't give a shit.

"Bye Brylee. It was good seeing you." Megan's smile is sweet and genuine.

"You too, Megan, and your little girl is beautiful." She thanks me, and then Chase leads me out of Frank's and into his truck.

Silence surrounds us as we make our way over to the movie theater. The parking lot is full, so we have to park toward the back. Side by side, we head inside and stand in line. "Do you care what movie we see?" Chase asks as we scan the titles.

"No, you can pick," I tell him, and so, of course, he

picks the action movie, which I don't care. With our tickets in hand, he leads us to the concession stand and orders popcorn and two drinks. While we wait for our treats, I hear my name being called and spot Kaylee and a good-looking man coming toward us.

I plaster on a smile and prepare for her to hug me, but when she reaches us, she moves toward me then stops, backing away slightly. It's my fault because last time I was stiff and awkward with her. My stomach sinks as the man with her looks at me curiously. "Baby, this is Brylee and Chase." She turns to me. "Brylee, this is my husband, Giles."

I hold my hand out, shaking his hand, and he does the same with Chase. They are such a cute couple, and I'm sure their child will be just as, if not more, from being a combination of them both. I ask her what movie they're going to see, and she tells me they're going to see Brad Pitt's latest movie.

Once we have our snacks, I stand in front of Kaylee and say quietly, "It was really good seeing you." My eyes blur and my nose burns.

She grabs me and pulls me into a hug, and this time I wrap my arms tightly around her. "I've missed you so fucking much," she whispers.

"Same."

Kaylee pulls back and looks at me. "Please, let's get together before you go home." I nod, and she gives me her number before Chase leads me to the line with our snacks and tickets while Kaylee and her husband step up to the counter to order their snacks.

"She was your best friend?" Chase asks as we sit down in our seats.

"Yeah, I've missed her so much." I stare at the

previews on the movie screen even though I feel his eyes on mine. I'm able to relax when he shifts in his seat and faces the screen.

The movie's been playing for at least an hour, and it's good enough to keep my mind off of stuff. The hero just rescued his woman from the bad guys, and now they're at his secret hideaway. I start to feel flushed as the hero puts the heroine in the bathtub, washing her bruised body. The tenderness fills me with longing.

After he bathes her, he puts his shirt on her and then blow-dries her hair, brushing it slowly and tenderly, and it makes me want to cry. Oh God, now she's kissing him and he's picking her up carrying her to his bed. My skin is on fire as I watch them make love. I wasn't expecting this or for it to be so graphic. The hero's bare ass pumps between her legs, and I can't help but press my legs together to ease the ache there.

They make the art of having sex look beautiful and passionate. I have no frame of reference since I've never done anything with a man before, but most sex scenes I've seen have been intriguing and beautiful. Out of the corner of my eye, I see that Chase is looking at my legs. He takes me by surprise when he reaches over, grabbing my hand in his.

The credits roll, and the lights go back on. I expect him to let go of my hand. Instead, he keeps hold of it and leads me outside. The night has cooled off slightly, and goose bumps break out over my skin. The scent of popcorn lingers in the air. We reach his truck, and he lets go of my hand as he helps me inside. The smell of our pizza makes my stomach growl so loud I let out a nervous laugh.

"Still hungry?" Chase asks as we pull out of the parking lot.

"Yeah, and I really am not used to this. Can we heat some of this up back at your place?"

"Of course. We'll heat it up in the oven so it crisps back up a little bit."

That's what we do when we get back to his house. While we wait for the oven to warm up, we go outside and share the joint that he rolled earlier. I hit it twice and hand it back to him.

"How do you feel? Any anxious feelings or anything? That can happen after doing a bunch of blow."

I shake my head because honestly, I haven't felt bad at all except that night. Maybe I feel fine because of my meds and how well he took care of me. Maybe smoking weed has helped. I looked into it for medicinal purposes a while ago for any alternative to get me off of the meds I take now.

It was surprising to see that different strains can help with different ailments. Of course, I won't do anything until I talk to my doctor because quitting my meds cold turkey would be extremely bad for me. When Chase had kidnapped me, I'd only missed them for just a few days, so I had yet to feel any of those effects.

His oven beeps, so I head inside and throw the pizza and cheesy bread on a cookie sheet and then stick it in the oven. I set the timer and then step back outside, taking my seat across from Chase.

"Have you ever had a boyfriend?" His question startles me, his eyes searching my face for what I don't know. I shake my head, and he asks, "How come?"

I shrug my shoulders. "I don't know. I guess it was just easier to be alone than to drag anyone else into my life and my issues. Plus, I didn't want to have to tell someone or explain what I did." I look out across Chase's darkened backyard. "Being alone is easier."

"It may be easier, but is it better?"

How do I even answer that? I mean, I know it isn't better because I'm so lonely most of the time, but alone I don't have to worry about people finding out what a horrible person I am.

"You're not a horrible person." *Oh shit*, I said it out loud. "No more negative talk, Brylee, I mean it. If I hear you talk bad about yourself anymore, then I'll paddle your ass."

I stand up. "You most certainly will not."

He follows suit and moves until he's right in front of me.

"I will do whatever I have to do to make you see."

"Make me see what?" I ask as he moves forward until we're almost touching. My heart pounds a rapid rhythm in my chest because he's staring at me with soft eyes. I want to melt into a puddle of goo, but I don't. Instead I stand firm even though my knees are wobbling. His hand comes up, cupping my cheek, and his thumb softly strokes my skin.

Licking my lips nervously, I don't miss the way his eyes drift to them, and my belly does a little dip. Ever so slowly he begins to lean into me, and my eyes flutter shut. I feel his breath tickle my lips as I wait for my first real kiss, but the timer from the oven blares, causing us to pull away from each other.

FIFTEEN
CHASE

Fuck, talk about the worst timing ever. Brylee's eyes flutter open, and I don't miss the look of disappointment on her face. "Stay right here. I'll be right back."

Inside I pull the pizza out of the oven and shut it off. I hurry outside as nervous anticipation fills me, but I find her right where I left her. Right now I feel like a guy who's never gotten his dick wet before. I'm fucking nervous, and I don't know what to do with that. I've always, always been confident with women, but Brylee's got me all screwed up. It's definitely not a bad feeling, just unfamiliar.

I stand right in front of her, cupping her cheek again. Her eyes dilate, and her cheeks turn a light shade of pink. Moving in slowly, I place my lips against hers. At first, it's just a slow glide until she begins kissing me back. It's not hard to see she's not experienced because her lips move tentatively against mine.

Bringing my other hand up, I begin to kiss her harder, my tongue licking the seam of her lips until she understands what I want and slowly opens her mouth for me.

The first touch of my tongue to hers has us both moaning into the other's mouth. My hands slide into her hair, gripping it in my grasp, and I pull her head back to deepen the kiss.

Her hands rest against my chest and I'm afraid she's going to pull away, but instead, they slide up my chest and around my shoulders. With her body flush against mine, my cock is so fucking hard that I'm afraid it's going to punch a hole through my jeans. I don't want to scare her with it, but she's got me so turned on right now.

Any worry about scaring her vanishes when Brylee pushes her hips against mine, rubbing against my dick. I want more than anything to carry her into the house and fuck her on my bed, but I won't. She's not ready yet, and I don't know if I'm ready to take the next step with her either.

Reluctantly, I pull away from her, and I don't miss the dazed look in her eyes. I rub my thumb back and forth over her swollen lips, and she gives me a smile so brilliant that it changes her entire face. I haven't seen it since I saw her in the hall the week before the accident. She'd been talking to one of her teachers—about what, I don't know—but her smile lit up the hallway and had every guy around her watching her with rapt attention.

I wonder when the last time she smiled like this was.

"I like seeing you smile," I whisper. She dips her head as her cheeks turn a deeper shade of pink. Her hands slide from around my neck down to my stomach, and she grabs hold of my T-shirt.

"That was nice," Brylee whispers before looking back up at me.

"Just nice, huh? Hmm…maybe I'm losing my touch." Her eyes widen when I grab her face and kiss her…hard.

This time there is no tongue because things could get too heated, and if we get to that point, then we need to take our time. I need to ease her into it.

There is one question I do have, and I pull away. "When do you go back to Chicago?" I honestly don't want her to go back. She's all alone there, and I don't think that's a good idea. She belongs here where I can keep an eye on her, take care of her, and show her all of the reasons she needs to forgive herself.

Brylee clears her throat before she speaks. "A week from tomorrow." Is it disappointment I hear in her voice?

The moonlight shines in her eyes, illuminating them. She's so fucking breathtaking right now. It kills me knowing what I did to her. There's no way I can ever make up for it, but I'll die trying. I know it hasn't been long, but she already looks like she's put on a little weight. Her face doesn't look nearly as gaunt, she's not as pale, and her eyes are naturally brighter, or they have been the past couple days.

All I want is to forgive her fully—I swear I'm trying. I know until I can fully forgive her it'll be hard for her to forgive herself.

"Okay. I want to spend time with you if you'll let me."

She nods. "I'd like that." Brylee lowers her head but then looks back up at me. "You know I would never tell anyone about what happened, just in case this is to butter me up and convince me not to tell anyone."

"I get that you would think that, but this wouldn't happen if I didn't want it to. Don't take this the wrong way, but I could go to the clubhouse right now and fuck any girl there." There's a fire in her eyes when I say that, and it makes me want to smile. At least I know she's got some feelings for me.

I pull her until she's flush against me, and she tries to push me away. "That was really rude." She gives me a disgruntled look.

"Hey, don't be like that." I laugh. Grabbing her face again, I kiss her, wanting to get her used to my touch because honestly I want to do a lot more touching. Again I pull back. "Let's go eat."

———

Four days have gone by since the night Brylee did blow at the clubhouse. When I knew she wasn't going to have any issues because of it, I reluctantly took her home the day before. It was selfish of me to keep her away from her parents. The past couple of days we've run together in the mornings and then we'd have coffee together at my place before I had to get to the shop.

Since the night of our date, we've kissed a few times, but that's all it's been. I feel like until I can completely forgive her, I shouldn't even approach a sexual relationship with her. Of course, that's if she'd even want that with me.

Now I'm on my way to pick her up to go to my mom's for lunch. I know Brylee is freaking out about it, and I wish she wasn't, but I can understand why. My mom called me earlier and wanted to know if I knew Brylee's favorite foods and drinks, and hell, I wouldn't be surprised if the woman put together some sort of gift basket for her. All she wants is for Brylee to feel comfortable.

I stop my bike in front of Brylee's parents' house and

climb off. Reaching the steps, the front door opens, and she steps out. My breath leaves me in a whoosh because she's so fucking beautiful right now. Her light brown hair hangs in loose waves around her face. She's wearing makeup even though she doesn't need it, but it's light and natural-looking.

She's wearing capri pants that are form-fitting and are a light gray color. Her shirt is soft pink and hangs off one shoulder with a white tank top underneath, and on her feet is just a pair of black Nikes. It's a simple outfit, but it fits her.

"Hi." I can hear the trembling in her voice.

I move up the steps to her and wrap my arms around her. Pulling her toward me, I gently kiss her lips. "It's going to be okay. She's really looking forward to seeing you."

She nods her head, and I lead her down to my bike. After she climbs on, we take off down the road. I love the feel of her on the back of my bike, her tits pressed against my back and her hands resting on my abs.

We pull up in front of my mom's white bungalow, and I help Brylee off before climbing off myself. I grab her hand, and we make our way up to the door, and before I can pull it open, my ma throws it open and greets us with a huge smile.

"Oh, Brylee, I love what you've done with your hair. You look beautiful." She approaches her and pulls her into a hug. "Thank you for coming."

"T-thank you for having m-me."

"Hey, Ma." She kisses my cheek and gives me a squeeze.

"Hi, honey. Come in, come in." We follow her into the house, and something seems off. I look around the living room, and that's when I realize that a lot of Kyle's pictures are missing. My ma has never taken them down...ever, but for Brylee she did. Of course, when you look closely at the walls, you can see the marks on the wall where it's obvious that pictures were hung.

It's not lost on me that Brylee is uncomfortably stiff and awkward as my mom leads her out back to the patio. My mom ignores it, but I know she can tell because she chatters on about nonsense as she pulls out a chair for Brylee. "I'll get the lemonade," she says and disappears inside.

I pull out my seat next to her and whisper, "Are you okay? Is this too hard for you?"

She chews on her bottom lip as she shakes her head. "I'm okay. I promise." She turns to look at me. "Did she take pictures down? I could tell the paint was faded in spots that looked like picture frames." Looking down at her hands, her voice breaks my heart. "Please go tell her to put them back up. I don't want her taking them down because of me."

"I'll go talk to her." I kiss her lips before getting up and walking inside.

"Hi, honey. Is she doing okay?" My ma is a fucking angel. She could write a book on the power of forgiveness, and it'd be a bestseller.

"She knows you took down Kyle's pictures. She doesn't want you to hide them from her."

My ma's eyes go soft, and she gives me a small smile. "Okay, I'll put them back up. I'll be out in a few minutes." She hands me two glasses. "Take this to Brylee."

Back outside, I sit back down next to Brylee, handing

her glass of lemonade to her. "Is she going to put them back up?"

"Yeah, baby she is." She nods her head before taking a drink.

A few minutes later, my ma joins us with a tray of sandwiches and a bowl of chips. I watch her disappear inside and then return with plates and a bowl of fruit. My mom and I both fill our plates, and I stick a sandwich on Brylee's plate and some fruit. I know she's a little uncomfortable, so she'll try not eating, but I won't let that happen.

"Brylee, what do you do in Chicago?"

"I'm a waitress at an Italian restaurant." Brylee almost looks embarrassed.

My ma, of course, doesn't pay that any mind. "Have you thought about going to college?"

Here we go, my ma is going to try and convince her to go back to school. Out of the corner of my eye, I see Brylee rubbing at her wrist, and my stomach dips because I can see the white raised lines on her arms.

"Not really, I mean, when I was younger I wanted to be a nurse, but I don't know why I never did."

"Oh, that's a wonderful profession to go into. You're still young enough to go to school." I wouldn't be surprised if my mom got information for her on nursing programs in Chicago. Of course, a part of me wants to grab info for the schools around here. We have two, one at the community college and one that's part of one of the local hospitals.

"I don't know, maybe."

Luckily, my mom changes the subject. "Honey, how are things at the shop? Are you staying busy?"

"They're good. Business is great, and we've got a

pretty quick turnaround and we've been able to expand. I've got a little more work to do on the bike I've been rebuilding, and I should be able to put it up for sale soon."

"That's great. Make sure you send my love to Loco and Tiffany and the boys. Tell Grayson I expect him to stop by and say hello to me, and if he wants to bring Katie to see me, I would not say no." My ma loves watching Katie for Megan. She doesn't do it often, but she's always thrilled when she gets asked.

"Honey, how's your dad doing?"

"Um…he's doing a lot better. My mom has him eating healthy now, and he hates it. He swears she's doing it to kill him." I'm learning very quickly that Brylee does well when she doesn't actually have to talk about herself.

We talk about nothing heavy while we finish eating, and then I help my mom carry everything inside. The back door opens, and Brylee steps inside, closing the door behind her. "Can I help with anything?"

"No honey, why don't you two go have a seat in the living room, and I'll get the dessert ready."

With a hand on the small of Brylee's back, I lead her into the living room, sitting next to her on the couch. My eyes drift around the room, taking in the pictures on the wall. Pictures of me and my brother line the wall and cover the entertainment center. There are even a couple family photos that my mom kept up even after my dad split.

Brylee gets up off the couch, and I watch her walk over to the wall of pictures. I get up and move over until I'm standing next to her. The picture that she is looking at is when I was around ten and Kyle was five, and I'm pushing him on my old Big Wheel.

"I remember that day. Ma was having a garage sale and had that marked and out to sell, but Kyle saw it and wouldn't get off of it until I pushed him. He made me do it over and over until I'd had it."

"I remember that." My ma stands next to us, gazing at the picture. "He loved bossing you around, and you'd never told him no, so he never stopped."

"Mrs. Foster, where's the bathroom?" I don't like the sound of Brylee's voice.

"Honey, it's the second door on the right."

Before I can even do or say anything to Brylee, she's moving down the hall and closing the bathroom door behind her.

"I shouldn't have put them back up," my mom whispers as she looks down the hall.

"No, I want her to see them. It'll get easier and easier if she does." At least I hope it does. I don't know where this is going, if we have a future, but there is something there, and we need to be able to explore that.

A sigh slips past her lips, and then she walks down the hall, putting her ear to the bathroom door. She stands that way for a few minutes before walking back toward me. "I don't hear anything. We'll give her a couple more minutes, then I'll check on her."

BRYLEE

Sitting on the side of the bathtub, I stare at myself in the mirror. What am I doing here? Why did Chase think this was a good idea? I'm the reason his brother is no longer here. Did a part of him want to torture me? No, he wouldn't have kissed me like he has if he was setting out to destroy me. Thinking about the kisses we've shared, my fingers touch my lips. Wait, what am I doing thinking about kissing him when I'm in his mom's house, and there are reminders everywhere that Kyle is no longer with them?

I can't hide in here forever. Standing up, I wash my hands and take a deep breath before stepping back into the hall. Thankfully it's empty, but I hear their voices and follow them to the kitchen. His mom smiles at me as I round the corner.

"Come have some dessert, sweetheart."

Chase pulls out the chair next to him, and I have a seat. His mom passes me a bowl of ice cream with caramel and chocolate sauce drizzled on top of it. "Ma makes her own ice cream," he leans into me and says.

Scooping up a spoonful, I stick it into my mouth and moan softly because it's so delicious. The mixture of caramel and chocolate is so gooey and rich, and before I know it, the bowl is empty and when I look up, Chase and his mom are both smiling at me. "I'm sorry, it was just so good."

"Well, I'm glad you enjoyed it. It was my nana's recipe, and I used to make it for the boys when they were little," his mom tells me.

After we leave, he takes me to my parents' house because he's got club business to attend to and also has to work in the morning. Plus, I need to spend time with my mom and dad. I've been absent a lot, and I only have a few more days to spend time with them. It's time to mend our fragile relationship.

SIXTEEN
BRYLEE

Chase pulls his bike up in front of my parents' house, and climbing off, Chase follows suit. I hand him his spare helmet, and he puts it under his seat. He unhooks my bag from the back and hands it to me. "Thanks."

"Have a good time with your parents. I'll text you later." I nod, and he shocks me by pulling me into his arms, hugging me tightly to his chest. Chase even shocks me more when he pulls back again, but this time he leans down and kisses me. It's closed mouth, no tongue, but I feel it all the way down to my core.

I stand in a daze on the sidewalk as I watch Chase climb back on his bike, give me a smile, and then ride away. When he disappears around the corner, I head into the house.

I find both of them sitting in the living room watching the news. "Hi," I say as I sit down on the couch next to my mom. "I'd—I'd like to make dinner for you two tonight. Is that okay?"

"Honey, that would be wonderful. Do I need to take

you to the store?" My mom gives me a smile and then smiles at my dad. "Doesn't that sound wonderful, John?"

My dad's eyes turn soft as he looks at me. "That does sound good. What are you thinking of making?"

"I was thinking about making grandma's meatloaf, but using ground turkey because it's healthier." A laugh bubbles up inside of me before escaping out of me because my dad mutters under his breath that we're trying to kill him with healthy food. Of course a few curse words escape as he gets up and disappears down the hall. "Maybe I shouldn't have mentioned the ground turkey part."

Wrapping her arm around my shoulders, she gives me a squeeze. "Yeah, I wouldn't have mentioned that. We won't tell him we're making mashed cauliflower either."

"I heard that," he shouts from the back of the house.

After Mom and I go shopping, I start prepping the meatloaf. When I was younger, I used to love helping her so I could stick my hand in the hamburger, squishing it in my fists. My mom comes in and stands at the kitchen counter watching. She tried to help earlier, but I kicked her out.

It's only been a few hours since Chase dropped me off, but I miss him already. I haven't had time to analyze that between grocery shopping and cooking. I'll never admit to anyone that I've been checking my phone over and over to see if he's texted me. He said he was going to be busy, but I'm sure he'll call when he has time. A part of me wonders if he's going to sleep with any of those girls from the club.

He probably should, they're prettier than me, probably normal and lower maintenance. Shaking my head, I hate that my thoughts always go there. Getting back to the task at hand, I finish making the meatloaf and stick it into the bread pan. I pop it in the oven and set the timer.

My mom hands me a glass of sweet tea, and I take a sip. "The meatloaf looked great."

"Thank you. I'll let it bake for about fifteen minutes before I start the cauliflower."

We sit outside on the back patio while we wait to finish making dinner. Dad's in their room taking a nap. They shared with me today that he gets to return to work the week after I'm home. He's the managing director of a manufacturing plant that builds tractors. When I was a little girl, he'd take me to work with him, and I'd stand in front of the huge window in his office and watch them assemble huge tractors.

After dinner, which was a huge success and my dad loved it so much that he ate seconds of the meatloaf and the cauliflower mashed potatoes, we sat outside and drank coffee. We listened to the crickets singing and the leaves rustling. It was humid, making the air thick—the scent of wet earth surrounding us.

When the mosquitoes started biting, we went inside, which brings us to now. I've just finished cleaning the kitchen when my phone beeps. A little too eagerly, I pull it out of my back pocket and see that it's a text from Chase.

Chase
Hey. How's it going?

Okay, that wasn't what I was expecting, but I didn't know what to expect at all, so I should just shut up.

> **Brylee**
> Good, just getting ready for bed. Are you still at the clubhouse?

> **Chase**
> We just finished our meeting. Gonna have a beer with Grayson and then head home.

Why do I feel relieved? I try not to think about that.

> **Brylee**
> Okay, have a good night.

I don't know what else to say to him right now.

> **Chase**
> I'll call you tomorrow. Night.

> **Brylee**
> Goodnight.

I plug my phone into the charger and set it on my nightstand. In the bathroom, I wash my face and brush my teeth. Grabbing my brush, I run it over my hair and then set it back down. I lift my shirt up a little bit and look at my stomach from the side and straight forward and smile. My stomach used to be concave, but now it just looks flat, which might not seem like a big deal, but for so long I only ate enough to sustain me. The past few days I've eaten obviously for nourishment, but also for joy.

In my bedroom, I lie down on my bed and stare at the ceiling, reflecting on my trip home so far. I can only describe it as bizarre. First, the fact that I came home at

all was a miracle. I never had planned on coming home...
obviously. Second, facing Chase again and him kidnapping me and that whole humiliating mess.

A normal person would've stayed far away from the
person who grabbed them and kept them tied up in their
basement—where ultimately they were planning on
killing them. Not me though, and maybe it was because
Chase and I had a history and that I had crushed on him
so hard back in school. Since our first encounter, things
have changed between us. I've heard him talk to his
friends, and I know he thinks he can "fix" me, but I feel
like I'm too far gone.

Oh sure, I'm eating more and I drove once, but when
I get back to Chicago, it'll be like it was before, or maybe
it doesn't have to be. Am I strong enough to make those
changes—to live the life someone my age should be
living? I guess time will tell.

———

My phone taunts me from the kitchen counter. I pace
back and forth in front of it knowing what I need to do,
or what I want to do, and I'm just being a freaking baby
about it. My parents are gone—they went out for the day.
They'd invited me to go along, but I told my mom that
my plan was to see and spend time with Kaylee if she
was available.

She was so excited about it that when they left she
was smiling widely at me. I can't let her down, plus
Kaylee was my best friend, and if I'm truly trying to
move past what happened, then I really should be making
the effort to make positive changes.

Before I can chicken out, I pick up my phone and pull

her number up and hit the green button. It rings and rings, and I'm beginning to think she's busy, but right before I pull it away, she answers. "Hello?"

"K-Kaylee, it's B-Brylee."

I don't miss her swift intake of breath. "Brylee, it's great to hear from you. How are you?"

"I'm good. I wanted to see if you wanted to go out for lunch."

"That would be great. I just got done working so I could come by and get you. We could go to Szechwan's and share some dumplings like we used to." We went there all of the time when we were younger. On the weekends, she and I would walk there and order two steamed dumplings and Mongolian beef. We'd gorge ourselves and then walk home.

"Okay, that sounds great." We hang up, and I hustle into the bathroom to get ready. I already showered, so I just do my makeup and put my hair into a loose bun on top of my head. Szechwan's isn't a fancy place, so I throw on jean shorts and a black camisole with a royal-blue fitted T-shirt. I stick my feet in my black Nikes and tie them quickly before heading back into the living room.

I'm just sticking my phone in my purse when I hear Kaylee pull into the driveway. Taking a deep breath, I put a hand on my stomach—I will the nerves to fade, and thankfully they do...sort of. Before I step outside, I grab my phone to send Chase a text, but I stick it right back in. I don't want to appear desperate and cause him to stop hanging out with me.

Stepping out onto the front porch, I smile when I see Kaylee is driving a minivan. I open the passenger side door and climb inside.

She turns in her seat. "Don't laugh—I know I always said I'd never drive one of these, but just look at the room in the back. Giles and I have gotten really familiar with how much room we have." Her eyes are bright and she's smiling so big I bet her cheeks ache. I want to smile like that.

My cheeks heat up because images, albeit vague ones, come to mind because I've got no frame of reference of Chase and me together, but I push those thoughts out just as quickly as they appeared. "It's super fancy," I tell her as I look at the touchscreen and then the TVs in the back.

"Yep, Giles and I made a deal. If I had to buy the mom-mobile, then I was getting the one with all of the bells and whistles. Luckily my hubby loves me and agreed with my wishes."

We reach the restaurant, and once inside, the hostess leads us to a booth. She tries to give us menus, but Kaylee waves her hand. "No, we don't need menus. Just our waitress or waiter when they're available." The hostess looks at me and I nod, signaling that I don't need one either.

After we place our orders and get our drinks, she looks at me, and I swear she's going to cry. "I'm so glad you called me." She looks down, then back up at me. "To be honest, I didn't think you'd call."

"Well…if I'm being honest too, it took me giving myself a pep talk before I actually picked up the phone, but I'm glad I did. Tell me how you met Giles."

She blushes. "We actually met when he came in to get his hair cut. We started chatting about the fact that he just moved here and what places he should see or visit. I was feeling rather brave and asked him if he wanted me to show him around. He agreed, so the next day he picked me up at the shop, and I took him around. We had dinner together and then went back to his place, and I had the best sex of my life.

"I chalked it up to a one-night stand, but he wasn't having any of that and started sending me flowers and candy to the shop or surprising me by bringing me lunch. It was pretty sweet, so after about a month, I caved and agreed to a date. That was all she wrote. We got married six months later in Vegas. That was two years ago. He wanted kids right away, but I asked if we could please wait and really work on solidifying what we had."

"That's really amazing. I'm so happy for you, and he seems like a nice guy."

Kaylee reaches across the table and grabs my hands. "He really is. I'd love for you to get to know him better."

Before I can answer, our food arrives. My mouth immediately starts to water as I stare at all of it in front of us. "I don't know if I can eat this entire meal, but for some reason, I really want to try." Kaylee throws her head back and laughs. I don't miss the way her belly shakes when she does it, and I smile at her, and it feels good.

"I just can't believe we ate this much when we were younger with no problem. Lately, I'm not able to eat as much." She pats her belly.

"Do you know what you're having?" I ask before biting into a dumpling.

She shakes her head. "No, Giles wanted to find out, but I loved the idea of being told as soon as the baby came out. Of course the nursery isn't quite ready yet because I didn't want it painted until we knew, but the baby will sleep in a bassinet in our room for now."

Kaylee looks at me from across the table. "Why wouldn't you talk to me or answer my letters?"

My stomach dips because I knew this was coming at some point, but a part of me was not ready for this today. I can't blame her because we were like sisters, and I shut her out of my life completely. "I wasn't in a good place back then." I lay my hands on the table and flip them over so she can see the scars. A cry leaves her lips as she rubs her fingers over the white lines. "In the past ten years, I've tried to kill myself three times." A shiver runs down my spine thinking about the last time, which was in Chase's bedroom.

"I didn't want you to look at me like you are right now, but it's okay. It was hard shutting you out because you were my sister from another mister and I didn't want to drag you into the middle of my disastrous life."

"Brylee Eilene Whitmore, you know that I would've done anything for you. What happened was an accident, and you'll never convince me otherwise." We're both silent as we continue eating.

We finish and I pay for both of us, even though Kaylee tried to fight me on it. "Do you want to come to my house? We can sit on my back patio and talk some more, and I promise we will only talk about what you want to talk about. I'll tell you this right now, that I want to know what the hell is going on with you and Chase Foster."

I nod as we head to her minivan, and we're silent as we make the drive to a cute subdivision of newer homes. She pulls into the driveway of a ranch-style home that's part brick, part siding. Flowers and shrubbery decorate the front, giving it a little extra flair than some of the other homes. "Did you plant all of this stuff yourself?" I ask as we walk up the sidewalk toward the front door.

She doesn't answer right away, and I turn around. Kaylee is rubbing her belly, taking a deep breath. "Are you okay?"

"Yeah, it's just Braxton Hicks contractions. Not the real deal, but they still can sometimes take my breath away." She starts walking again. "Okay, I'm good now." She walks past me to the front door and lets us in.

Her place is decorated just how I imagined. She was always super girly, and I'm not surprised her home is decorated with dusky pinks, soft tans, and grayish blues. I walk over to the wall and smile as I look at their wedding photos. I knew she'd make a beautiful bride, but the pictures are proof. Her dress was a white trumpet-slash-mermaid off-the-shoulder sweep train dress that had a bit of lace overlay up top. Giles wore a fitted black suit with a thin black tie.

"You were such a beautiful bride."

She stands right next to me. "Thank you, but there was just one thing missing from my wedding day." Kaylee grabs my hand. "I didn't have my maid of honor there."

Tears fill my eyes. "I'm sorry I wasn't around to share in your special day."

"I know." Kaylee takes a deep breath. "Okay, no crying. If I start, I won't stop. Come, let me give you a tour." Her home is gorgeous but homey. It's a place where you want to just kick off your shoes and relax. "This is the nursery."

She opens the door to the room, and there's a crib, changing table, and dresser, but they're in the middle of the room. Tarps are folded up in the corner. "It doesn't look great yet, but it will once it's finished. Most of the clothes we have so far are gender neutral, but if I'm being honest, I think it's a little girl. It's just a feeling I get." Kaylee grabs her stomach again. "Ooh…damn these Braxton Hicks contractions suck.

"Now let's go outside."

We stop in the kitchen, and she hands me a bottle of water before leading me out to the deck. We get comfortable in a couple of chairs, and my eyes drift around the yard. It's big and spacious, and I can definitely see it being the type of yard children would have fun running around in.

"Tell me about Chase. How did that happen?"

What do I tell her? I can't tell her that he had kidnapped me and kept me tied up in his basement. She'd lose her mind about it. Kaylee had a temper when we were younger and always stuck up for the little guy, so she'd probably go after Chase herself.

I don't want to lie to her, but that's exactly what I'm going to do. "Um…I was at Kyle's grave and Chase showed up. We talked all night long, and I don't know, we've just started hanging out. It's just a friendship, I mean he's kissed me a couple of times, but I think he just wants to be friends."

"Honey, I don't think he wants to just be friends. I saw the way he was with you at the movies. He's definitely into you in a big way."

My face heats up, and I stare at my lap. I'm trying to not get my hopes up because maybe Kaylee was wrong in what she saw. "I don't know, maybe he is." Although I haven't heard from him at all today.

"He'd be stupid not to be into you. I know it's been ten years, but it doesn't change the fact that you're a good person and always have been. It's not unusual for there to be an attraction, and plus you were both into each other before the accident, so there has always been some sort of feeling there. You share a history, a connection."

"Yeah maybe, but maybe he's just trying to fix me."

"Oh shit." My eyes fly to Kaylee. "Brylee, my water just broke." Sure enough, a little puddle forms between her legs.

Panic consumes me as I jump up from my chair. "Oh God! What do you need me to do?"

"Um…can you help me change into some dry clothes?"

I help her into the house and follow her to her bedroom. Growing up, we'd seen each other naked enough that when she strips out of her wet clothes, I don't bat an eyelash. She grabs dry panties, and I pull a maxi dress out of her closet, helping slip it on over her head.

"Can you grab the baby's bag? It's in the nursery by the door."

Rushing to the nursery, I grab it, throwing the strap over my shoulder. She meets me in the hall, and we head toward the front. Kaylee grabs her cell phone and purse and hands me the keys. "Do you remember where St. Mercy is?"

"Yeah, but shouldn't we wait for Giles or call an ambulance?"

Kaylee starts to laugh. "That's funny. Giles works a half hour away, so I'll call him on our way." She pauses by the door with a hand on her belly, and she starts panting.

"Maybe we should call an ambulance, I really think we should."

Kaylee grabs my hand in hers. "I'm seriously okay."

I can't tell her that I don't have a license, that I'm terrified to drive—so I don't. I walk outside and help her into the passenger seat and then climb in the driver's side. I'm taller than she is, so I scoot my seat back a little bit. Taking a deep breath, I close my eyes, whispering, *"I can do this,"* to myself over and over again. I go over the rules of the road in my head to distract me from my fear.

Slowly I back the van out of the driveway and head in the direction of the hospital. My hands shake as I grip the steering wheel so tight that my knuckles are white. As I head down the street, Kaylee calls her husband, and tears fill my eyes. I don't know what he says to her, but Kaylee rests a hand on her stomach and softly cries, "I know. I can't wait to meet our baby either. Okay, I love you, baby." She wipes her eyes and gives me a smile. "He's leaving now."

I know I'm driving extremely slowly, but luckily Kaylee doesn't seem to notice. We reach the hospital a few minutes later, and I drop her off at the main entrance while I park her van. I let out a sigh of relief, closing my eyes and resting my head on her steering wheel as I shut her van off. I grab the bags and take off through the parking lot until I reach the automatic doors. I find Kaylee inside them waiting. "Why didn't you go get checked in?"

"I didn't want you to have to hunt for me."

I help her stand up, and we stop at the main desk. While they get her registered, I stand off to the side and pull my phone out, shooting Chase a quick text.

> **Brylee**
> Hey, I was with Kaylee today and her water broke. I just brought her to the hospital. Kaylee's having her baby!!

I immediately see the little bubbles appear, which means he's answering me right now.

> **Chase**
> That's great. Do you need me to come get you?

He does stuff like that, and it makes me feel like maybe he does have feelings for me.

> **Brylee**
> Yeah that'd be great. I'll text you when her husband gets here.

> **Chase**
> Sounds good, babe.

They wheel her upstairs, and in her room, I help her get changed into her gown. After that, they hook her up to a machine that lets us hear the heartbeat. The nurse starts her IV, and then they check her. She's already dilated to five centimeters. Kaylee refuses pain meds, opting to do it naturally.

I'm in the middle of rubbing her back when her husband comes running into the room. I step back while they embrace and feel myself get just a tiny bit jealous. I wish I had what she did. Giles turns and thanks me for getting her here safely. That's my cue to leave.

Walking over to the bed, she holds her hand out to

me. "I'm going to leave you to it. You're going to be a wonderful momma, this baby is lucky."

She shakes her head. "Please stay. We were always supposed to do this together."

"I don't want to intrude." I look at Giles. I don't know him, so I don't know how he'd feel about this.

"Whatever my baby wants, she gets." He smiles warmly at me, but then our attention is drawn to Kaylee as she begins to moan.

It's four hours later when I'm finally leaving. Kaylee, Giles, and their son Christian are resting comfortably. Kaylee was a rock star and handled labor and delivery like a boss. She said it was yoga that helped her be able to handle the labor and then when it was time to push. It was after she'd delivered the baby that her parents showed up. Giles's parents passed away when he was a teenager. Her mom and dad were amazing, and at least this baby would have one amazing set of grandparents.

When her mom saw me standing in the room, she grabbed me and pulled me into a huge hug and began to cry, which made me cry. I promised her I'd stop by to see them before I went home.

I step out of the automatic doors and find Chase in his truck waiting for me. I wasn't sure that the offer would still stand when I texted him four hours later than planned, but he immediately responded that he'd be on his way to get me. I climb in and shut the door behind me.

"Well?" he asks. I pull out my phone and show him the pictures I took of Christian. "He's a good-looking boy." He swipes and freezes. I look at my phone, and it's the picture of me with Christian in my arms. I almost don't recognize myself because my smile is so bright. "You're breathtaking," he whispers.

I look up at him, and his face is close to mine. He grabs it in his hand and pulls me to him. Our lips meet in a slow glide, and his tongue peeks out, licking the seam of my lips. Opening to him, our tongues dance and my fingers find their way into his hair, and I moan into his mouth.

A knock on the window has us pulling away from each other. A security guard is at Chase's window. "Move along," he says, and Chase nods before starting his truck and pulling away.

We pull out of the parking lot ,and my stomach chooses to growl loudly. "Are you hungry?"

"Yeah, kind of, it's been a while since I've eaten."

He pulls into the parking lot of El Mexicana, which was my favorite Mexican restaurant when I was younger. We get seated at a table in front of the windows at the front. I don't bother looking at the menu. "Okay, you've obviously eaten here. What's good?"

"Um...the carne asada tacos are amazing or the shrimp fajitas." When our waitress comes, I order the tacos, and he orders the fajitas. He says it's so we can share.

He grabs my hand. "What was the whole birth thing like?"

"It was amazingly beautiful but so fucking scary I thought I might pass out. Kaylee was a champ. I'm sure it helped that Giles knew when to comfort her and when to back off. I was surprised she asked me to stay, but that had always been the plan when we were younger. We always swore that we'd share the birth of our children together."

"Do you want kids?"

I shake my head, my throat feels thick. "Not anymore, not after what happened." Thankfully our food arrives, and I don't have to talk about it anymore. I lied to him, I want kids—I want them more than anything, but I'm scared. Karma could try and take them away from me, and I just can't chance it. Plus, up until now, I've kept my distance from others. ,

"You may change your mind someday."

I shrug my shoulders and go back to eating. Luckily he doesn't bring it up again. When we finish up, we leave and he takes me home. He pulls up in front of my parents' house, and I'll never admit I'm a little disappointed that he didn't take me back to his place, but he doesn't owe me anything. "Thanks for picking me up."

"Sure, I'll call or text you later."

He leans toward me and kisses me quickly. I hop out of his truck and give him a wave before heading inside to tell my mom all about Kaylee and the baby.

SEVENTEEN
CHASE

I pull away from the curb and head toward the clubhouse. Dropping her off and leaving her at her parents' had been hard. I want nothing more than to spend time with her, but I needed to step back to see if the feelings that I'm developing are real or just guilt for kidnapping her. It's not fair to her if it's just the guilt talking.

Pulling my truck into the lot outside of the clubhouse, I hop out and make my way inside. Loco is sitting at the bar with a bottle of beer sitting in front of him. "What's up, old man?"

He turns to me. "Who you calling old? I'd kick your ass in two seconds." I won't even test that theory because he could. He'd have me on the floor before I knew what was even happening. "How's Brylee?" I was with him when she had texted me that Kaylee was having her baby.

"She's good. I think she was riding the high of watching her friend's baby being born."

"Why aren't you with her now?" He takes a sip of his beer, and I go behind the bar, grabbing my own.

"Because I'm starting to have strong feelings for her, and I want to make sure that the feelings I have are real and not some weird sense of guilt."

"That's probably the smartest thing I've ever heard you say." He chuckles while he lights a cigarette and passes it over to me.

"You're an ass," I tell him while sticking the cigarette in my mouth and lighting it. "I could tell she was hurt that I was dropping her off at home, but I didn't want to tell her why. It would hurt her feelings."

"Not to get all deep with you, but isn't that your answer right there? I mean, you didn't want to hurt her feelings—since when did you care about anyone's feelings but your own?"

He's right. I sit down next to him. I'll finish my beer and cigarette then go see her, and we'll talk.

Arms wrap around my shoulders—it's Kelly. "Hey, baby. Do you want to have some fun with me tonight?"

I grab her arms and lift them off of me. "Sorry, babe, I'm taken." Am I? Yes, I am. I need to go right now and see Brylee. I don't know if Kelly pouts or what, but I yell over my shoulder to Loco that I'll talk to him later.

Outside in my truck, I pop a piece of gum in my mouth and drive across town to Brylee's parents' house. It's still early enough that I know no one is asleep as I park in front of the house. I climb out of my truck and make my way up to the front door and ring the doorbell. A moment later Brylee answers the door.

"Chase? What are you doing here?"

"I thought that maybe we could go for a walk."

"Okay, let me tell my parents and grab my shoes. Do you want to wait here?" I nod so she disappears inside and returns a couple of minutes later. She sits down on the steps, slipping her shoes on. Once that's done, she stands up, and we walk down the front steps to the sidewalk. I grab her hand, lacing our fingers together, and we make our way down the street.

With my free hand, I shake a cigarette out of my pack and grab it with my teeth. I light it and hold it between my lips while I shove the pack back into my back pocket. Pulling it out of my mouth, I blow out the smoke. She looks up at me and smiles. "Is the smoke bothering you?"

She shakes her head. "No. What's on your mind?" I stare at her in shock because she's right, I do have stuff on my mind. How is it she can read me already?

"I have feelings for you." She freezes. "I don't want to lie to you, but I don't know how I feel about it. For so long, I felt like I hated you, but then it changed, and now I don't know what to fucking do about it." I take a drag of my cigarette and blow it out. "One thing I do know is that I can't stay away from you."

She doesn't say anything, and after my confession, I don't either, but now she knows, and she knows that I have no clue what I'm doing or what I should do about it.

We're a couple blocks down when she finally speaks. "I'm heading back to Chicago in two days, then you won't have to think about me again."

I grab her by her upper arms and turn her to me. "Do you think that's what I want because it's not. Truth is, I don't know if I can forgive you yet." She tries to pull away, but I hold her tighter. "I'm trying to, I swear to God I am, but I need you to forgive me for what I did to you too."

Brylee turns away from me, and I know there's got to be a part of her that doesn't forgive me, and until we can forgive each other, how can I expect her to forgive herself?

"You are so, so pretty." My hand reaches up, and my thumb rubs back and forth across the apple of her cheek that has turned the most adorable shade of pink. Pulling my hand away, I grab her hand in mine. "We should head back." Turning around, we head back down the street toward her parents' house.

I watch her out of the corner of my eye as she plays with her hair with her free hand. It sucks that I've made her uncomfortable, but it needed to be said. Brylee needed to know how I felt and that I'm conflicted.

Giving it a go with her could prove to be very bad for us, but it could also be something fucking amazing, and that's why I think we owe it to ourselves to do it...or at least try.

I walk her up to her front door and pull her into my arms. She fits perfectly against me, and with a little extra meat on her bones, she'll fit even better. "Can I take you to breakfast in the morning?"

Brylee nods, her forehead against my neck. "Yes."

"Good. I'll be here at nine." I pull back enough to lean down and kiss her softly on the lips. "Bye." I kiss her cheek before turning and walking back to my truck and climbing back in. Pulling away, I look in my mirror and find her standing on the front stoop with her fingers on her lips, and I fucking smile.

———

BRYLEE

I'm silent as Chase drives us toward the airport. When he'd taken me to breakfast the day before, he'd asked my parents if he could drive me to the airport and they both hesitantly said yes, but with the promise that I'd have dinner with them and the next morning, today, I'd have breakfast with them.

My heart is full and happy that a relationship, or a new one between us is possible. I don't expect things to be better overnight, but we all need to make an effort. I want to make the effort. I never realized how sad and lonely I really was. The heart attack could've killed my dad, and then what would have happened? I'd be riddled with guilt because I didn't heal that breach.

Had I not made the effort that I have so far, I would've missed out on the hugs that my parents seemed to love dishing out.

Chase places his hand on my thigh, bringing me back to the present. "Where'd you go?" he asks, giving my thigh a squeeze.

"Just thinking I was glad that I spent time with my folks and tried to shorten the gap between us. I've made a promise to myself that I'll make more of an effort with them. You know, calling them and stuff." I chance a glance at Chase, and he's got a small smile on his lips.

All too soon, we pull up in front of the airport. We climb out of his truck, and he grabs my suitcase out of the back and comes around to meet me on the sidewalk. For the first time in my life, I don't want to be alone anymore. I don't want to say goodbye, but I have to. I know I have nothing or anyone waiting for me, but I'm hoping to change that—I'm hoping that there are things that I can attempt and succeed at. I want to be worthy of Chase's forgiveness. I want to work toward forgiving myself.

"Call me when you land. Let me know you got back to your place safely." I nod my head. "Be safe."

He wraps his arms around me, hugging me tightly. Chase's warmth seeps into my body, chasing away the ever-present chill. "I'm going to miss you," I whisper into his neck. If I'm being honest, I'm surprised I even said it at all.

Chase pulls away and kisses my lips slowly, causing tingles to start in my belly. I wish I would've had the chance to do more with him physically, but it just wasn't meant to be. At least I've gotten to share some really beautiful kisses with him. He pulls away all too soon and smiles down at me. He opens his mouth, then closes it before he tells me. "I better let you go so you can get checked in."

Disappointment fills me, but what did I really expect? He'll probably be glad when I'm gone so he doesn't have to remember what I did.

Giving him a smile, I pull the handle out so I can roll my suitcase behind me. "Yeah, I should go. Thank you for the ride."

I make my way toward the automatic doors, and when I'm halfway to the door, I turn and find Chase standing there watching me walk away. Lifting my hand, I give him a small wave. I get the obligatory chin lift, and then I head inside the doors.

My eyes flutter open, and I see we're preparing to land. I open my bottle of water and take a huge drink.

I'm not sure why, but earlier I was hit with this insatiable thirst. I drank two bottles of water while I waited for my flight, and then I drank the one in my hand while I waited for the plane to take off, but then I fell asleep.

After landing and pulling up to the gate, I power my phone up and send a quick text to Chase letting him know that I've landed. Down at baggage claim, I grab my suitcase and then make my way toward the L.

Hopping on, I stare blankly out the window as we begin to move along the tracks. My apartment is only two stops away, so it doesn't take that long before I'm stepping off and making my way down the stairs. My apartment is three blocks away, and I flag down a cab anyway. I get dropped off and make my way inside.

The first thing that hits me about my tiny little studio apartment is that it barely looks like someone lives here. Nothing hangs on the walls, and nothing sits on top of my end table or coffee table. My full-size bed sits in the corner with its plain white comforter and plain white sheets. I throw my suitcase on my bed and quickly unpack.

Luckily, I did laundry last night, so all of my clothes are clean, and now I won't have to worry about doing laundry anytime soon. In my bathroom, I put my toiletries away, and again I'm hit with just how dull my apartment is. My towels and bath mat are all mono-chrome, a plain light tan color.

Zipping my suitcase up, I stick it in my closet and wonder if I'll ever have the opportunity to use it again. In my little galley kitchen, I grab some ibuprofen—my head hurts all of a sudden. I swallow down the tablets with a huge glass of water.

Climbing into my bed, I lie on my back and stare at the ceiling. Am I brave enough to make changes? Can I start living the life I should've had ten years ago?

Maybe or maybe not, but I owe it to myself and my parents to try.

EIGHTEEN
BRYLEE

It's been a week since I've been home. I made a promise to myself that I was going to do something new each week. This week I'm going to make an effort to get to know my coworkers. I know it might not go well because the whole time I've worked there, I haven't made the effort, but all it takes is one person to talk to me then the others will follow...I hope.

I talked to Chase last night. Our contact has mainly been texts, and that's okay, it was just nice to hear from him at all. I decided against telling him my plan, mainly because I didn't want to let him down if I was unable to do it. Sharing with him that I've made friends is what I really want to do.

I button up my white dress shirt, rolling up the sleeves to my elbows. Grabbing my leather bracelets off of my dresser, I slip them on both wrists, hiding the scars. The ends stick out from under the leather, so I use this amazing cover-up I found that doesn't come off easily. I slip into my black dress pants and notice when I go to zip them up that they're a tad bit snug.

The day after I got home, I went to the market and stocked up on groceries. Every day I ate five small meals a day. If I ate too much, then I didn't feel well. I don't own a scale, but I'm sure I've gained some weight.

Slipping my feet into a pair of black ballet flats, I grab my purse and my keys before heading out to the restaurant. Maggio's is a pretty well-known Italian restaurant, a family-owned place. It's a father-son duo and treats all of us like family...even me, and I don't ever come to any of their parties or hang out to chat after work. They're still good to me and treat me just like everyone else.

I walk the two blocks to the restaurant and enter through the front door. Casey, another waitress, is putting her stuff in her locker when I enter the break room. "Hi, Casey." She jerks her head up and looks at me.

"Um...hey, Brylee. How are you?"

Keep it cool, I think to myself. "Good, thanks. How are you?" *Ugh*, I sound like a robot.

"I'm good." She looks at me closely. "You look great. I don't know what it is, but you look fantastic."

My cheeks heat up, and I whisper a *thank you* before grabbing a stick of gum and popping it in my mouth before stuffing my purse in my locker.

The whole night went well. I didn't talk a whole lot because I didn't want to freak them out or something. We were busy, and people were feeling generous with the tips. It was nice to actually let myself enjoy talking to the customers.

Casey offered to drive me home, and I actually said yes for a change. We didn't really talk a whole lot in the car, but it was nice to not feel so lonely.

Now I'm sticking my tips into a little fire safe that I

EVAN GRACE

keep under my bed. I shove it back under there and move the box back in front of it. In the kitchen, I make myself some chicken and chicken-flavored Rice-a-Roni.

When it's done, I sit on my bed with my plate of food and my laptop and get caught up on episodes of Masterchef. I'd never make it on a show like that. I would cry the first time Chef Ramsay yelled at me.

After I eat, I stick my plate in the sink and go sit back down on my bed. I pick up my phone and see that I have a friend request on Facebook, and it's from Chase. I normally don't even use social media. Oh sure, I signed up for it, but it was merely so I could get a glimpse of Kaylee's life, and I didn't or couldn't make contact.

I shake my head as I open the app, and my thumb hovers over the accept or decline button. "Stop being a baby," I whisper harshly to myself. Before I can talk myself out of it, I hit the accept button.

I open my texting program.

> **Brylee**
> Hi!

It takes a couple more minutes before I see the little conversation bubbles pop up.

> **Chase**
> Hey you. Did you work tonight?

> **Brylee**
> Yeah, it was a good night. I made some killer tips.

196

Chase
That's great. I hung out at the clubhouse
tonight. Drank some beers with the
guys, and now I'm watching the
Cardinals.

I lie down while I wait for him to respond, but my eyes drift shut.

I open my eyes and see that it's dawn. Out the window next to my bed, I see the sky is a purplish red, and soon the sun will be up. Rolling over in bed, I close my eyes and fall back asleep.

The sun is shining brightly in the sky when I finally wake up. I grab my phone and see that it's ten thirty. I also see that I have an unanswered text from Chase. Why do butterflies take flight in my belly when his name pops up on my screen?

Chase
Hello????

Another one came in ten minutes after that.

Chase
I'm guessing you're asleep. G'night, and
I'll talk to you tomorrow.

I send a quick text to him.

Brylee
Sorry about last night. I guess I was
exhausted. Talk to you later.

After climbing out of bed, I use the bathroom and then brush my teeth. In the kitchen, I make some coffee and throw two pieces of bread in the toaster, and when it's done, I smear Nutella on it along with some sliced strawberries.

Once I'm done eating, I clean up my kitchen and start walking around my little studio. I need to brighten up the space, but how should I do it? I change out of my pajamas and throw on yoga pants and a fitted T-shirt and slip my feet into my flip-flops. I brush out my hair and throw it into a ponytail, skipping the makeup until it's time to get ready for work.

There are a couple different stores that are within walking distance that sell used goods, maybe I can find some pieces for my place. I grab some money out of my safe and stick it into my wallet.

Locking up, I make my way outside, stick my earbuds in, and listen to my music while I make my way toward the first shop. The sign for *Nostalgia* is up ahead. It carries a lot of vintage pieces. I spin in a slow circle inside as I take in all of the pieces. The scent of cinnamon hits my nose, and Elvis plays softly in the background.

My flip-flops slap against the black-and-white tile as I slowly move through the store, looking for pieces to buy.

"Can I help you?" I turn and find an older woman smiling at me.

"I was just looking. I'm trying to find some decorative pieces for my place." I scan the items around me.

She clasps her hands in front of her. "Do you have a color you'd like to use? What color is your sofa?"

"Um…well, it's dark tan. I like the color lavender a lot."

The woman gives me a sweet smile. "That's a lovely color. It's nice and soft."

She takes me around the shop and shows me a picture in a light wood frame. It's of the Eiffel Tower, and the sky is a beautiful shade of purple. I tell her I want it, and then I pick out an old pitcher and glass set. It'll be more for decoration. It's clear, but when the light shines on it, so many bright colors appear.

I pay for my purchases, and she suggests another shop that's not too far that sells decorative pillows, blankets, and towels—all brand new, but eclectic designs. After I leave, I decide to take the stuff I bought home before hitting that other store. I set my bags on the coffee table and then turn around and walk out.

The shop is lovely, decorated in a soft rose color and different shades of cream. This time it's the scent of roses that hits my nose. A picture across the store draws my attention, and I move across the room toward it. It's two small boys, one chasing the other. Tears fill my eyes as I remember seeing the picture of Chase and his brother and how this picture reminds me of it.

I have to buy it, whether I give it to Chase or his mom or keep it for myself. I grab it and take it to the register and then go over to the decorative pillows. Once I'm finished picking several out, I pick out a couple of throws to lay on my bed and drape over the couch.

Once I'm home, I toss some of the pillows on my bed and some on my couch. I take the throw that is swirls of creams, lavender, and rose-pink and drape it across the back of the couch. Then I grab the dark lavender throw and drape it across the end of my bed. The wall next to my bed is where I end up hanging the Eiffel Tower picture, and for now, I hang the picture of the two boys above my couch.

I set up the pitcher and glasses on my little table in

the little dining room I have. It's amazing how just a few decorations can really spruce a place up. I pick up my phone and snap a couple of pictures. I had taken some earlier that were the before pictures.

I send them to my mom with the caption, I decorated a little.

It doesn't take long before she replies.

> **Mom**
> Oh honey, I love it. What a difference a little color can do. Are things good?

> **Brylee**
> Yes, things are good. How's Dad?

> **Mom**
> He's great. Today he was back at work, and so far so good.

That makes me feel better knowing that my dad is getting back on track with things. It's one less thing to worry about while I try to fix the fractured mess my life has become.

> **Brylee**
> I'm going to lie down for a nap before work but tell Dad I'll call him tomorrow.

> **Mom**
> Will do, honey. I love you.

> **Brylee**
> Love you too.

I grab my Kindle and lie down on top of my comforter, turning it on and pulling up the book I've been reading. It takes only minutes before I'm lost in my fictional world, and then shortly after, I drift off to sleep, proud for once that I've made a positive change in my life.

———

After cashing out my last table, I head into the break room to get my purse and head home. It was a long day, and my feet hurt. All of my shift I tried to be more sociable with my coworkers. It's sad that they all seem to be in shock that I'm trying to talk to them.

Brian, one of the bartenders, comes into the break room. "Hey, Brylee, we're going down to Charlie's at the end of the street. Do you want to come and have a drink with us?"

I give him what I hope is a relaxed smile. "Sure, that'd be nice." I close my locker and put my purse over my shoulder.

"Great, Sam and Carly are already there, and Casey's coming as soon as her last table leaves. Come on, you can walk down with me." On our way, he talks the whole time about his wife and his kids. I smile looking down at the sidewalk as we walk. "Sorry, I talk a lot." He's silent for a minute. "It looks good on you."

"What does?" I ask.

"Your smile, you don't do it enough."

What does one say to that? I simply tell him thank you, and we reach the bar before I have to say anything else. We're greeted with smiles, and I pull out my chair, sitting next to Carly when we reach the table.

"I'm glad you came," Carly leans into me and says. "How was your night? Your section was hopping."

"It was good, but b-busy. What about you? The bar

was always full." Ugh, I suck at small talk. When I was younger, I would never stop talking, now, or at least up until recently, I talked sparsely.

"It's the midweek blahs, hump day. They're about over their work week." She takes a drink of her beer. "I heard about your dad. How's he doing?"

"He's doing great, thanks for asking. Now he's back at work, which is good for him. He likes to stay busy."

I only stayed a couple of hours, but I'm happy to admit I had a great time. A lot of the talking was not done by me, but I got to know the others really well. The stories they shared made me miss that closeness with others. It made me miss Chase, which is fucked up because, let's be honest, he kidnapped me and wanted me dead. I won't deny, though, that I turn to mush when he kisses me, and that's so fucked up and confusing. I'll never admit that I want him—I want him with every fiber of my being.

I hate that it bothers him that he has feelings for me and that he doesn't know what to do with them. But there's nothing I can do or say that will help him with his decision. I want him to come to whatever decision on his own without me swaying him one way or another.

It's still early enough that I feel safe walking home alone. Of course I have my pepper spray at the ready just in case. When I step inside my apartment, I lock the door and toss my purse on my table. I change out of my work clothes and into shorts and a T-shirt.

I grab my phone and sit down on the bed.

Brylee
Hi. How are you?

I'm not sure if he'll even respond, he seems to be spending more time at the clubhouse. I'm sure he's been with those women, and I know I don't have a right to be upset or care, but I do. For a short time he made me feel special and like maybe a man could find me desirable.

I send another text.

Brylee
I went out with a few coworkers tonight, and it was nice—I had fun.

After plugging my phone into the charger, I grab a bottle of water. Before I climb into bed, I turn on my TV and lie in bed watching reruns of *The Big Bang Theory*. It's more for background noise as I stare at the ceiling thinking about the past ten years. I've wasted so much time hating myself and merely existing, and those are my thoughts as I fall asleep.

I begin to cough over and over again. Sitting up, I reach for my bottle of water and chug half of it down. My cough finally stops and I lie back down. *So weird*, I think to myself. Maybe I'm getting sick. This isn't the first coughing fit I've had lately. In the morning I'll make an appointment with my doctor and just make sure that it isn't anything to be worried about.

NINETEEN
CHASE

I pick up my phone from the bar at the clubhouse and see it's a text from Brylee. Opening the message, I can't help but smile. She actually went out with some coworkers tonight. A sense of pride fills me because I know that it had to have been hard for her, but she did it anyway.

Grabbing my beer off the counter, I take a swig, ignoring Kelly, who has been trying to hop on my dick this past week, but I've constantly turned her down. I'm fucking horny, but I've been using my hand—not wanting to fuck anyone else until I figured out what I was going to do about Brylee, which is a first for me. I've never cared about hurting some chick's feelings, but I care about hurting hers.

She's been on my mind a lot, and all it's left me is confused. I want her, but I don't. When we kiss, I forget all rational thought, and I just want to bury my dick as far inside her as I can. What's wrong with me? I'm beginning to think less and less about the accident and about my brother dying. Instead I'm thinking of her and the pain she's lived with for the past ten years.

I pull up her number to call her, but Grayson sits down next to me. "What's up? You've been quiet, and Kelly won't stop whining about you ignoring her. Is this about Brylee?"

"She texted me tonight that she went out with some coworkers, and I'm really proud of her. I know that wasn't easy for her."

"That's good, right?"

I nod my head.

"Okay, so what's that got to do with fucking Kelly?"

I grab a cigarette and place it between my lips and light it. The smoke fills my lungs before I blow it out. "I can't, no, I won't, do anything until I know for sure what I plan to do about Brylee."

"So...is she your girlfriend?"

I shake my head.

"Well, what is she then, because let's not forget you were going to hurt her or whatever the fuck it was that you had planned?" He says the last part in a harsh whisper.

"I don't know what she is, and yes, I'm very aware of what I almost did, but things have changed, and I need to figure out what I'm going to do. I don't need some random pussy clouding my mind."

He looks at me closely. "Okay. I get it. I'm sure it can't be easy developing feelings for someone who you share the kind of history that you guys do. I'll make sure the girls know that you're not available and to stop bothering you."

"Thanks, man. Sorry, I'm not trying to be a prick."

Grayson raises his brow.

"Yeah, okay, maybe I like being a prick. Sue me. I'm gonna take off." He pulls me into a back-slapping hug, and I shove him away and flip him off as I make my way outside. Climbing on my bike, I pull out and make my way toward home.

After parking in my garage, I head inside and pull my phone out of my pocket and call Brylee.

"Hello?"

"Hey, it's me. Tell me about your night. That's really great, by the way." I can't hide the pride in my voice.

"T-thanks. Well, the other day I started talking to Casey just a little bit, it was awkward, but I did it. Once she started talking to me, the others slowly started talking to me too. I know a few of them go out sometimes after work, and I happened to be in the break room when Brian was in there and had asked me if I wanted to meet them all for drinks."

Why do I not like that it was a guy who asked her to go? I try not to analyze it right now.

"He's a bartender, so he's really chatty, telling me about his wife and kids. I didn't really have to worry about talking because he did enough of it for the both of us. They all talk a lot, but they were really nice." She sounds excited, which fills me with something I haven't felt in a long time—joy.

"That's great, babe. Just be careful." I pack a bowl and sit out back smoking it while she tells me about decorating her place.

She sends me the before and after pictures, and it's amazing how just a little bit of color really changes the look of a place. It's been a few weeks since she's been there, and already the changes are monumental. Maybe not to other people, but knowing her history, these steps are all big.

"Your place looks great."

"Thanks, I guess I never realized how plain it was. The stuff I got was super cheap too. How are things with you?" Her voice turns awkward and stiff.

It makes me smile, and well, maybe it's the weed too. "Things are good, babe. Just working on the bike I'm rebuilding and being busy at the shop. I've been hanging at the clubhouse a lot more just because I miss you being around." I pull the phone away from my ear, close my eyes, and tilt my head back. I've been trying to keep things neutral for now, but her happiness is doing all sorts of things to me.

I put the phone to my ear. "—miss you too." I catch the tail end of it.

"Have you thought at all about getting your driver's license?"

Her sigh comes through the line. "I-I don't know. Maybe."

"I can understand why you'd hesitate, but please think about it."

"Yeah, okay, maybe. I promise I'll think about it."

We don't talk much longer before we hang up with the promise we'll talk later. I finish smoking my bowl, and closing my eyes, I lean back in my chair. The euphoric buzz settles over my body, and I smile up at the sky.

————

I'm leaning over the engine of a Camaro. My mind wanders to the past couple of weeks. She's changing, every day, little by little. I've loved hearing about it, but then a small part of me hates that I love hearing it. A part of me still wants her to be the sad, lonely woman I

EVAN GRACE

kidnapped. Then of course I'm pissed at myself for even thinking that. I want to be a part of these new experiences she's living.

She's been out shopping with girls from her restaurant, and she's been hanging around the vintage shop she got some stuff at. The owner has apparently taken a liking to her and has been mentoring her, which is great. Brylee having as many positive people in her life is for the best. The positivity will continue to rub off on her.

This past weekend I texted her to see what was up, and she and the wife of a coworker were getting their nails done. Brylee had texted that she was going to call me later, and I didn't hear from her until late that night. Don't get me wrong, I was happy she was out doing stuff, but I was starting to feel left out. It was crazy to even go there, but that was how I felt.

The boys and I have been keeping an eye on her folks and making sure they didn't need anything. Her dad has been friendly to us, and her mom is nice but leery, which was completely understandable. She may not know what happened originally between Brylee and me, but given our history, she's always been watchful. Again, it's completely understandable.

My mom's been grilling me for information every time I'm over there. When I would tell her details about Brylee, she'd wear the sweetest smile on her face. I know my ma has refrained from asking questions about Brylee and me, which is good because I don't know how to answer her.

"Chase?" I'm back to the present and turn to find Loco standing in the doorway. "Did you still want a ride to the airport in the morning?"

Earlier this week I made the decision to surprise

Brylee with a visit. I want to see her and see for myself the progress she's made. Plus, I fucking miss her, and I just want to hug her and to hold her. "Yeah, that'd be great. I need to look at Ma's car when I get back, it's acting up again. Hers wouldn't make it."

"Don't worry about that. I'll have Grayson get it and bring it back to the shop." He slaps me on the back before disappearing into the back.

I turn back to the engine and get back to work.

———

I disembark the plane and make my way out of the airport with my bag slung over my shoulder. Nervous anticipation fills me as I arrange for an Uber to pick me up. Moving through the crowd, I make my way toward the exit.

This morning I had made sure to find out where Brylee was going to be without her knowing why. I hope she doesn't care that I plan on crashing at her place. Three days is all I have time for due to the shop being busy.

My driver pulls up, and I climb inside, giving him the address for Maggio's. Brylee is working the lunch shift this week, so she's only on until four. I look at my phone, and it's three fifteen. I figure I'll go order something to eat and then hang out until she's done. Fuck, I hope she's not mad that I'm just going to show up like this.

We reach the restaurant; I get out and take a deep breath before walking inside. The place is really nice. It's decorated in reds, black, and white. The man at the hostess station is wearing a fitted suit. "Just one today?"

"Yeah, and could you sit me in Brylee's section?"

The guy's eyes light up before he grabs a menu and leads me to a table in the corner. I look around and don't see Brylee anywhere yet. I set my bag in the chair across from me before sitting down.

"Would you like me to let her know you're here?"

I shake my head. "It's actually a surprise."

He nods and then hands me a menu. "She'll be right with you. Enjoy your meal."

The host disappears up front, and that's when I see her making her way toward me, stopping to talk to a couple of her tables. It gives me the chance to watch her without her knowing. The smile on her face is breathtaking, her hair looks a little longer, and she looks curvier, but maybe it's all in my head. It hasn't been that long since I've seen her. My dick immediately begins to perk up, but I will it to go down. I don't need to be sporting wood in her place of employment.

I hide my face from her as she moves toward me. "Hi there, welcome to Maggio's. I'm Brylee, and I will be your server. Can I start you out with something to drink?"

Lowering the menu, I give her a smile. "Hi."

"Oh my gosh. What are you doing here?" She smiles at me, and I make a split decision, standing up and pulling her into my arms. Her light floral scent wraps around me as well as her arms. I don't miss the way she fits better against me, and I fucking love it.

"I wanted to see you and surprise you…obviously. Is this okay?"

She nods her head enthusiastically. "It's great. Really. Sit and look over the menu. Do you want a beer? We've got a couple different Italian beers. I could bring you one and surprise you."

"That'd be great, and honestly, why don't you pick your favorite meal for me?"

Her teeth bite into her lower lip. "Okay, I can do that. Is there anything you won't eat?"

"Not really. I'm not a huge fish fan, but other than that, I'll eat anything."

She gives me a small smile. "Okay, I'll take care of you, and I'll be back with your beer in a few minutes." She goes to walk away but turns back toward me. "I'm really glad you're here." She says it quietly, and it causes warmth to spread through my chest and gut.

A few minutes later she brings me my beer and a glass of water. I drink it as I Google places to go that are within walking distance of Brylee's place. Her dad had given me the address to her apartment, so I plugged her address in and points of interest. If we take the L, we could be in the heart of downtown and at Millennium Park within fifteen minutes. The entrance to the L is only a couple of blocks from her apartment.

"Here you go." Brylee returns and sets a plate down in front of me loaded with food. "This is my personal favorite, chicken piccata. It's served with our own red-skinned mashed potatoes."

My stomach growls, and Brylee starts to laugh. It's a melodic sound that I hope to God I get to hear more of, and I want to be the one that makes her laugh.

She starts coughing, covering her mouth with her arm. I stand up and grab her upper arms. "Baby? Are you okay?"

Brylee nods her head. "Yeah, sorry, I've had this nagging cough that comes and goes. I've been to the doctor, and everything checks out. I'm not sure what the deal is, but as long as I guzzle water down, then I don't start coughing." My eyes must betray the calmness I'm showing because she cups my cheek with her hand. "I'm fine, I promise. Now eat your food, and I'll be done shortly and I'll come sit with you."

She disappears into the back and worry washes over me. I didn't realize she'd been dealing with a cough. Maybe if it happens again, I'll have to take her to the hospital to get checked out. I turn back to my food and cut into a piece of chicken and try to control the moan that wants to slip past my lips when I pop it into my mouth.

Before I know it, my plate is empty and my beer is gone. A short, slightly heavy-set dark-haired man comes toward me with a broad smile on his bearded face. "You must be Chase. I'm Brian—my wife Erica has been hanging out with Brylee a lot lately." I stand up and take his offered hand in mine, giving it a firm shake. "I'm guessing you're the reason why Bry has started opening up and talking to us."

"I may have given her the nudge, but it was all her. How long has she been doing that coughing thing?"

"Uhh…I'm not sure, maybe a week or two that we've all noticed, but before that, I don't know. Sorry."

"It's cool, I just didn't like the sound of it. I'm here for the next three days, so if it gets bad I'll make her go to the hospital."

"Good idea. I've got to get back behind the bar, but nice meeting you, and I hope we get a chance to hang out before you head home." He walks back behind the bar, and I'm just sitting down when Brylee comes out with a white slip of paper.

"Here's your bill, and just FYI, my manager, Roberta,

let me give you my employee discount since I don't use it a lot, or more like ever."

I pick up the bill and turn it over. Jesus, they practically give away meals to their employees. I'll just have to leave Brylee a big tip. I hand her my card, and she disappears with it. Once that's all done, I step outside to smoke while she finishes up her side work.

After snuffing out my smoke, I step back inside and stop in the bathroom to take a piss, and wash my hands. I head back out to my table and finish my water while I wait. A few minutes go by, and she comes walking out with her purse over her shoulder.

"You all finished?"

"Yep, I'm all done."

I stand and grab my bag before grabbing her hand in mine. We head in the direction of what I'm assuming her apartment is in.

"What made you decide to come see me?"

"I wanted to see for myself how you've been doing. You know I've missed you." Out of the corner of my eye, I can see her cheeks turn an adorable shade of pink.

"I'm glad you're here. My place is really small, and my bed is only a full-size, but we'll fit." I let go of her hand and wrap it around her shoulders.

We reach her apartment, and it looks a little run-down, and the locked entrance is questionable. She lets us in, and the inside smells a little musky, but I ignore it as we walk up the flight of stairs. Brylee unlocks her door, and I follow her inside. The last pictures she sent, the place was a little spruced up, but this is so much better.

The walls are covered in colorful prints, not my taste, but they totally looked like Brylee. Candles decorate the end table, entertainment center, and bedside table. The smell of citrus fills the space. She takes my bag from me and sets it on the end of her bed. "Is there anything you want to do?"

"I wouldn't mind a quick nap. I got up early today."

"Sure, go ahead." Brylee grabs the decorative pillows and throws them onto her chair.

I crawl onto her mattress, and she surprises me by climbing on and lying next to me. "Is this okay?" she asks, and instead of answering her, I wrap my arm around her waist and pull her until her back is snuggly against my chest.

My lips touch the back of her head, and the scent of raspberries wafts into my nose. "Should we go have a late dinner and see a movie?"

"That sounds good."

I yawn widely. "It's a date."

Before I fall asleep, I feel her body relax, and her slow, steady breathing fills the room, and only then do I fall asleep.

TWENTY
BRYLEE

I climb out of the car, followed by Chase. He thanks the driver and grabs my hand as we walk toward The Potsticker House. I've never been here before, but I've heard others rave about it, and I love authentic Chinese food.

Earlier I had only slept for about thirty minutes, but when I woke up Chase was still asleep, so I took the opportunity to watch him while he slept. He's twenty-eight, but in sleep, he looked so much younger. I reached out and stroked his bearded face. I don't know what he puts on it, but it always feels so soft.

The lines around his blue eyes were smoothed out, and his mouth was soft. I felt such a thrill when he showed up at the restaurant. It also gave me a thrill when he said it was because he missed me and wanted to see for himself how I was doing. It filled me with so much pride that he really seemed proud of me.

Hell, I've been proud of myself too. Lately I've been making friends and going out. It was nice to not feel so lonely anymore. It's been easier opening up to people, but I'm still not ready to tell any of them about the accident, not yet at least. The past couple of weeks I haven't been going to bed or waking up hearing that *thump, thump*. Sometimes I felt guilty about that, but sometimes I didn't.

When Chase's eyes had fluttered open, we didn't speak, we just stared at each other. It was weirdly intimate and no words were spoken, but it was like we didn't need them. Chase and I finally got up and got ready for dinner.

Now we step inside the restaurant, and the scent of some delicious food hits me and my stomach growls. Another plus is I've become a pig. I can't seem to eat enough most days. I've tried to keep healthier stuff stocked at home. I want to put on weight, but I want to do it healthily. I still run almost every day, but lately, it hasn't been to drown out bad thoughts. It's because I just love to run. All of that stuff has made a difference physically as well as mentally.

My hair looks a lot healthier, my eyes are bright, and I've got a healthy glow. I still take my meds every day, but my doctor has thought about lowering the dose. Her hope is that over the next year I might be able to get off of everything. God, that would be so great, and I have Chase to thank for all of this.

Him kidnapping me was probably the best thing that could ever happen to me. How fucked up is that? It's true though, and I've been trying to figure out a way to thank him, but I'm not so sure how to do it. One thing that keeps coming to mind is that I want to give him my virginity. It's crazy, I know, but how do you thank someone who has made you feel again? It's not gratitude, I've realized it's love. I'm in love with

Chase Foster, but then again a part of me always has been.

"Brylee?" My eyes fly to Chase, who's giving me a questioning look. "Are you okay?"

"Yeah, sorry I spaced out there for a second." He looks me over closely. "Really, I'm fine. I promise."

Chase reaches out, stroking my cheek. "If I haven't said it before, let me just say that you look fucking beautiful."

"Thank you." He leans down and kisses me quickly before grabbing my hand and pulling me toward the hostess stand.

Dinner was delicious and conversation was light. I got to know so much more about Chase's love for motorcycles. It was after he got his first bike and he rebuilt it himself, and he told me about Loco sending him to school to learn how to fix bikes.

He gets offered big money for the bikes that he rebuilds. Chase showed me a couple of pictures of the bikes that he's done, and they're gorgeous. It was easy to see the pride he takes in his work.

After Chase pays for dinner, we walk outside, and Chase lights a cigarette. He grabs my hand, and we walk down the street toward the movie theater. I turn to look at him. "When I was younger, I always wanted a scooter. Just something I could ride around town." I hold my hands up to my head. "I wanted a helmet like yours but in a cute girly color, like pink or purple."

"A scooter, huh? Like the new ones that are more like motorcycles or like a Vespa?"

"They look old school, but I think it's the Vespa."

He nods his head, and then we head inside the theater. Hmm...I wonder what was going through his mind.

I finish brushing my teeth and brushing my hair and step out of the bathroom. My body freezes at the sight in front of me. Chase is in a pair of blue boxer briefs that mold to a muscular butt and muscled thighs. He turns toward me, and I can't help it when my eyes drift to his penis. I may be a virgin, but I know enough to know that he's got a large dick. The sound of Chase clearing his throat startles me, and then he starts to laugh.

I don't miss that his dick is getting hard right before my eyes. "Baby, stop staring at him. It's obvious he likes you."

Embarrassment takes hold of me, and I shut my eyes. I feel his body heat as his body brushes mine. His fingers sift through my hair as his lips softly brush against mine. He kisses me with soft brushes of his lips. My hands reach out and touch his bare chest, and his skin is soft, warm, and hard all at once. I run my hand hesitantly up his pecs until my hands wind around his neck just as he deepens the kiss.

His tongue licks the seam of my lips until I open my mouth, and my tongue brushes his. I feel his hands moving until they're cupping and squeezing my breasts. I whimper into his mouth when he strokes my nipples with his thumbs.

There's heaviness between my legs that I want to rub to ease it. He begins plucking at my nipples, and I want to have an orgasm right now. My hands slide down his body until I let one hand rub over his erection. This time he groans against my mouth, and I do a full-body shiver. I hesitantly grab it like I've seen in the porno movies I've watched. It jerks in my hand, and I pull my mouth away from his. "Am I doing this right?" I ask as I stroke it up and down over his underwear.

"Fuck, yes. God, that feels fucking amazing, but do it like this, and it'll feel even better." He reaches inside his boxers and pulls his dick out, and I bite my lip. Chase grabs my hand, wrapping it around his stiff length, and has me squeeze it as my hand pumps up and down. "Just like this, but first." He pushes me down on the bed, covering my body with his.

Chase grabs my hand and again wraps it around his dick. I begin pumping it up and down. He groans against my mouth, and I squeeze him a little harder until he grunts into my mouth. I feel him lift up slightly before his hand reaches inside of my panties, and he begins rubbing my clit.

"Shit, you're so wet. I fucking love it." He thrusts his tongue into my mouth as he pushes one finger inside of me, and embarrassingly enough, I begin to come immediately.

My head tips back, and my mouth opens in a groan as my pussy squeezes his finger, and I ride his hand. His hips start moving faster, and then they turn erratic as I feel something warm and sticky hit me on my stomach. Chase kisses my lips before pulling back. "Let me get you cleaned up." He tucks his softening length back in his underwear and climbs out of bed. I reach down and run my finger through his cum and then bring it to my mouth. It's salty, warm, and a little bitter.

Chase climbs back on the bed and wipes me off with a wash rag and then throws it into my hamper. He lies down and then pulls me until I'm practically on top of him. "How was that?"

A sigh slips past my lips, and I snuggle further into

him. "That was amazing." I don't recognize my voice. It almost sounds dreamy.

He chuckles and then kisses my forehead. "Let's get some sleep, and I'll make you breakfast in the morning." It doesn't take any time at all before I am sound asleep.

————

All too soon, and it's time for Chase to head home. These have been the best three days of my life. We've been to Millennium Park, Navy Pier, and the Skydeck at Willis Tower. I'm not sure how he got me to go out on the Ledge, but he did.

The minute we had stepped onto it, he fit his front against my back and his arms wrapped tightly around me. Neither of us spoke as we gazed out on all of Chicago—words weren't needed. We were just in the moment... together. The view was breathtaking, and as long as I didn't look directly down, I was okay. His one thumb rubbed back and forth across my stomach, causing goose bumps to pop up all over my skin, and he must've been able to feel them because he laughed softly against my ear. His minty breath hit my cheek in puffs, making me want to turn in his arms and kiss him with everything I had.

Chase asked another couple to take our picture while we stood there. His arms were wrapped around me, and my front was plastered to his chest. In the first picture we were smiling at the camera, and in the second we were smiling at each other, but still so close together. I was glad to have those images where I could look at them whenever I wanted.

We didn't stay there long after that. Before we went

back to my apartment, we stopped at the market and got stuff to make dinner, which we did together. Being with him was becoming my addiction, and I hated that he was leaving because what if he decided I wasn't worth it or he couldn't forgive me?

He'd admitted the second night he was conflicted about taking things further than what we've done. It hurt to hear him say it, but I understood, and causing him stress was the last thing I wanted to do. He did surprise me when he told me he wasn't going to sleep with anyone else. Not while whatever this was was going on.

I wasn't sure if I totally believed that because he is so good-looking, and I didn't miss how the girls at his club looked at him. They all wanted him, desperately. Heck, most of the girls there had him, again something else I hated, but he's a grown man, and it wasn't my place to judge.

This morning while we snuggled in my bed, I asked questions about Kyle, and he didn't hesitate answering them. It was hard hearing everything, and by the time we finished talking about him, I was sobbing against Chase's chest. My heart was breaking all over again, but it was like I needed to hear this stuff. If anything was going to last with Chase, I needed to be able to hear stories because I never wanted him to forget his brother.

Chase ended up making me take half a Xanax because I had been so upset. Now I was better, just sad he's leaving. We've just stepped out of my building when his Uber car pulls up. He sets his bag down and pulls me into his arms and hugs me tight. I do the same even as the tears begin to fall again. "No tears, baby. We'll see each other soon."

My goal is to work as much as I can the next three

weeks and then go home for a long weekend. "I know. I've just had an amazing time with you."

"Same." He grabs my face, tipping it back to look at him. Leaning down, he kisses my lips, causing my toes to curl. The driver honks the horn, and Chase pulls back. "I'll text you once I get home."

I nod my head. "Okay, have a safe flight."

He kisses me one more time before picking up his bag and jogging down the steps to the awaiting car. I watch Chase as he climbs in the backseat and waves to me just before the car drives away. I stand frozen on the steps until the car disappears down the street.

Back inside my apartment, I fling myself on my bed, and a fresh wave of tears fall. How pathetic am I that I miss him already? I wanted to tell him so many times over the past couple of days that I'm in love with him, but it hasn't felt like the right time. Maybe because he's unsure about things between us, and confessing to him that I love him for him to just turn around and reject me.

Before I fall asleep, I say a little prayer that Chase gets home safely and that I'm able to get home to visit my parents and Chase.

I fly up in bed, gasping and coughing. My hands fly to my throat because I swear someone just had their hands wrapped around it. My heart stops racing, and I climb out of bed on shaky legs, making my way into the bathroom so I can splash cold water on my face. Gripping the basin of the sink, I stare at myself in the mirror, and there's nothing on my neck. Maybe the sheet had found its way around my neck, or maybe it was just a bad dream.

In my kitchen, I fill a glass of water and slug it down before crawling back into bed. Of course I'm wide awake now, so I grab my Kindle and pull up the new book I've been reading. Before long I'm nice and relaxed and able to go back to sleep.

———

Brian called out sick today, or his kids and his wife are all sick, so he stayed home to take care of them. I offered to go over and help, but he said they were contagious, and it was better to stay away. Roberta had me help cover the bar during my shift, and to be honest, I'm making more money than I do just waiting tables. Carly is working with me, so I've tried to be flirtatious like she is, and it seems to be working. Of course then I feel bad, like I'm betraying Chase or something.

It's silly and irrational, especially since I don't plan on doing anything, of course, but still, I don't think he'd be happy if he saw these guys flirting with me. "How's that hottie of yours?" Carly says as she comes to stand next to me as I put glasses away. "He reminds me of a younger Ragnar from *Vikings*."

It's still weird to have people actually want to know about me or my life, but it's also nice. "He's good. I'm flying home next week for a long weekend. It'll be good to see my parents and Chase."

"Ahhh…so that's why you've been working so much lately." She leans into me. "I know you have a not-so-great past." My eyes widen, and she quickly adds, "I can read people. I'm very sensitive to emotions, and I can just see it inside you—this sadness, this pain that you're trying to get past. I'm not asking you to tell me about it today, but whenever you're ready to trust me with that secret, that pain, just know I'm here for you."

I don't even know what to say. I'm touched by her sweet words. "Thank you." That's all I say because nothing else really needs to be said, but I give her a smile that I hope conveys how much her words mean to me. It's been so long since I've had a good, solid friendship, and now I'm developing several and can't help but get teary-eyed, but I quickly blink them away.

"No tears. Just know that I'm here when you're ready." I shoot her a smile before I turn away and get back to work.

TWENTY-ONE
CHASE

I pull up in front of my ma's house and hop out of my truck. Not bothering to knock, I push open the front door and call out, "Hey Ma, I'm getting ready to head to the airport to get Brylee. Do you want us to stop by and say —" My words die in my throat when I step around the corner to find my dad sitting at the table with my ma.

My dad stands up. "Brylee? *The* Brylee? What are you doing with that murdering bitch?"

"Thomas, stop that. It was an accident," my mom says from behind the man who sired me and then split when shit got too real. "Chase, go get her and take her back to her parents' house or yours, okay?"

I give my ma a chin lift, and when I turn to leave, my dad stops me with a hand on my arm. "You are not going to bring that girl anywhere around us. She destroyed our family—that bitch should be in jail."

Before I can stop myself, I've got my dad by the throat against the wall. "You shut the fuck up about Brylee. You're the one who shouldn't be around us. A fucking coward is what you are, running when the going gets tough. Leaving Ma to grieve alone unless you decide to fucking come back and confuse her. Ma's forgiven her, and so have I." My body locks up tight. I forgive her? *Fuck, I forgive her*.

A heaviness that has always been on my shoulders is suddenly fucking gone. I look at my pathetic excuse of a father. "You stay away from Brylee. She does not exist for you, do you hear me?"

"Y-yes. I-I'll stay away from her."

My ma places her hand on my arm. "Let him go, honey. It's okay, you go get Brylee. Your dad will be leaving soon."

I nod and let go of him, backing away. The pussy won't look at me—good, because I don't want that fucker making eye contact with me. "See ya, Ma."

Storming out of the house, I climb in my truck, but I don't head toward the airport like I should, instead I head toward the clubhouse to talk to Loco. I'm fired up right now, and I need to cool off. I still have plenty of time to get to the airport as long as I head in that direction in an hour.

I pull into the parking lot and hop out of my truck. The place is quiet inside, which during the day isn't that unusual. I head down the hall toward Loco's office. Talking and giggling comes from his office. I peek around the corner first just to make sure I'm not going to walk into something I don't want to see, but when I look, all I see is Loco in his chair and Tiff sitting on the end of his desk.

I knock on the doorframe, and they both look toward me. They both must be able to tell that something is wrong because Tiffany hops off Loco's desk and comes toward me and kisses my cheek. She disappears down the hall.

Turning toward Loco, I say, "Sorry, I didn't mean to interrupt you guys." I sit down across from his desk and scrub my hands over my hair.

"You didn't, Tiff was actually on her way out. She'd brought me lunch. So tell me what's going on. I figure you'd be on your way to the airport to get Brylee."

I lean forward. "I stopped by Ma's to see if she wanted me to bring Brylee over, and lo and behold, who is there but my fucking dad. That piece of shit had the nerve to tell me to keep her away from us, and then he called her a fucking murdering bitch. I got so pissed I shoved him and pinned him against the wall. Fuck, I'm so pissed right now I didn't want to head toward the airport until I calmed the fuck down. Brylee has made such amazing progress, and I don't want this to cause her to backslide."

"We'll keep an eye on your dad. I'll make sure that he doesn't go near Brylee while she's here. You need to tell her, though—that isn't something she should be surprised with. Go—go get her. Make sure you bring her by, I want to see this new version of Brylee."

I stand up, and he comes around, slapping me on the back. "Thanks for letting me vent, man. The man is something else. He disappears for years at a time and thinks he gets any say in any part of my life or Ma's."

"I know, brother. He's fucked up, and he needs to quit projecting his shit onto you. You're in a good fucking place right now. Your bikes have never looked better, and I have to believe that part of the reason is because of Brylee."

I nod my head slowly. "You know what. The only

good thing that happened today seeing my dad was that I realized something." My hand scratches at my bearded face. "I forgive her. I fucking forgive her."

"What made you come to that decision?"

"I don't know for sure when it happened. All I know is that when he called her a murdering bitch, I wanted to punch a hole in his face, and all I wanted to do was shield her from ever getting hurt because of it."

Loco comes toward me and pulls me into a bear hug. "That is so fucking great, brother. You didn't see it, but we all did. You were drowning in that grief, even ten years later. Never forget Kyle, but fucking celebrate his life, man. Now go get Brylee before she thinks you forgot about her."

He slaps my back before letting me go. I look at my phone, and Brylee's flight is supposed to land in twenty minutes, and it takes at least thirty to get there. "Shit." I rush out to my truck and break several laws getting to the airport. Once I reach it, I have two texts from her. One was twenty minutes ago, and one was ten.

Parking my truck, I jump out and run toward the automatic doors. I look around, and that's when I spot her. She's sitting with her back against the wall, her arms wrapped around her bent legs, her cheek resting on her knees, and her eyes closed. I call her name, but she doesn't move, but that's when I see she's got earbuds in.

I move toward her and stop when I'm standing right in front of her. Getting down on my haunches, I tap her knee. Her head jerks up, and she pulls her earbuds out. "Hey." She smiles at me. "I was afraid you forgot about me."

I reach out and tuck her hair behind her ears. "Nah…I had to stop and talk to Loco, and I just lost track of time."

Grabbing her hands, I help her stand up and then wrap my arms around her. She squeezes me tight. "I missed you so much." Brylee's lips touch my neck.

"Missed you too." Pulling back, I bend down and kiss her lips quickly. "How was your flight?"

I grab her hand in mine and lead her outside. "It was good, quick."

"Good. Any more coughing fits? Did you get checked out?" I've never been in a relationship before where I truly cared about that other person. Call me selfish, but I was more concerned about myself.

"I went, and they couldn't find anything. He said it could be allergies and maybe just post-nasal drip. I'm taking allergy meds to see if that helps." We get in my truck and head toward the exit. "I've got some exciting news."

"Oh yeah? What's that?" She surprises me by reaching out and grabbing my hand.

"They're going to start weaning me off my meds. I've been on them for a long time now, but he says that within this next year I could be off of them all. I'm excited but scared."

"That's great, babe. How do they do it? You can't just quit taking them altogether, right??"

I pull her hand to my mouth and kiss it. "No, I have to be careful about withdrawal and slipping back into a state that I don't want to ever be in again."

It sucks what I'm about to tell her, and I don't want this to be a setback. "That's good. Listen, I wanted to talk to you about something. This isn't going to be easy, but just listen, okay?"

She stiffens next to me, and I just need to get it out. "I stopped by Mom's today to double-check that she wanted us to stop by after I picked you up, and my dad was there." Brylee tries to pull her hand from mine, but I won't let her pull away from me. At her sentencing, my dad was charged with contempt because he kept screaming vile things at Brylee. Her dad had to be restrained because he went after my dad.

Not that I could blame the man. My dad didn't hold back, and it mortified my mom.

"Brylee, I swear to you that he will not come anywhere near you. He'll be gone soon anyway. That's why I was late. I went to talk to Loco, and he said he's going to keep an eye on my dad. He's not going to hurt you."

She rips her hand from mine. "I shouldn't have come. How did I think this could possibly be a good idea?" Brylee mutters to herself.

I pull over on the side of the highway. She turns toward me with wide eyes. I hate that the sweet, carefree look that was on her face is now gone. Now she looks withdrawn and fucking sad.

Grabbing her face, I look her straight in the eye. "Baby, I don't care what he thinks or what he said. That man abandoned his family because he's a fucking coward. It has nothing to do with you. He'll disappear again out of our lives, and we won't have to worry about him. Please don't let this ruin your visit. I've fucking missed you, and I won't let him ruin your visit home."

She opens her mouth to respond, but I pull her toward me and kiss her lips...hard. When she finally sinks into the kiss, I pull away. My thumb strokes her lip, and I can't help but smirk at the dazed look on her face. "It's going to be all good. I promise."

Nodding her head slowly, she whispers, "Okay. I won't let him ruin my visit." I kiss her one more time before pulling away, putting my seat belt back on, and pulling back onto the road. At least she lets me hold her hand all the way back to my house.

Once we pull into my driveway, I grab her bag and lead her inside. She follows me back to my bedroom, and she freezes. Two weeks ago, I finished paying off the bedroom set that I bought. I hated her sleeping on a mattress on the floor. I want her to be comfortable when she's here. Sure, I could've had her stay at her parents' house, but call me selfish, I wanted her with me.

After we relax for a little bit, we get ready to go have dinner at her parents' house. I've never, in my twenty-eight years, ever been to dinner at my girlfriend's house. Her mom has warmed up to me slightly, and that was only when I brought a couple of the club members' sons over to mow their yard, trim the hedges, and clean out the gutters. It was one less thing her dad had to worry about.

We make our way toward her parents' house. We're both quiet, but it's a comfortable silence. She's not like one of those bitches that goes on and on about nothing. Brylee doesn't talk unless I make her or she's got something to say.

Pulling up in front of her parents' house, we climb out. I come around the front end and grab her hand in mine. As we approach the front door, it flies open, and her mom appears in the doorway. She gives her daughter a big smile and holds out her arms as we approach.

"Hey, Mom." Brylee wraps her arms around her mom. I watch the interaction between the two of them. It's so natural between them now, no awkwardness at all.

Her mom looks around Brylee and smiles at me. "Hello, Chase."

"Hey, Mrs. Whitmore."

Her mom loops her arm through Brylee's and looks back at me. "Chase, I told you to call me Paula."

Inside, her dad Mike greets us, hugging his daughter extra tight. I shake his hand and then follow him into the kitchen and take the beer he offers me. He signals for me to follow him with a jerk of his chin. We take them out to the back deck and he leans against the railing, staring out at nothing. Fuck, is he sick?

Moving to stand next to him and copying her dad's posture. "Everything okay?"

"I never thought I'd see her again." His words are pained.

My body locks tight. Shit, does he know? "Uh, what do you mean, Mike?"

"That girl in there is the daughter I lost ten years ago. For once when I look at her, I'm not scared she's going to fucking die on us." He turns to look at me. "What happened was awful, and as a parent, I can't imagine what it was like to lose your brother, for your mom to lose her son. The first time she tried to kill herself, we were in shock. She convinced us it was a mistake and it wouldn't happen again, but it did. My child, my child was desperate to die."

"Fuck, sorry, I don't know where I was going with this. It's just really good to see my Brylee back, and I have you to thank for it." I watch the lone tear run down his cheek.

A knot forms in my throat, and a burning sensation begins in my gut. "Don't thank me," I choke out. "You don't know what happ—"

He cuts me off with a hand up. "I'm not stupid, son. Don't think I don't know that something happened between you two that I more than likely would not like. I thought about going to the police, but she denied anything happened. I didn't know if she was protecting you or maybe what she said happened really did. All I know is that since the day she came back home, she's been changing and becoming more like her old self. I was beginning to forget what my beautiful daughter looked like." He looks at me. "I don't care what you think. Thank you for that." He says it with so much conviction I feel it deep in my gut.

Mike disappears inside, and I close my eyes. *What the fuck*, I whisper to myself. What do I do with that? How do I take his thanks? I take a swig of my beer, and the scent of fresh-cut grass hits my nose.

"Chase?" I turn toward Brylee, who I didn't hear come out. "Are you okay?"

I grab her and pull her to me; wrapping my arms around her, I bury my nose in her neck and breathe in her soft floral scent. My lips touch the warm, delicate, sensitive skin behind her ear, and she sighs. "I'm okay, I promise. We just had a nice talk."

She must believe me, which was what I wanted because her arms wind around me, holding onto me tightly. "Good. I thought something was up when Mom dragged me into the kitchen to 'help' her with something."

I can tell she's waiting for me to give her more, but I can't, not right now while I process her dad's words. "Let's go inside."

She nods, and I wrap my arm around her shoulders and lead her inside.

Dinner went well, followed by dessert. With full stomachs, we leave shortly after that, and we decide to head to a little coffee shop downtown and sit outside drinking our pussy-ass lattes, and I will never admit to anyone that it's so fucking delicious and that I'm trying very hard not to moan after each sip.

Maybe I'm not hiding it well because Brylee is watching me, and I swear there's a twinkle in her eye. "Okay, it's good. You were right."

"I told you. They're my favorite. A shop by the restaurant makes one similar to this, and it's my weekly treat."

After our coffee drinks, we decide to go back to my place and watch a movie. On our way home, we stop and get snacks. Once we get back, we sit outside and smoke a joint. The night air is slightly cool, which means that fall is just around the corner. The air is far less humid, which means not as many bugs.

Brylee takes the joint from me and hits it twice before passing it back to me. "What did my dad say?" She holds my stare and waits.

"What does it matter? It's not important." Of course that's a lie. We haven't fully talked about what happened, and I'm nervous about doing it. What if she's just pushed it out of her mind, and if I bring it up, it'll bring those bad feelings back?

"It's important to me, and we shouldn't keep things from each other. If this is going to work between us, we have to be honest."

God, I'm so fucking proud of her right now. I've had to always coax her to share her thoughts or feelings with me, and I like this side of her. She's standing up for herself and what she wants. Hitting the joint in my hand,

I hold the sweet-tasting smoke down in my lungs before blowing it out. "Your dad suspects that something happened between us when you first came home. He said that he wanted to go to the police, but you kept denying that anything bad happened."

"Even though he suspects something happened, he's happy that you've started to change and seem more like you used to be."

She sucks in a breath and leans back in her chair staring up at the sky.

"I've put them through so much," she whispers. Brylee sits back up and looks at me. I don't miss the way her eyes are bright with unshed tears.

"Hey, hey, hey. No crying." I hold out my hand to her. "Come here, baby." Thankfully she takes it and lets me pull her to me, and she sits across my lap. "We need to talk about what happened in the basement. I know now is not really the best time, but the more I think about it, I know it to be true. The things I said, the things I did, I can never take back, but I need you to forgive me. I wasn't in a very good place after I found out you were back, and then I saw you. I-I hurt you." Fuck, this is harder than I thought.

Flashes fly through my mind of the day I dragged her down into the basement while she was tied to the chair and scared out of her mind. She'd been upstairs because she had to be cleaned up because I left her alone in the basement all night and she'd had an accident. Then there was catching her as she was trying to hang herself in my fucking closet.

Image after image assails me, and my stomach turns. Brylee surprises me by wrapping her arms around my shoulders. "We're fucked up, aren't we?" she asks.

235

I shouldn't do it, but I can't help it. My head flies back and I begin to laugh. We're talking full-body shaking laughs, and then I realize that she's laughing too. She buries her face in my neck as her body jostling in my lap has my dick getting hard. Brylee freezes because I know she can feel it. She pulls her head back, and her eyes lock with mine. Any laughter that was there has died.

I stroke her cheek with my thumb. Her eyes go soft, and she whispers, "I forgave you a long time ago for what happened."

My eyes widen, and I'm shocked by her words—I'm humbled by them. "Thank you for that. You have no idea how much that means to me. There's something that I wanted to tell you too. It hit me earlier today that I forgave you."

First the tears slip down her cheeks, then a sob rips from her throat, and she buries her face in my neck. Her whole body shudders as she cries and cries and cries. I'm beginning to worry until she wraps her arms around me. "Thank you," she whispers over and over again.

I stand up with her in my arms and carry her into the house. Moving down the hall, I take her into my room and lay her on the bed. "I'm gonna lock up real quick."

She looks up at me with her tear-filled eyes and nods her head. Brylee grabs my pillow and hugs it to her chest. I quickly lock up the house and head back down the hall and find her curled up and fast asleep.

In the bathroom, I quickly take a leak, wash my hands, and then brush my teeth. Back in the bedroom, I strip down to my boxer briefs and then pull back the covers, crawling in next to her and pulling her into my arms. She rolls to me even in her sleep, and I love that she loves cuddling. Before her, I was never much of a cuddler. It's a little early for us to be going to sleep, but then it's been an emotionally exhausting day.

Hugging her to my chest, it doesn't take long before I feel my eyes get heavy and I drift off to sleep.

TWENTY-TWO
BRYLEE

Chase and I are on our way to meet Loco and Tiffany for breakfast at the diner by the shop. When I woke up earlier, Chase had been wrapped around my back like a spider monkey, but I loved waking up with him practically covering me with his body and pinning me to his bed. It took some wiggling before I was able to turn until I was facing him.

I leaned forward, placing my lips against his, and reached between us to rub my palm against his hard length. We haven't done much more than we did that night in Chicago, and I'm ready for more—I want more…with him.

He awoke slowly, and I should've been worried about morning breath, but he didn't seem to care as he took over the kiss and moved us until I was on my back with him in between my legs. His hands found their way under my shirt, and in one swift motion, my breasts were bared to him. Chase's mouth left mine, and he began the descent down to my breasts. First he took one nipple into his mouth, licking and sucking it while I moaned, and then switching to the other.

Chase then started moving lower, and I felt my pulse begin to race. That was something we hadn't done yet, and I was really nervous. Of course the nerves quickly vanished at the first swipe of his tongue. My hands flew to his hair as my hips moved of their own volition. He sucked my clit into his mouth and caused me to arch my back and cry out.

Pressure began to build, and I knew I was close to orgasming. "Oh god, Chase. I want you inside me." I moaned.

He pushed one finger inside me, and my hips thrust, trying to chase my orgasm that looms just out of reach.

Chase lifted his head and flashed me that cocky grin of his. "Not yet, baby. This is just a preview, and you'll get the good stuff tonight." He lowered his head and attacked me again with vigor. He pulled out his finger and added another, pushing them back inside of me, stretching me. It didn't hurt, but it felt slightly uncomfortable until he rubbed his fingers against a spot inside of me that made me shudder violently.

Embarrassment hit me when I could hear the sound my body was making since I was so wet, but then my orgasm crashed over me. I gripped his hair, arched my back, and moaned his name loudly.

His lips traveled back up my body until he reached my lips and kissed them ever so gently. I moaned because I could taste myself on his lips. It was different, but not unpleasant. All too soon, he pulled away. "What about you?" I looked down at the massive erection in his boxer briefs.

"I'm good, baby. I don't want to cum until I'm buried

inside of you." He moved and situated us so he was on his back, and I was practically on top of him. We ended up falling back asleep.

Now he parks his truck, and I hop out, meeting him at the front, and he grabs my hand. We walk down the sidewalk and spot Loco and Tiffany standing out front. Of course, Loco is so big that he's not hard to miss. They spot us, and my cheeks heat up. Can they tell that we've messed around? Do I look okay? When they look at me, do they see the girl who got really messed up at their clubhouse? I run my free hand down my hair, smoothing it.

"Hey, guys!" Tiffany calls to us and makes her way to us. She pulls me into a hug. "My god, honey, you look fan-fucking-tastic." Holding onto my upper arms, she pushes me away and looks me up and down. "You've got some curves going on. I like it."

"Thanks. I had to buy a whole new wardrobe. It's nice to have so much more energy now." I don't know what it is about that woman that can cause me to open my mouth and let the verbal diarrhea fly.

"I bet it is." We follow the men inside and then follow our waitress to a booth.

After we eat, we sit for a little bit and drink coffee. "I wanted to thank you for helping, or arranging help with Chase taking care of the stuff around my parents' house," I say, looking at Loco.

"It's our pleasure. He seems to be doing well."

"He is. I think he's happy to be at work and feeling like he's contributing. Plus, I think he was starting to drive my mom crazy being around all of the time." They both smile at me from across the table, and Chase places his hand on my thigh, giving it a squeeze.

I've never been this happy or content in my whole life, well, at least for a very long time. A part of me feels guilty—like maybe I don't deserve to feel the way I do, but I'm beginning to learn that's not true.

After breakfast, Loco tells us to come to the party at the clubhouse tonight, but I think we were planning on it anyway. We walk out with them, and I accept Tiffany's hug goodbye and then give Loco a wave. He leads her over to a huge black truck, and to be honest, I'm not surprised he's got one.

I wave goodbye to them before letting Chase lead me down the street to his truck. "Are you sure you're okay coming to Kaylee's with me? You can just drop me off if you want." I haven't seen her since she had the baby, and I'm excited to get to hold Kaylee's precious son, Christian.

"I told you it was fine. We both knew she'd want to see you while you were here." I climb into his truck, and he rests his hand on my thigh.

Ten minutes later, we're walking up the sidewalk to Kaylee's front door. Before we even reach the door, it's flung open, and Kaylee greets us with a huge smile on her face. I move up the steps, kissing her cheek when I reach her. She hands me a sleeping Christian, cradling him to my chest, and I carefully carry him into her living room. I'm so busy studying the handsome little boy in my arms, I don't know if Kaylee and Chase even followed us inside.

I want more than anything to be a mom, but I just don't think that it's ever going to happen for me. I've come to terms with and have accepted that. I'm afraid I'd be one of those mothers that don't let their child do anything out of fear of something happening. I'll just have to get my baby fix by coming to see Kaylee and Christian.

Staring down at the sweet boy, I stroke his cheek with my finger, and he opens his mouth and yawns widely. He brings both of his chunky little fists up to his mouth and begins sucking on them. I can't help it and smile down at the sweet boy. I always hear people talk about smelling the tops of babies' heads and decide to take a whiff myself.

Sure enough, he smells like baby powder and milk.

"Did you just sniff my son?"

My head flies up, and Chase and Kaylee are both standing in front of me. Kaylee's got a huge smile on her face, and I don't want to analyze the look on Chase's face. I always assumed I was safe from ever having to tell my partner that I did not want children.

"I've heard how good babies are supposed to smell, and I had to see if it was true. It is, so there." I stick my tongue out at them and look back down at Christian. "Is he starting to sleep through the night for you yet?" Last time we talked, she said he was getting up every two to three hours to eat.

"We're slowly working up to where he's up every four hours, which is better. Giles usually gets up with him before work and feeds him his bottle before putting him back to bed. That way I can usually squeeze out another hour or two of sleep." I feel the couch compress as she sits next to me, stroking a hand over her son's head. "He's such a good baby. He only cries when he's hungry. If he needs his diaper changed, he just does this little whiny sound, but that's it."

"You look fantastic." She doesn't look like she was ever pregnant, well, except for her boobs that are bigger.

Where I am tall and more willowy, she's fairly tall and has a more athletic frame. Even with no makeup on and her blonde hair up in a messy knot, she still looks beautiful. She's got that new mommy glow, or what I assume is the new mommy glow.

"Thanks. This little guy has been my walking partner, and as soon as I get the go-ahead, I can start teaching and practicing yoga again. Do you still run?" We used to run all of the time when we were younger.

"Of course I do."

"How about we run together tomorrow? Of course, I don't want to take time away from you and your plans."

I leave the day after tomorrow, so I am limited on time, but never too busy for Kaylee. I know I have a long way to go before I can heal that breach between us, but we're definitely heading in the right direction.

Chase sits down next to me on the other side and looks at Christian. He surprises me when he reaches out and rubs his large hand over the baby's little head. Christian's eyes flutter open, and he opens his mouth in a huge yawn again, and this time he grabs Chase's finger and tries like hell to pull it close enough so he can pop it in his mouth.

The baby gets super angry when Chase takes his finger away, and I look up at Kaylee. "Is he hungry?"

She takes him from me, and he immediately tries to latch onto her breast through her shirt. I start to laugh. "Okay, we'll leave you to it. He's not going to wait too much longer. Call me or text me about going for a run. I can certainly come to you if you plan on bringing Christian."

Kaylee stands up. "I'll text you later and let you know." I hug her and kiss her cheek before leaving.

Chase doesn't kiss her, but he does give her a half hug sort of thing.

In the truck on the way back to his place, he grabs my hand. "Do you think you'll ever want kids?" I was hoping we wouldn't be having this conversation for a while, but I guess it's better to do it before either of us gets too attached.

I shake my head. "N-no. I won't ever have kids." The words hurt so much to say, and I want to fucking cry right now.

"Why not? You looked like a natural with Kaylee's boy."

Staring blankly out the window, I try to come up with the right words to say. I don't want to come across as a crazy person, or at least no more crazy than I really am. "I'm afraid that if I have kids, I'll be super protective over them and ruin their lives because of it. What if I'm afraid to let them out of my sight? It could prove to be so toxic for an innocent child, and I can't do it. Plus, what if karma pays me back for Kyle by taking my child?"

Chase doesn't say anything, and I'm nervous. We get back, and I climb out of his truck and follow him to the front door. He lets us in, and he walks silently into the kitchen. I hear him rooting around in the cupboard and then hear the back door open and shut.

My stomach turns as I move through his house into the kitchen. Out the back window, I watch him pace back and forth as he smokes a cigarette. Do I go to him or let him stew in whatever it is that's bothering him? But I'm not a dummy. It's because I don't want kids.

I decide to put on my big girl panties, which I've been doing a lot lately, and step out the back door. He's on me so fast it scares me, and Chase leans down until we're eye to eye.

"You would be a great fucking mother." I open my mouth to argue, but he gives me a look that has me closing my mouth. "I don't want to hear it. Karma doesn't work that way. You didn't hit Kyle on purpose, it was a goddamn accident. I don't want to hear you say that kind of shit again." Grabbing me by the shoulders, he gives me a little shake.

He backs away from me and takes a drag from his cigarette. I watch him snuff it out and throw it into his little fire pit. Again he moves toward me, brushing my hair out of my face. "I hate that you think you don't want children. You deserve to have a big, loud, loving family."

A tear slips down my cheek, and he reaches out, wiping it away before I can hide it from him. "I'm just too scared and just assumed that I'd never even have the opportunity to think about kids." I realize it sounds like I think he's possibly the one to do it. "I don't mean that I would have them with you or that you want them with me."

Chase pulls me toward him again and wraps his arms around me, hugging me tightly. His laugh vibrates against my chest. "What do you say we just stay in tonight, order Chinese, watch movies, and make out on the couch?"

I nod against his neck. "That sounds great."

"Good. Now let's go nap." That's exactly what we do. We strip down to our undergarments and crawl under his comforter. He situates us, and I lay my head on his chest. I kiss the tattoo that says Kyle that's right over his heart and close my eyes.

My eyes flutter open, and I roll over, finding Chase's

side of the bed empty. Climbing out of his bed, I throw my clothes back on and then go into the bathroom to relieve myself. After I wash my hands, I brush my teeth and brush out my hair. I throw my hair up into a bun and then head down the hallway in search of Chase. I hear his voice and step into the kitchen.

He's standing outside. I shouldn't be eavesdropping, but I hear my name. "She's good." A pause. "Yeah, Ma, I told her about Dad. How do you think she took it?" Chase stares up at the sky. "Good, I'm glad he left. You don't need his shit. Brylee doesn't need his shit." He laughs. "No, you don't need to come over and see how she's doing for yourself. We'll stop by tomorrow." Another pause. "We're staying home tonight. Okay, I love you too."

He turns to the window. "Come on out, baby."

Oops, I think it's safe to say that I'll never be a good spy. I step outside and move toward him. He opens his arms, and I walk right into them. "Your dad's left already?"

His hands rub up and down my back. "Yep. After I left to get you, my mom let him have it and told him next time he showed up that he better bring divorce papers so she can start moving on. Dad threw a fit, so she told him if he didn't leave, then she was calling the cops and having him arrested for trespassing and harassment. He left about two minutes after that."

"I'm sorry."

"Nope, stop saying that shit right now. You have nothing to be sorry about. If he wants to hold on to the past…" He pauses. "Shit, that's what I did. It was why I grabbed you that day, because I was holding onto my grief and anger and I didn't want to part with it. Now I know what it feels like to feel free of that bullshit. It's no longer weighing on my mind, on my shoulders, and on my heart."

I grab his face, pulling him down for a kiss and licking the seam of his lips until he opens and lets me into his mouth. Our kiss is slow and sweet, and it ends far too quickly. "Go order our food, find us a movie, and I'm going to run and get us drinks and dessert."

"Okay, that sounds good." As I walk away, his hand strikes my ass. "Hey…what was that for?" I rub the sting out, trying to give him my best disgruntled look. Of course he isn't bothered by it because he just laughs at me.

I step inside, and before I shut the back door, I flip him the middle finger and then blow him a kiss. His response is to shake his head and give me that smile of his that I love. That one that's so slow and sensual you get that ache in the pit of your stomach while you watch it be directed at you.

My body shivers thinking about the fact that maybe tonight will finally be the night when he claims every part of me because, let's face it, he totally owns my heart and my soul.

TWENTY-THREE
CHASE

Brylee lies in front of me on the couch while we watch *The Godfather*. She'd never seen it, which is a crime. It's one of my favorite movies, and she was agreeable to watching it.

Earlier we pigged out on chicken lo mein, Mongolian beef, egg rolls, and crab Rangoon. At one point I fed her, and she didn't mind at all. In fact, every so often she nipped my fingertips, then moaned around each digit as she sucked them into her mouth. Fuck, if we were out and she moaned like that, I'd have to beat lots of guys' asses off her. My dick definitely responded.

I'm okay with fighting. It's been a while since releasing the pain that resides in my chest—or at least the pain that used to live there. Now, I want to brawl because it's fun. Maybe once she's gone to Chicago, I'll see if any of the guys at the clubhouse want to go to the gym and spar with me.

Focusing back on the movie again, I watch Michael's sister marry that piece of shit. Needing to feel her warmth, I wrap my arm around Brylee's waist and pull

248

her tighter to me. She rubs up against me, burrowing into me.

I slip my hand under her shirt, then stroke her stomach. Instead of a laugh, she sighs, which makes me smile. Not done yet. I dance up her stomach until I find her breasts. They're a little fuller than before. I cup one in my hand and then pinch her hardened nipple through her silky bra.

Her ass grinds against my aching dick, making me want to strip her bare and pounce. Brylee's hair is in a braid so her neck is exposed to me. Leaning down, I kiss her softly behind the ear, not missing the goose bumps that pop up all over her skin. I shove the hand cupping her breasts under her bra and the feel of her smooth flesh.

In all my life, I've only ever fucked women. I didn't make love. Hard and fast, then kicked them to the curb. Never have nerves played a role until now. Brylee's hinting around that she's ready for sex has turned me into a teenage boy again. It matters to me that she enjoys it, and that's a first. Once we cross that line, there will be no coming back. Now that I've had a taste, I want more. I'm an addict, but an addiction to her is one that I'd welcome.

Brylee demands my attention back to her neck, cocking her head to give me better access to her neck. I flick my tongue out tasting her skin and dragging it to her earlobe giving it a playful nip. She whimpers, egging me on. Her arm wraps around the back of my neck while she grinds against me.

Somehow she turns around so we're facing each other, and her lips are on mine. I wrap my arms around her and move her around until she's straddling me. Our kiss turns urgent, and her mouth opens, and our tongues duel. She pulls back. "Make love to me…please?"

I stare up into her ice-blue eyes, and all I see is love shining brightly in them. It scares the fuck out of me, but it also exhilarates me. With Brylee wrapped around my waist, I hold her and amble to my room.

On my bed, I watch her bounce. She bites her lip as I crawl onto the bed and over her. I grab the rubber band and pull it out of her hair so it fans across my pillow.

She's like a dream come true, and she's trusting me with a gift I don't really deserve. I'm gonna make it worth it to her. First I need her naked, and getting her that way is exactly what I do. I slide my hands under her shirt and don't stop until I'm dropping it off the side of the bed. Her bra clasps in the front, I pop the hook and peel the cups off slowly.

My mouth waters, but I refrain from doing anything just yet. I want to savor the moment. I make quick work of peeling down her panties and shorts until she's completely bare to me. I climb off the bed, pulling my shirt up and over my head, and throwing it on the growing pile of clothes. I'm wearing shorts, so I quickly take them and my boxer briefs off.

My dick sighs in relief, then I give him a quick squeeze before crawling back up on the bed. I surprise her by lying down next to her and not on top. She turns to look at me, and I can tell she's confused. "Are you sure you want to do this?" I stroke her hair from her face.

"I've never been more sure of anything," she admits without hesitation.

I pull her body toward me until it's flush against mine and brush my lips to hers. Our tongues do that familiar dance and my body screams at me to enter her. She wraps her long, slender leg up over my hip, pulling me even closer to her.

Rolling us, I get situated on top of her. I press kisses down her body. She moans when I reach her breasts, sucking one tip into my mouth and applying just enough pressure to have her squirming under me. I switch to the other side, giving it the same treatment.

Brylee pulls my hair, holding me to her chest. While I suck the tip, I run my fingers through her wetness, then rub her clit. She moans, and I love it.

In no time at all, she's grinding against my hand. Moving my hand, I push one finger inside her and then two, trying to stretch her so it doesn't hurt when I bury my dick inside of her.

I move until my lips are aligned with hers again, and I kiss her hard, forcing her lips open with mine. My tongue licks against hers as I rub her clit. She cries out against my mouth, and I know she's close. "Let me hear you let go." Her head arches back and she moans against my mouth. I reach down, pushing two fingers inside of her, rubbing that sweet spot that prolongs her orgasm.

After wringing two orgasms from her, I push up and let her watch me as I lick the wetness of her from my fingers. Her eyes are dazed, and she licks her lips. I bend down, placing my lips on hers. "Are you ready?"

She nods her head. "Yes." Her voice is a mere whisper. I reach into the nightstand next to my bed and grab the box of condoms, taking one out. With shaky fingers, I manage to get it on my cock without totally fucking it up.

"We'll go slow. If at any time you need me to stop, just tell me, and I will."

She reaches up and cups my face. "I trust you."

I graze her cheek with my knuckles. "That means more than you'll ever know. I'm going to make this so good for you." I bend down and kiss her quickly before pulling away.

"You already have." She sighs, and the smile she gives me makes my heart thud loudly in my chest.

"Spread your legs, baby." She slowly opens them, and her chest rises and falls quickly. I grab her ankles and spread her open just a bit more. I grab my aching cock and line it up with her opening.

Fuck, I can feel the heat coming from her already, and it's sweltering. Pushing in just the tip, I give her a few seconds to get used to it before pushing in a little bit more. In and out I move further inside her until I hit her hymen. "This is going to hurt, but I'll try to make it quick."

She nods, and I kiss her lips before pulling almost all of the way out and then thrusting inside until I'm buried to the hilt. Brylee cries out, and I groan because she has the tightest, hottest pussy I've ever had the privilege of being inside. A tear slips from her eye, and I lick it away. I have to move, but I can't until I know she's okay.

"Did I hurt you?" I whisper against her lips.

"No, I just need you to move." Pulling almost all the way out, I thrust back in, picking up the pace and a rhythm that has her moaning against my mouth. I tip her hips up and begin rolling my hips as I thrust in and out of her. She wraps her arms around my shoulders.

"Are you going to come again for me?" I whisper.

She nods her head. "Look at me." Her gaze is heated, cheeks flushed, and her mouth is slightly open. Fucking breathtaking. "You feel that, baby?" She sweeps her tongue across her lips. I feel her squeeze the fuck out of my dick, and I kiss her.

She pulls her mouth from mine. "Oh god!" Her hips

thrust against mine erratically, and I take over, gripping her hips as I thrust into her over and over until that tingle starts at the base of my spine, and I come, and come fucking hard.

I collapse on top of her, and she wraps her arms and legs around me like a spider monkey. Kissing her neck slowly, I enjoy the feel of her stroking her hands up and down my back.

"Let me get rid of this condom. I'll be right back." I slowly pull out of her, not missing the whimper that slips past her lips. Throwing the sheet over her naked body, I climb out of bed and make my way into the bathroom. When I peel the condom off and wipe myself off, I don't miss the streaks of blood and know what they mean.

After I grab a washcloth, I get it wet under the tap and turn the water off. I'm completely humbled by the fact that she chose me to share the gift of her virginity with. We share such a tumultuous history, but together we have the opportunity to start a new chapter...together.

I step back into my room and find her lying on her side. "Are you sore, baby?"

She shakes her head.

"Good, I'm going to clean you up." I pull the sheet from her body and don't miss her flushed skin. I spread her and wipe between her legs. When I finish, I throw the dirty washcloth into my hamper and then pull her to me.

"Thank you," she says against my neck. "That was everything I thought it would be."

I situate us so her head is on my shoulder, then stroke her back. "Thank you for letting me be the one to give it to you." I press my lips to her forehead and don't miss the dreamy sigh leaving her lips. "Sleep, baby."

She sinks further into me, and not long after, her soft snores fill the room.

———

I jerk awake with a start. Brylee is coughing so hard her lips are blue. Grabbing her shoulders, I call her name over and over, but she's not responding. "Fuck, baby! Wake up! Brylee…Brylee! Brylee!" I shake her so hard her head thuds against the mattress. "Brylee! Fucking look at me! Look at me right the fuck now!"

TWENTY-FOUR
BRYLEE

My eyes fly open. Shock, sadness, and dread fill me. I frantically look around, then realize I'm in Chase's basement and still tied to the chair. My heart beats a rapid staccato in my chest. Nausea pools in my belly as he gets in my face. His cigarette breath hits me. "What the fuck is wrong with you? You fucking crazy bitch." He wraps his hands around my throat, squeezing it until the air is cut off.

I wriggle under his weight, clawing and kicking, but his strong hands squeeze tighter. Staring up at him, the man from my dreams is gone. Was he ever really there? Have I hallucinated some sort of happily ever after? Oh god, I'm crazy.

Tears stream down my heated cheeks as under-standing sinks in: this is how I die.

Finally, *finally*, his fingers slip off my windpipe, and air floods into my lungs. Spittle flies everywhere as I cough and cough.

"Please, just let me go." My voice is hoarse and raspy. My throat aches, and I just want to rub it or hold it.

"I won't tell anyone what happened. Please, I'll leave town, and you'll never have to see me again." My words are barely audible, but I continue. "I promise I won't come back. Please, just please let me go, Chase."

He bends down until we are at eye level. A part of me wants to reach out and touch and hold him, but I can't because what's in my head isn't real. I've always been able to go to my "safe place" when needed. In that reality I learned how to be happy, fall in love, and share my life with the man that I've always loved. Tears leak down my face because the man in front of me now is not him.

It was all a lie.

This Chase, the real one, may look like him, but it breaks my heart that he's not. I close my eyes and try to slip back into my "safe place," but he grabs me by the shoulders, shaking me so violently my head jerks back and forth. "Don't you space out on me again! Open your goddamn eyes."

I do what he says and gaze up at him. His blue eyes are bright, and he looks slightly maniacal. He grabs me by my face, and I cry out. "You killed Kyle. You took him away from me." This is it, this is where my life ends.

Before I can react, he wraps his hands around my throat again and squeezes, cutting off my air. A blinding pain rams into my head, but I can't cry out. My vision is murky. I try to take a breath but can't, and my fight response kicks in. My leg flies out, then the other. Trying to get loose, I thrash in the chair. The pressure lets up around my throat, but then I'm falling backward in the chair. Chase wastes no time moving on top of me, his hands move back toward my throat.

"N-no, please!"

His gaze is dead, unfocused, and glossy in his deadly

pursuit. Can he even hear me? My heart scrambles faster and faster as he succeeds a third time, wrapping his hands around my throat and squeezing. I try to get free so I can fight him, but I can't. He doesn't stop, and my vision is splotchy, black-and-white spots dancing. I try to shut my brain off but think about my parents instead. At least they won't have to worry about me anymore. This is the end, and I'm finally paying for my mistake.

A weird sense of peace comes over me, and I quit fighting and allow myself to fade into the nothing.

———

CHASE

The moment Brylee stops moving, I bend over and throw up on the floor. With two shaky fingers pressed to her neck, I realize her pulse is gone.

"Fuck, fuck, fuck!" On my hands and knees, I pinch her nose, put my lips to hers, and blow into her mouth. What am I doing? "I don't know fucking CPR!" I try to remember the week we learned first aid back in health class in the eighth grade. It clicks, and I pump her chest, but nothing is happening. "Shit!" I breathe into her mouth again and again, but her body is eerily still.

"No!"

Panic hits, and I grab the bucket and throw it against the wall with a roar. "What have I done?" Back on my hands and knees, I crawl across the floor until I reach her. My hand shakes uncontrollably as I stroke hair away from her beautiful face. I'd forgotten how beautiful she is. "I'm sorry. So, so fucking sorry. What did I do?"

Tears drip from my eyes and onto her face. Should I

call the cops and turn myself in? Should I call Grayson and Loco? They'd know what to do. Wait, maybe I should call my mom? No, I can't. It would destroy her.

I'm unsure of how much time passes before I dazedly look at Brylee's still form. Images flash through my mind: seeing her for the first time at school, catching her watching me with that sweet smile on her face, and the day I was finally going to talk to her, but one of my friends had intercepted me.

Her last thoughts, her last feelings, were fear, and it's because of me. What was I hoping to gain from this? Kyle's never coming back, and now I'll go to prison for the rest of my life. Mom would have to deal with a son who is a murderer—no, I can't leave her to watch me rot in prison.

On autopilot, I go up to my room, and in the back of my closet, I find the cold metal box hidden under a loose floorboard. The weight is heavy in my hand as I rush down the stairs to be with Brylee.

In the room, I sit next to her body and open the box. A picture of Kyle and me sitting on the front steps of my parents' house, the last one of my brother and me before he died, greets me. Two days later, our lives were changed forever.

As I lay the picture next to Brylee's mussed hair, something I haven't seen in a long time catches my eye: a vial of white powder, a spoon, and sterile water. I stare at the contents. I never told anyone I kept an emergency stash hidden in my closet, not Grayson, not Loco…not anyone. I never planned to use again. I bought the heroin last year when dealing with life got too hard. Why'd I keep it? Fuck, I'm not sure why I kept the container. I try not to think as I dump the contents onto the spoon, then mix in the sterile water.

I wipe my sweaty palms down the front of my jeans.

I mostly snorted and only shot up a couple of times because the release of the high scared me. Pleasure like no other was immediate. Too good and too sweet.

Like an old friend, the thrill of it greets me, and sickening excitement pumps through my veins. I find a cotton ball and add it to the spoon, then grab a syringe and tourniquet.

My heart thunders against my ribcage.

Focusing, I submerge the tip of the needle into the cottontail and withdraw. I swipe my tongue across my upper lip as the syringe fills with cloudy liquid. My hands don't shake as I use my teeth to fix the tourniquet around my bicep.

In the bend of my arm, a vein pops up to attention. Before I dive into bliss, I lean over Brylee's body and touch my lips to her warm forehead.

"I'm so sorry, so fucking sorry," I whisper. Tears fill my eyes, but I don't brush them away. Instead, I close my eyes and inhale her scent. A final goodbye.

Sitting up, I clench and unclench my fist until tingles dance up my forearm. Satisfied, I grab the syringe and slide the tip of the needle into my vein. Pulling the plunger back, I watch blood mix with yellowish liquid. Sweat drips down the sides of my face. Inhaling deeply, a musty vomitus scent hits my nose.

The tingles in my forearm spread to the rest of my limbs. A whirling sensation reaches my ears, and I lie down and stare at the picture of Kyle. Will I see him again? Maybe he's waiting for me on the other side.

Numbness washes over my body, and before my eyes flutter shut, Brylee turns her head. Her beautiful gaze latches onto mine. Her chest is shaking. Is she coughing? I blink, but it takes what feels like several minutes for my eyes to open. Brylee tries to move over to me. I want to smile, to touch my lips to her moving ones, but I can't move.

Then everything fades away.

EPILOGUE
BRYLEE

FIVE YEARS LATER

I pull my car up under the tree at the edge of the road before climbing out with the flowers I picked up. The tombstones appear up ahead, and I take a deep breath as I make my approach. Even five years later, it's still painful to be here. I read the names *Kyle Jason Foster* and *Chase Alan Foster,* and tears fill my eyes as I remember that day.

I'd never seen someone OD before, and I never wanted to see it again. When I came to, Chase was lying next to me. I watched as his lips turned blue and his tanned skin turned an ashen white. His body twitched and shuddered, but watching him vomit then start to choke frightened me the most. I fought against my ropes to get to him. And I did, but I dislocated my right wrist in the process.

The moment he was gone, I swear I felt his spirit leave his body. Don't ask me how, but it was like I suddenly felt very alone. Then two sets of footfalls ran down the stairs a short time later, or it could've been hours for all I knew. Grayson, and later who I gathered was Loco, emerged seconds later.

They called an ambulance for me, and Loco held me close while Grayson mourned over Chase's body. I wanted to mourn, but I wanted to mourn a version of Chase that I seemed to have invented in my head and who really didn't exist anymore.

I spent two days in the hospital while they monitored my injuries from him choking me.

My parents stayed by my side the whole time, and I had been thankful for their support. What surprised me more was that members of Chase's motorcycle club stood guard outside my hospital room since reporters kept trying to get me to do an interview knowing my history with Chase. The day I was discharged home, my parents drove me back to their place, and Chase's mom waited for us on the front steps.

"I can send her away. You don't need to talk to her," my mom had said.

But I needed to.

"It's okay, Mom. This is something I need to do." Mom gave me a worried stare but nodded and left me alone with Mrs. Foster.

She stood as I approached. All I wanted was to tell her how sorry I was that I couldn't save Chase, but I cried instead. Rushing toward me, Mrs. Foster hugged me close. Even though I didn't, really, I rasped out, "I'm so sorry."

"No, honey. It's me who's sorry."

We sat together for a long time on the steps, neither

of us saying anything. She just wrapped her arms around me and held me close. Her cries were silent, but I could see the tears rolling down her face. We stayed like that for a long time, both of us needing the comfort.

Before she left, she handed me a picture of Chase—the boy I remember from high school—and Kyle. "Loco found this next to you on the basement floor." Her chin wobbled.

I hugged the photo to my chest knowing what it meant for his mom to give it to me. "Thank you. This means a lot."

Next to her car, she said, "We're having a service for Chase." She glanced over my shoulder, then back at me. "I'd like you to come, but if going to his funeral would be too difficult, I understand."

"You don't owe them anything! You need to heal and move on." Mom's red, blotchy face broke my heart, but she refused to appreciate why I needed to go. Regret, anger, shame, and hatred brought Chase and me together. It was time to let the past go and allow in peace, love, and forgiveness.

Against my parents' wishes, I went to say goodbye to Chase alone.

The first thing I noticed was all of the bikes lined up outside the funeral home when I walked up.

Men in leather were everywhere. Nervously I rubbed my sweaty palm, the one without the cast, down the skirt of my dress as they turned and stared at me. Most knew who I was, I think, because I got a lot of chin lifts, and soft smiles, which was surprising coming from big scary dudes.

Once I stepped inside, Loco greeted me with a sweet

hug. "You're the bravest woman I know," he whispered into my ear.

I shook my head. "I'm not brave. I'm just trying to find peace."

"You got up and came. You're forgiving and finding a new path." He smirked. "I'd sure in the hell call that brave." I opened my mouth to protest, but he cut me off. "Don't argue. I'm older and bigger than you."

When he pulled away with a hand to the small of my back, he led me inside. The casket was up at the front and open, but I didn't think I was brave enough to go until Mrs. Foster saw me standing there.

Weaving through the crowd, I made it to her, hugging her tight. "I'm so glad you're here," she said. I still couldn't talk above more than a whisper, so I gave her a smile and nodded. After everything we've been through, no words were ever really going to be needed between us. She led me to the casket and, when I looked down at him, I started to cry because he looked just like the Chase of my dreams. Everyone assumed I hated him for what happened, but I could understand his pain and grief because I lived with the same. Maybe my pain and grief were different, but not really.

I didn't go to the burial because I was too emotionally raw, but I watched from across the street as the entire group of motorcycles drove by. Loco and Grayson led the pack, both giving me a chin lift as they followed the hearse. Once all of the bikes and cars passed by, I walked home.

I never went back to Chicago, well, I went long enough to move out of my apartment and quit my job. My boss knew a little about what happened to me and my desire to be close to my family. My first year home was one of rebirth, you could say. I should've died in the basement that day, but I didn't. I was given a gift, a second chance at having a life, and embraced that.

In a surprising turn of events, the Jackals MC welcomed me into their circle with open arms. Grayson helped me pass my driver's test so I could get my driver's license. Loco's old lady's name was actually Laura, and she helped me study for the entrance exam for the small private college on the edge of town. She actually worked in the admissions office, so I think she had a lot to do with me getting in.

During that year, I went to therapy, which helped me deal with the overload of emotions I ignored all those years ago. Guilt was hardest to let go, but as time went on, I learned to process things better. It took time to repair my relationship with my parents, but we all worked hard to get us where we are now.

Grayson has been such a huge support for me, and I'll never be able to repay him for what he's done for me. He's my best friend, which is so weird, but we share a sort of weird bond.

He's still single and loving it, or so he says, but I told him it's because he hasn't met the right girl yet—when I say that, I usually get an eye roll.

Kaylee actually moved away after college. She lives in California with her husband Giles. I've reached out on social media, and we've talked a little bit, but it might be too late for us to fix what I broke, but I won't ever stop trying. Megan is single with no kids and has become a good friend, and I think I have Grayson to thank for that.

Two years ago I finally got my nursing degree and found a job in the mental health unit of one of our local hospitals. It's the most rewarding yet challenging job I've ever had, but I feel like I make a difference every time I go to work.

In that time, I fell in love and got married. He's amazing, sensitive, funny, and just a little badass. I've never laughed so much in my entire life. He's been around since the beginning, so he knows every ugly detail of my life, which is a good thing. I'm still not a big fan of the dark, and when we bought our house, it couldn't have a basement. He understood that, and we looked and looked until we found our home. Even five years later, some days are better than others.

A twig snapping has me turning. "I thought you were going to wait in the car," I say with a smile.

"I know, but our little princess woke from her nap, and when she saw Mommy, she wouldn't take no for an answer." Cooper gives me those puppy dog eyes and sticks out his lower lip. And he wonders where our daughter gets it from.

He's tall and lean, has shoulder-length brown hair, and a beard he keeps trimmed short. He's a biker and a computer programmer, which is the strangest combination ever. Grayson introduced us at a party at the clubhouse three years ago. Friendship was all I could manage while getting my life together, and school kicked my ass, too, so that didn't help my nonexistent love life.

Thank goodness Cooper didn't give up, and my parents absolutely fell in love with him. Couldn't have picked a better man to fall in love with and have children with.

I place a hand on my belly, knowing this child will be just as loved. Our daughter, Sadie, reaches for me, and I snuggle her close. "Can you stay with Daddy a little longer? Mommy will be right there, then we'll get ice cream."

She nods, her curly brown hair falls into her eyes, and she gives me the most beautiful smile.

Sadie lunges for Cooper, and he kisses me before heading back to the car. He gets me and knows why I have to come here every year, and when we're done and my husband and daughter are asleep, I'll write my yearly email to Chase and Kyle's mom.

Mrs. Foster moved to Florida a year after Chase died to live with a cousin of hers. She's happy, or as happy as one can be with both of her children gone.

Chase and Kyle's dad never resurfaced, and nobody knows if he knows that his eldest son is gone. Grayson hopes he never comes back, for everyone's sake, but I guess only time will tell.

I lean Kyle's flowers against his tombstone, then I kneel next to Chase's. After laying his flowers just like his brother's, I grab the picture out of my purse. It's the one of the two brothers that was taken so long ago. I stick it in the little picture holder on Chase's tombstone as the tears start to flow.

"I should hate you. I should, but I don't. You don't know it, but you gave me a second chance. I've promised myself over and over again that I will not squander what I've been given. I just wish you would've been given one, too." I blot the wetness from my cheeks. "A part of me believes that had things been different, you and I could've had something amazing. Don't get me wrong, I love Coop so much, and the life we've created is better than any dream, but you and I were destined to be in each other's lives. I hope you've found peace and that you and Kyle are together. I'll always wish things had been different, but if I've learned anything over the past five years, it's that we can't change the past. We can only learn from our mistakes and grow from them."

I place my hand on his name on the tombstone. "I'll see you next year." I stand up and walk toward the car that holds my husband and my daughter and I smile.

IF YOU LIKED THIS, YOU MIGHT LIKE:
THE LIES BETWEEN US BY YOLANDA OLSEN

The truth can set you free—or destroy everything you've ever known.

Gracie Blackburn swore she'd never return to her hometown, but when news breaks that her estranged father, Hoyt, is on death row for the murder of her mother, she can't stay away. Haunted by questions and unresolved memories, Gracie sets out to confront Hoyt before it's too late. She doesn't want to believe he's capable of such violence, but the past has a way of twisting even the purest love into something unrecognizable.

Jori Davidson has always been Gracie's rock. Her childhood best friend—and the one person who knows all her secrets. But Jori is hiding a devastating lie of his own, one that could tear apart the fragile trust between them.

As the truth about that night slowly unravels, Gracie is forced to face the lies buried in her family's past and the forbidden feelings she's long-suppressed for Jori. In the end, she must decide what's worth saving: the love she's always yearned for or the answers she's desperately seeking.

AVAILABLE AUGUST 2025

ACKNOWLEDGMENTS

First and foremost, I want to thank God because without him, I wouldn't have realized what I was meant to be doing. I feel very blessed to be doing something I love so much.

To my husband Jim and our boys, thank you so much for supporting me and loving me when I'm on a deadline —pretty much ignoring my responsibilities at home. Jim, you stepping in and taking care of the house and cooking dinner so I can write has meant so much to me.

To Angela, thank you for all of our nightly writing sessions. Your encouraging words have gotten me through a lot while I was finishing this book. You kept me going, especially when I was scared with the direction the book was taking.

Thank you to my fantastic editor, Ellie McLove!! Thanks for making this story the best it could be, and your emails made me smile and get extremely giddy! I can't wait to work together again.

Judi Perkins, from Concierge Literary Designs. You made me the most beautiful cover and captured exactly what I wanted it to be. You were so easy to work with.

To Diane, my fantastic PA, thank you for always being my rock as my book releases draw near. Thank you for making the best teasers, helping make my release day so successful and fun. I'll never be able to thank you enough for all of the hard work that you do for me, and

I'll always be grateful that you came into my life. We make a damn good team.

To my review team, thank you for taking time out of your busy lives to read and review my books, whether you love them or not, it means a helluva lot.

To my street team, we really need a cool name, but for now, thank you for always sharing my releases, teasers, and sales. You guys are amazing.

To Linda at Forward PR & Marketing, thank you for being my cheerleader behind the scenes and for being just as excited for my stories. Words can never express how thankful I am to you for coming into my life and making my releases phenomenal.

Lastly, thank you to my readers. Your love and support means the world. Thank you so much.

ABOUT THE AUTHOR

Evan Grace was a Midwesterner and readaholic for most of her life until one day an idea came to her and a writing career was born. She's a sucker for happily-ever-afters and loves creating fictional worlds that others can get lost in.

When the voices in her head give it a rest, which isn't often, she can be found with her e-reader in hand. Some of her favorites include, Aurora Rose Reynolds, (the queen) Kristen Ashley, Kaylee Ryan, and more. She finds a lot of my inspiration in music, movies, TV shows and life.

Grace is a wife to Jim and mom to Ethan and (the real) Evan, a show re-watcher, a long-time healthcare worker, and constant worrier. How does she do it all and write? She has no idea.